ZERO BREAK

A Mahu Investigation

NEIL S. PLAKCY

mlrpress

www.mlrpress.com

Published by
MLR Press, LLC
3052 Gaines Waterport Rd.
Albion, NY 14411

Visit ManLoveRomance Press, LLC on the Internet:
www.mlrpress.com

Cover Art by Victoria Landis
Editing by Kris Jacen

Print format ISBN# 978-1-60820-591-2
ebook format ISBN#978-1-60820-592-9

Issued 2012

Zero break refers to the deep-water location where waves first begin, often far offshore. For Honolulu homicide detective and surfer Kimo Kanapa'aka, it means his most dangerous case yet.

A young mother is murdered in what appears to be a home invasion robbery, leaving behind a complex skein of family and business relationships, and Kimo and his detective partner Ray Donne must navigate deadly waters to uncover the true motive behind her death and bring her killer to justice.

Kimo is also in trouble at home, as he and fire investigator Mike Riccardi consider fathering children themselves.

MLR Press Authors

Featuring a roll call of some of the best writers of gay erotica and mysteries today!

Derek Adams	Z. Allora	Maura Anderson
Simone Anderson	Victor J. Banis	Laura Baumbach
Helen Beattie	Ally Blue	J.P. Bowie
Barry Brennessel	Nowell Briscoe	Jade Buchanan
James Buchanan	TA Chase	Charlie Cochrane
Karenna Colcroft	William Cooper	Michael G. Cornelius
Jamie Craig	Ethan Day	Diana DeRicci
Vivien Dean	Taylor V. Donovan	Theo Fenraven
S.J. Frost	Kimberly Gardner	Michael Gouda
Kaje Harper	Jan Irving	David Juhren
Thomas Kearnes	Kiernan Kelly	K-lee Klein
Geoffrey Knight	Christopher Koehler	Matthew Lang
J.L. Langley	Vincent Lardo	Anna Lee
Elizabeth Lister	Clare London	William Maltese
Z.A. Maxfield	Timothy McGivney	Tere Michaels
AKM Miles	Reiko Morgan	Jet Mykles
William Neale	Cherie Noel	Willa Okati
Brynn Paulin	Erica Pike	Neil S. Plakcy
Rick R. Reed	A.M. Riley	AJ Rose
George Seaton	Riley Shane	Jardonn Smith
DH Starr	Richard Stevenson	Liz Strange
Marshall Thornton	Lex Valentine	Haley Walsh
Mia Watts	Missy Welsh	Stevie Woods
Ian Young	Lance Zarimba	Mark Zubro

Check out titles, both available and forthcoming, at
www.mlrpress.com

To my beloved Samwise—thanks for all the years of unconditional love, and for inspiring Kimo and Mike to adopt Roby.

"Kanapa'aka, you and Donne are up," Lieutenant Sampson said, walking up to my desk in the Criminal Investigation division on the second floor of police headquarters in downtown Honolulu. He handed me a piece of paper with an address on Lopez Lane, in the shadow of the H1 Freeway. "Home invasion robbery-homicide."

His polo shirt that morning was a shade of emerald green that reminded me of *The Wizard of Oz*. Yeah, I'm a friend of Dorothy, and proud of it, though it hasn't always been easy being the only openly gay detective in the Honolulu Police Department.

I took the paper from him and pushed my chair back. "Your turn to drive," I said to Ray Donne, my partner.

A blast of hot air assaulted us as we walked from the air-conditioned building into the garage. "Jesus, it's only ten o'clock," Ray said. "And it's March, for Christ's sake. Back in Philly I'd still be freezing my nuts off."

Ray was an island transplant, and even though he'd been in Hawai'i for nearly three years, he still had some of the wide-eyed innocence of your average tourist. "You and Mike do anything fun this weekend?" he asked, as we got into his Toyota Highlander SUV.

I loved the way Ray was so accepting of my relationship with Mike Riccardi. Around some cops I had to be careful not to say anything that could be construed as too gay—like mentioning my partner by name.

"We went out on my friend Levi's boat," I said. "He wanted to show off his latest investment, generating energy from wave power."

"That's pretty controversial, isn't it?" Ray asked, swinging out of the garage and onto South Beretania Street, narrowly avoiding a collision with a clueless tourist in a rented convertible.

"Especially for surfers, right?"

"Yeah." I'd been surfing since I was old enough to stand on a board, and I had a proprietary interest in the ocean and its ability to generate killer waves. "He makes a good argument—the waves are a regular source of power, and it can reduce our dependence on fossil fuels. I'm not convinced, but hey, he's dating one of my best friends." I stretched my legs and said, "How about you and Julie. You do anything?"

"Trying to make a baby. What can I say? It's a tough job, but somebody's got to do it."

Ray and Julie wanted to have kids. She had finished her MA in Pacific Island Studies the year before, and was slogging through the last courses for her PhD in geography, focused on the islands of the Pacific. They were hoping to start a family when she was working on her dissertation.

I laughed and said, "Better you than me, brah," and we joked around until we pulled up in front of a small bungalow with attached carport, painted a bright yellow, with red trim around the windows and doors. The house stood out in a row of drab single-story homes with peeling paint and overgrown postage-stamp sized yards.

I knew the neighborhood from my years driving a squad car. It was a mix of retired servicemen who had landed in the islands after Vietnam, recent immigrants from Asia living in multi-generational family groups, and long-time islanders in service jobs, often working two shifts just to make ends meet.

The responding patrol officer was Lidia Portuondo, a beat cop I've known for years. She was standing outside the house in the bright sunshine, next to her patrol car. A light breeze whipped the hem of the flowered muumuu worn by the heavyset *haole*, or white, woman she was talking to. The woman's miniature pinscher, on a red leash, yipped and jumped around in a frenzy as we got out of the SUV.

"This is Mrs. Robinson," Lidia said.

I smiled and Ray started whistling the Simon and Garfunkel

song. Lidia gave the woman our names, then stepped back.

I knelt down to pet the min pin. "And who's this?" I asked. He skittered back from me, sniffing nervously.

"This is Little Caesar," Mrs. Robinson said proudly.

"Like the pizza," Ray remarked.

She glared at him. "Like the emperor."

I motioned us all over to the shade of a big kiawe tree. "Were you the one who called the police?" I asked.

"I certainly did. I went out to get the paper this morning, and Little Caesar slipped between my feet. He knew something was wrong. He went right across the street and into the back yard."

I could see a hint of a smile playing on Lidia's face. She's a pretty haole woman in her early thirties, with dark hair pulled into a French twist. Her family went back to the original Portuguese immigrants from the island of Madeira, and when I looked at her I could see the no-nonsense attitude her ancestors must have had to survive in the fields.

"I ran after him," Mrs. Robinson said. "I don't like him to be out without a leash. You should see the way people drive around here."

I suppressed a chuckle at the picture of the tiny black dog with pointy ears racing across the street, the big woman in the flowered muumuu in hot pursuit.

"When I got to the back yard, I saw the sliding glass door to the lanai had been smashed. I grabbed Little Caesar and came right back here and called the police."

She shook her head. "This neighborhood is falling apart, between all the immigrants and the teenagers who run around in packs, their pants falling down. The police don't do anything to protect us. I don't know what I'd do without Little Caesar."

Lidia picked up the narrative. "I responded about half an hour ago. I rang the front bell of the home across the street and got no answer, so I walked around to the rear of the residence, where I observed the broken door Mrs. Robinson reported."

Ray was taking notes. "And then?"

"I looked in the door and saw a Caucasian woman in her early thirties lying on the living room floor. I entered the residence and established that she was no longer breathing and that there was no one else inside."

Mrs. Robinson gasped and tightened her hold on Little Caesar's leash. "This neighborhood just isn't safe anymore," she said. "My son wants me to move out to Mililani where he lives."

"Thank you, Mrs. Robinson," I said. "I'm sure we'll have some questions for you in a little while. Can we find you across the street?"

She nodded, and tugged the dog's leash. "Mommy has a treat for Little Caesar, back at the house." The dog recognized the word 'treat,' and started jumping up and down again as she led him back to her house.

I turned to Lidia. "Lead the way."

We checked the front door and found it locked. The two living room windows were locked, too, and an air conditioner blocked the only other window on the street. Ray and Lidia went left, while I went right. When we met up in the back yard we compared notes. No signs of forced entry on either side.

A hibiscus hedge with yellow blossoms that matched the paint job marked the boundaries of the back yard, separating it from its neighbors, but there was no fence to keep out predators.

Lidia pointed at the smashed door and then stepped back. A metal lawn chair lay sideways on the small paved lanai next to the door; it looked like that was what had been used to break in. We stepped up and peered into the living room.

As Lidia had described, the body of a slim woman in her early thirties lay on the floor, curled into the fetal position, facing the windows. Her shoulder-length dark hair swirled on the carpet next to her, a single strand falling across her forehead. She wore an oversized UH Warriors T-shirt in dark green. It looked like she'd been stabbed, multiple times. Her blood had soaked into the faded beige carpet and dried the shirt to her skin in places.

The air inside felt almost as hot as it was outside as Ray and I stepped gingerly through the broken door. I'm no pathologist, but I've seen enough bodies to know that she had been dead for at least a couple of hours. The blood had settled toward the side of her body on the floor, and her skin was as pale as a TV vampire's. I phoned the ME's office while Ray called for a crime scene tech. Then we both put on rubber gloves to avoid contaminating the scene with our own prints.

Lidia stayed out front by her cruiser as we evaluated the house. The first thing we did was begin taking pictures, before we touched or moved anything, beginning with exterior shots of the lawn chair and the broken door.

The living room décor was a real contrast to the gruesomeness of the dead body on the floor. Kids' toys were scattered over the sofa and coffee table, and framed photos of two women and two small girls hung on the walls. One was the haole on the floor, though her brown hair was longer in the pictures and she had more of a tan. The other woman was somewhat slighter, most likely Chinese, with dark hair pulled back into a ponytail. The girls looked like they were a mix of both races.

In one of the photos, the haole woman was perched on a surfboard at Makapu'u Point, the lighthouse in the background of the shot. The picture had been taken with a telephoto lens, and the woman smiled exuberantly. Her evident happiness reminded me of how I felt when I was out on the water.

Somehow that made it worse, knowing that a fellow surfer had died.

At my friend Harry's urging I had bought a netbook a few weeks before, and started using it to keep my notes. When I finished photographing the scene and the victim, often at multiple angles and from wide to narrow shots, I popped the memory stick from the digital camera and plugged it into the netbook. I transferred the photos from the stick to the same folder I had created on the case, which would grow to hold my notes, as well as relevant websites, the autopsy report, copies of all the forms we had to fill out, and so on.

Once the crime scene was documented, Ray went right, toward the kitchen, and I went left, into the master bedroom. The walls had been painted with a beautiful seascape that stretched around the whole room. The artist had captured the sense of a beach at dawn, with a few shorebirds, a dolphin's fin just offshore, a couple of palm trees and lots of sand.

The room was dominated by a king-sized bed with a rattan frame. A duvet patterned with palm trees had been thrown off to the side. An old air conditioner, turned off, filled the window that faced the street.

The bureau drawers had been dumped out, their contents strewn across the floor. A jewelry box had been turned over on the bureau top. A couple of earrings and a pewter necklace lay next to it. I took photos of the disarray.

In one corner, a plain door had been laid on top of two low filing cabinets to form a desk. The drawers had been pulled out, and papers and manila folders were scattered on the floor. I glanced through the ones I could see without touching anything. Mostly paid bills and articles on childcare.

I went back into the hall and turned into the second bedroom, which had been painted with a mural of jungle animals and brightly colored tropical birds. Two tiny beds took up most of the room. They had both been made and piled with stuffed bears, lions, and other animals of indeterminate species. The closet was hung with shirts and pants in sizes that ranged from two to three years. The old-fashioned upright chest that held their other clothes had been turned over, all the tiny undershirts and panties dumped on the floor.

"Ray," I called. He was at the door of the small bedroom a moment later. "The little girls in those photos have been living here."

"Yeah. I found a bunch of kid food in the kitchen, little plates and silverware and stuff."

"But where are they? If they were here when their mother was attacked…"

Neither of us wanted to say out loud the gruesome possibilities. "But these beds haven't been slept in," Ray said. "Little kids like this, they'd have been in bed long before their mom would have gone to sleep." He shivered. "Reminds me of some fairy tale."

"One with an evil ogre," I said.

Ray's our expert on kid stuff; he grew up babysitting his little brothers and sisters. I was the youngest kid in my family and I was always too busy surfing or reading to worry about taking care of any neighbor kids.

Lidia appeared at the back door. "I called in for the home ownership records," she said. "Two women are co-owners. Anna Yang and Zoë Greenfield."

"Anything about two little girls?" I asked.

She shook her head. "Want me to check birth records?"

"Yeah, please. See if you can come up with anything that matches either woman."

She went back to her squad car and Ray asked, "So where are the kids? They've got to be priority one. Think we should call out a Maile alert?"

Back in 2002, after a little girl disappeared, the state set up a program to notify the public of an abducted child through radio and television bulletins and electronic highway billboards. "Let's see what we can find first," I said. "Maybe Anna Yang has the girls with her, and she's got a cell phone."

I wiped the sweat from my forehead. The ME's team arrived then, one male tech and one female, and we spent a couple of minutes with them. We couldn't turn the air conditioning in the bedroom on until the ME had finished with the body, because we didn't want to disturb the ambient temperature of the house, so we had to suffer with the heat and the humidity.

As soon as the ME's team was situated, I walked back into the bedroom, plugged the Bluetooth gizmo into my cell phone and called my best friend, Harry Ho. Harry can do the kind of computer searches in minutes that would take me a day, or take our police computer techs, who like their paperwork, even longer. I gave him Anna Yang's name and address. "Can you see if she's got a cell phone?"

"This is too easy." I heard Harry's fingers at his keyboard as Ray and I put on rubber gloves. We found a wallet in the bedroom debris; our deceased was Zoë Greenfield. There were more pictures of her, the Chinese woman, and the two kids in her wallet.

We sweated as we searched, stopping frequently to wipe our foreheads with paper towels. A couple of minutes into our search I heard Harry's voice in my ear. "Got a pen?"

"Better. Got the netbook." I picked out the number Harry read off to me on the keypad. "Thanks, brah."

I hung up and dialed the number Harry had given me. When a woman answered I asked, "Is this Anna Yang?"

"Who's this?" a woman asked, with a strong Chinese accent.

"My name is Kimo Kanapa'aka," I said. "I'm a police detective. Is this Ms. Yang?"

"Yes. Yes, that's me."

"Do you have the children with you?"

"Yes, it's my week. What is this about? Where's Zoë? Is she all right?

I gave Ray a thumbs up, and relaxed. It was good to know that the two little girls hadn't been kidnapped or killed. "I will tell you what I can, if you can just answer a few questions for me. Do you still reside at the house on Lopez Lane?"

"No. Can you please tell me what's going on?"

"I'm afraid Ms. Greenfield has been killed," I said. "Someone may have broken in during the night in a home invasion robbery."

"My God..." I heard her choke back a sob. "Who would do such a thing? Zoë is such a good person."

"I'd like to talk to you about her," I said. "Can I reach you at this number?"

"I have to see her. I'm coming right over." She ended the call before I could say anything else.

Ryan and Larry, two crime scene techs we often worked with, showed up to take fingerprints and look for trace evidence. Ray and I continued our search of the house, documenting everything we saw with notes and digital photos. There was no murder weapon evident, so I had the crime scene techs make sure to search the trash, inside and outside.

Ray and I could guess from the stab wounds that a knife had been used to kill Zoë Greenfield, so we inventoried all the knives in the household, then looked for evidence that might tell us more of what happened that night. Had the deceased eaten dinner at home? An empty microwave popcorn bag, an open DVD case on the player, a pair of wine glasses or beer mugs—all those are clues that can explain a sequence of events resulting in murder. There was a single glass in the sink, with the residue of what smelled like iced tea, and the TV section from the *Star-Advertiser* was folded open to Sunday night.

As the female ME's tech bagged Zoë Greenfield's hands and feet, I asked if she had an idea of time of death. "Doc Takayama will have to tell you that."

The male tech said, "Given the temperature in here, I'd say you're looking at six to twelve hours ago." She glared at him. It was obvious she was new, because he added, "We can give them a window so they know where to get started."

Ryan, Larry, Ray and I were all dripping with sweat by then. Working around the body, they began taking samples from the carpet as Ray and I went into the kitchen to consider.

Six to twelve hours before gave us a window of between 11 pm and 5 am the night before. "What do you think?" Ray asked. "She made herself a big glass of iced tea and settled down to watch TV in her T-shirt?"

"I think she must have finished her program, put the glass in the sink, and went to bed," I said. "She was either asleep or drowsing and she heard the door smash in."

"Why didn't she call 911, hide in the bathroom?"

I shrugged. "Who knows? Maybe she heard someone outside, went to the living room to check, and didn't have time to get away once the burglar broke the door in."

Lidia knocked on the front door. "Ms. Yang is here."

Behind her I saw the woman from the photos. She was smaller than I expected, barely five feet tall, in her early thirties, like Zoë Greenfield. She wore a dark sleeveless blouse that showed impressive muscles in her arms, and white shorts, with a tiny purse on a long strap over her shoulder. She tried to peer around Lidia into the house.

"Bring Ms. Yang to the back yard," I said. "We'll meet you there. I'd like her to identify the body."

We stepped back out through the broken door as Lidia led the woman around the corner. "Where's Zoë?" she demanded, her accent making the words sound harsher than I figured she intended. "I want to see her."

She moved quickly, darting to the broken door and looking in. "Oh, my God!" she said, and she burst into tears.

Lidia took her by the elbow and led her to the picnic table by the swing set. She fished a tissue from her pocket and gave it to the woman. I sat down across from her, Ray next to me, and I introduced us. "I'm sorry for your loss," I said. "Is the woman on the floor Zoë Greenfield?"

She nodded, dabbing at her face with the tissue.

"Can you tell us what your relationship was with Ms. Greenfield?"

"Zoë and I were partners for seven years," she said. "We met when I was starting my own business. She was doing some pro bono accounting work for an artists' cooperative that I belonged to. She helped me organize my books and set up a billing system." She spoke pretty well, but still had trouble with words like billing, which came out more like birring.

She blew her nose. "We were attracted to each other, and I moved into her condo. Three years ago, we decided we wanted children. Zoë was very businesslike about the whole thing. She found this house, and recruited a sperm donor, and she carried the twins. Their names are Sarah and Emily."

"Sweet names," I said. "But you're no longer together?"

"About a year ago, things started to go sour. Three months ago, Zoë finally decided it was over." Her speech was deteriorating the more upset she got, and the increased accent didn't make it easy to understand her.

Ray asked, "Can I get you some water? Iced tea?"

"Tea," she said. "There's always a pitcher in the refrigerator."

She crumpled the tissue in her hands. "I don't know what I'm going to tell the girls. You don't have to call the state, do you? They're my girls, too. Not just Zoë's."

"Where are they now?" I asked.

"When we split up, I moved to an apartment above a restaurant in Chinatown. The woman next door is like my adopted grandmother, and she babysits for us."

"The girls are with her?"

She nodded. "As soon as you called me, I took them next door and came right over here." She started to cry again. "They're so little. How do I tell them that Mommy Zoë is dead?"

Ray returned with the iced tea, and after she had a good long drink, she continued. "The girls are always our first priority," she said. "On her weeks, she drops them off on her way to work. I work out of my apartment, so I have them with me more during the day—but sometimes I go to the gym, or work on site for a client, painting murals. My grandmother takes care of them then, too."

I realized she had probably painted the murals in the house, and admired her talent. She looked like she went to the gym pretty often—she had a slim, sturdy frame, and strong arms. "So Ms. Greenfield was alone here at the house?"

She nodded. "When did this happen?"

"We'll have to wait for the medical examiner's report to know for sure." I hesitated. "But it appears Ms. Greenfield was killed between six and twelve hours ago. So sometime Sunday night." I looked at her. "Can you tell us where you were at that time?"

"Home. With the girls. I'd never leave them alone in the middle of the night, and I couldn't ask my grandmother to look after them so late." She looked straight at me. "We knew that the neighborhood wasn't completely safe, but we never imagined something like this could happen. When we bought the house, it was all we could afford. Zoë made a good salary, but my income went up and down."

That wasn't much of an alibi. Anna Yang had a motive, and with those strong arms she had the means to stab her ex. A knife was a woman's weapon, and there was a lot of passion in the number of stab wounds. But it was way too early to jump to any conclusions.

"Was there anything valuable in the house?" I asked. "Something someone could have targeted?"

She shook her head. "Nothing a thief would have wanted. But Zoë did have some nice jewelry, including a couple of Chinese pieces handed down from her family. Her great-grandfather, I think it was, did some business in the China trade, a hundred years ago. There was one special piece, though, a gold dragon pendant."

"I didn't see anything like that in the house. Can you describe it? We can put an alert out to the pawn shops."

"I can draw it for you." She pulled a piece of paper and a stub of a pencil from her tiny pocketbook and started to sketch. As I watched her, I remembered the case that had dragged me out of the closet, a few years before. The couple there had been male—one Chinese, the other haole, and I knew that part of the attraction between them had been that difference in races. Among gay men, a haole who likes Asian men is called a rice queen. I wondered if her family history and the jewelry she possessed made Zoë Greenfield the female equivalent of that term—and if it mattered to the case at all.

Looking at the page upside down, I saw the dragon take shape, in quick, sure movements. Anna's jaw was set, and her dark eyes focused on the page.

When she had finished, she drew thin lines to the eyes—rubies—and the claws—jade. At the bottom she noted that the jade on the dragon's hind claw had a tiny chip in it. She passed the picture over to me.

"Beautiful." I pulled out my camera and snapped a picture of it to add to the file. "The pendant—and the drawing."

She smiled.

"You keep cash in the house?"

That turned the smile into a laugh, which turned to tears and a hiccup. "We never had had more than a hundred dollars at a time, and that was spent almost as soon as we had it."

"How about appliances? Big-screen TV? Computer?"

"Zoë had a laptop. She kept it on the desk in the bedroom."

"That's gone," I said. "Do you think you could take a look around the house with us, tell us if there's anything else you can see missing?"

From my place at the picnic table, I looked across the small yard and through the glass doors. The ME's team had loaded Zoë Greenfield into a body bag and were lifting her onto a gurney. We gave them a couple of minutes to get out the front before we stood up.

"Are you still the co-owner of the house?" I asked. "We can give you the name of a company to replace the broken door. And then you'll need a cleaning company in here. I'm afraid it's going to get messier before it gets better. The crime scene techs will be dusting for fingerprints, and that gets dirty."

Anna Yang was still in shock, but she nodded. I turned the air conditioner in the bedroom up to high, but it wasn't much use, especially with the living room door busted open. Ray and

I walked her through the house, starting with the carport, but it didn't look like much of value had been stolen beyond the dragon pendant and a few other pieces of jewelry.

"Who would do this?" Anna was crying again, as we stood in the master bedroom and looked at the debris.

"Ice addicts often just look for a house to burglarize," Ray said. "Where no one's home, or maybe just one person. They aren't the most organized criminals."

We led her back to the kitchen, where we sat down at the table. "Did Ms. Greenfield have next of kin you would like us to contact?" I asked.

"She wasn't close to her family. Her parents are old hippies, and she grew up in a commune in northern California, near Mendocino. When she decided to study accounting in college, they looked at her like she was some kind of mutant."

That was a new one for me; when I met a gay or lesbian person who was estranged from family members, it had always been over sexual orientation. I guess there was no end of the ways that people could become estranged from each other. Anna found Zoë's address book and we copied out her parents' phone number.

I hesitated, trying to figure out the best way to ask what I needed to. I always try to bend over backwards when I deal with GLBT couples to respect their relationship. Though Zoë and Anna had broken up, they shared the two children, and a history. Finally I just plunged in. "Who'll be responsible for the burial arrangements?" I asked. "Will that be you, or her family?"

"I'll do whatever her parents want." Anna pulled her tissue out and blew her nose. "If they want me to bury her, I will. But if they want to take her home, I won't argue with them."

While I waited for her to gather herself, I pulled out my netbook and took notes on everything she had said. When Anna had recovered, I asked, "Where did Ms. Greenfield work?"

"For the state," Anna said. She fished in her purse and pulled out a leather wallet. "Here's her business card."

I put it down on the picnic table and snapped a picture of it. According to the card, Zoë Greenfield was an assistant director of audit for the Department of Business, Economic Development and Tourism. "We'll call down there," I said. "Is there anyone else you think we should talk to? A friend, perhaps?"

"A friend? But why? Wasn't this a robbery?"

"Burglary," I said. "But we have to look at all the angles. Someone could have been harassing her, for example. Or maybe she was frightened of someone."

"Zoë wasn't a friendly person. She said that there was never any privacy, never a place she could just go to be on her own when she was growing up in the commune. When she got to be an adult, that's all she wanted—time for herself."

"Tough to be in a relationship when you feel that way." I thought of Mike and me. We both liked our space, and it had been difficult for us at first, when we moved in together. I wanted to do the things I always had—surfing, reading, jogging, and so on. Mike preferred to veg out in front of the TV set; he needed to decompress from the stress of working in the fire department. We were still working those problems out, though in the eight months we had been living together things had gotten easier.

"You know how they say opposites attract," Anna said. "I think deep down, Zoë was more attracted to her parents' lifestyle than she was willing to admit. She liked that I was artistic, that the way I looked at the world was so different from hers. And I need a lot of time on my own, to paint. That suited Zoë just fine."

"Did Ms. Greenfield have a cell phone? Because we didn't find one in the house."

"She did. We called each other all the time about the girls."

"I guess it was stolen, then. I'm sure we'll have more questions for you once we have a better idea of what happened here."

She nodded as she folded her wallet and put it back in her purse. "I don't know what I'm going to tell the girls. They're so young." Before she left, she called the glass company and arranged to have the broken door boarded up.

Ryan and Larry were still working; they'd picked up some fibers from Zoë's body that might have come from her assailant's clothing, as well as some dirt on the floor. Everything had to be separately packaged and taken back to the lab for further analysis.

It was high noon by the time Ray and I started canvassing the neighborhood. Fortunately the breeze had brought some cloud cover, and that made it more comfortable to walk from house to house. Because of our geography, the island is full of microclimates—it can be sunny on Sand Island and showery at Schofield Barracks, windy in Waikiki, and dead calm in Kaneohe.

Most of the neighbors weren't home, but a plump young woman wearing a faded pink T-shirt that read SO MUCH TO DO, SO FEW PEOPLE TO DO IT FOR ME answered our knock next door. A small boy hid behind her legs.

Ray and I introduced ourselves. Her name was Hayley, and she was a stay-at-home mom. She looked like she had some Filipina in her, as well as some haole. "Is something wrong?" she asked.

"I'm afraid so," I said. "Did you see anyone come or go from the house next door this weekend?"

"I don't pay much attention. My little one keeps me busy most of the time. I used to swap babysitting sometimes with Anna, but then she and Zoë broke up and Anna moved out. Since then, I haven't seen or talked to Zoë."

She leaned down and picked up the boy, and swung him on to her hip. "She's not the friendliest person." She looked at us. "What happened?"

"Someone broke into the house over the weekend," I said. "That kind of thing been happening around her a lot lately?"

She frowned. "It's not a very nice neighborhood. Sometimes when I'm out walking the baby, I see homeless people on the bus benches. There's a girl down the street I'm sure is high most of the time. The house behind us was broken into about a year ago, and there's a house on the other street where the power was shut off on the people because they didn't pay. They trashed the house and then abandoned it."

She jiggled the boy on her hip, and he buried his head against her shoulder. He looked so sweet and happy that it touched my heart and I wondered for a moment if I would ever hold my own child like that. I saw Ray looking tenderly at the little boy, too.

Mike and I had talked once or twice about having kids, either adopting or donating sperm, but never seriously. Seeing the photos of Anna and Zoë's kids, and then Hayley's little boy, reminded me of those conversations, and I wondered if we should have another one soon.

Hayley patted her son on his back and said, "My husband and I are renting here, saving up money for our own house. But it's tough."

"I hear you," Ray said. "My wife and I are in the same position."

I was lucky that Mike already owned his half of the duplex he shared with his parents when I met him. I wasn't excited about living just a single wall away from my in-laws, especially when his father didn't like me, but I felt like a real grownup every time I pulled up in our driveway and walked up the walkway to our front door, where our dog was waiting to jump all over me.

None of the other neighbors we found had seen or heard anything unusual over the weekend, though a few mentioned break-ins in the neighborhood. We listened to Jake Shimabukuro's "Sand Channel" on our way back to headquarters, and the melancholy sound of his ukulele matched both our moods.

Our first step was to pull up records on past home invasions in the area. Our statistics are organized by beat, and the beat where Zoë lived had one of the highest rates of burglary, robbery and larceny in District 1.

As I'd pointed out to Anna, what had happened at the house on Lopez Lane was a burglary, not a robbery. The simplest way to break down the difference was to begin with theft – taking the property of another. That was the same as larceny.

When you add the threat of violence, you've moved up from theft to robbery. And when you enter a room or building with the intent to commit theft, that's burglary. So we had a homicide committed during the act of burglary at the residence on Lopez Lane.

All three crimes had been on the rise in the neighborhood where Zoë Greenfield lived, a group of small homes in the shadow of the H1 expressway. A simple check of real estate prices told me that it was a depressed neighborhood. Driving around it earlier in the day had confirmed that impression, and in areas that are plagued by poverty, crime rises. The criminal element takes on all the power, and the ordinary folks who live in the area pay the price. It's an unfortunate corollary to Darwin's laws of evolution. The strong survive and the weak suffer.

Part of the problem was political. The businesses and other large landholders in the area, like Honolulu Community College, got the attention, and the poor folks were overlooked.

Mike and I lived in Aiea Heights, a few exits down the highway from Lopez Lane, and farther from downtown. The property values were higher up there, but in the current economic climate, with people losing jobs and banks foreclosing on mortgages, nobody was safe from financial disaster. There was nothing to keep folks from poorer neighborhoods traveling a few miles to victimize ours—or our own neighbors from seeing us as prey.

I'd always felt safe there; the neighbors knew that Mike was a fireman and I was a cop. Anyone looking for a good mark might see that our house looked well-kept—but we had secured the property, and there were better pickings higher up on the hill. Nonetheless, the statistics were uncomfortable.

Could what had happened to Zoë Greenfield happen to us? Would I come home from a police conference, and find Mike dead in our living room? Or would we return from a getaway weekend on Maui to find our house ransacked, our dog lying dead on the floor? And what if we did have kids—I was sure I would always be worried about them, and their safety.

I remembered there was another set of parents involved in this case, and I picked up the phone to call Zoë Greenfield's, and let them know what had happened to their daughter.

The number I'd been given for Zoë's parents, in Mendocino, California, was some kind of community phone, and it took a few minutes for a woman to come on the line. "This is Sunshine," she said.

"Mrs. Greenfield?"

"You can call me that if you want. Who's this?"

I told her my name and rank. "I'm afraid I have some bad news for you. Your daughter Zoë died over the weekend." I explained that it appeared someone had broken into the home, possibly for the purpose of robbing it, and killed Zoë.

"We haven't been in touch with her for some time. She was still in Honolulu?"

"Yes. But the good news is that her daughters weren't in the house when she was killed."

"Daughters? Plural?"

"Yes. I thought they were twins?"

"I didn't even know she had children. How old are they?"

I had to call over to Ray and then come back to her. "They're two years old," I said. "Sarah and Emily."

"Sarah," she said. "That was my name, once. A long time ago. Are they with their father?"

"Zoë was involved with a female partner at the time the twins were born," I said. "Although they aren't together any more, they shared custody of the girls, and right now they're with her."

The news that her daughter had been in a lesbian relationship didn't seem to bother Sunshine, and I wondered if perhaps I had hit her with so much that she wasn't processing it all. Or maybe she had always known that her daughter was gay. In any case, I found her lack of emotion troubling. But there was no way she could have killed her daughter in Honolulu and made it back to northern California, where the nearest airport was hours away.

She sighed. "When Zoë left for college, she left her family behind. We disagreed on just about everything—politics, economics, the way we eat and the way we dress. Zoë chose to buy into the business and government power structure, which my husband and I rejected. But even so, we would have gone to her graduation, if she'd told us about it."

So the roots of Zoë's problems with her parents ran deep. It was interesting to see the ways in which parents exerted power, in small and large ways. You have to eat your vegetables. You have to go to school. All that. But there are more subtle ways in which parents control their kids.

Mine made me, and my brothers, go to Hawaiian school, where we learned bits and pieces of the language and culture. By the time I was thirteen I could repair an outrigger canoe, speak enough Hawaiian that it became a code with my friends, pound out a couple of rhythms on an *ipu* gourd, and weave a decent *lauhala* mat to use when my dad dug an *imu* in the backyard to roast a pig.

I did all that because my parents made me. Of course, I rebelled in small ways, refusing to eat poi, sneaking out to go surfing when I was supposed to be doing homework, and so on. But when it counted—when I was dragged out of the closet and I needed their help and support—they were there for me.

"Ever since she was a little girl, Zoë was different," Sunshine said. "When she was six years old, she told us that she didn't want to be called Fallopian any more. She picked the name Zoë out of a book."

I couldn't blame her. What little girl wants to be named after a part of her mother's reproductive system? "We let her be the person she wanted to be," Sunshine continued. "Even if she disagreed with us. We wouldn't buy her dolls, you see, because they perpetuate unreasonable stereotypes of women. So she used to collect broken or discarded ones from the trash. One of her Barbies had no legs, so Zoë announced that she was a paraplegic. Her brother Vas built her a little wheelchair."

It was always tough to learn about homicide victims, to see them as real people, as their families and friends did, because it made the tragedy of their deaths that much stronger. "She was a tough girl," Sunshine said. "If someone broke into her house, I'm not surprised Zoë would stand up and fight."

I told Sunshine I was sorry once again, and gave her the medical examiner's phone number so that they could make the burial arrangements. "If you'd rather not be involved, her ex will handle things."

"Colorado and I will take care of our daughter," she said, and that was the only time I heard some real emotion in her voice.

While I was on the phone with Sunshine Greenfield, Ray faxed the picture of the dragon pendant to all the local pawn shops. Then we started reading through cases in the neighborhood around Zoë's house, and in the adjacent areas, looking for patterns. We pulled up records on those accused of similar crimes, checking to see whether they were incarcerated.

The department kept detailed crime statistics, divided first between violent crime: murder, rape, robbery and aggravated assault; and property crimes: burglary, larceny-theft and motor vehicle theft. Since the crime at Zoë Greenfield's home fit into both categories, we had a lot of files to look at. They were further divided by adults and juveniles, and since we had no idea who our perpetrator was, we had to look at them all.

It was slow, dogged police work. Fortunately most of the records we were searching were online—but even then, we were hampered by the slowness of our city-provided computers and the network in general. We did find one good suspect: a seventeen-year-old named Ryan Tazo who had been picked up a couple of times for theft at Honolulu Community College, a branch of the state university system. He lived near the house on Lopez Lane.

Just before our shift ended at three, we met with Lieutenant Sampson. "Where are you on this home invasion?" he asked, as we stood in his office doorway like a couple of misbehaving schoolboys.

"We've got one lead," I said. "A teenager with a sheet for breaking into offices at HCC."

"We should go over to her office, too," Ray said. "See if anyone there had a beef with her."

"This sounds more like a crime of opportunity," Sampson said. "I can authorize you a couple of hours overtime this afternoon, but save looking into the victim's personal life until you've exhausted your leads."

Ray was glad; he was always happy to pick up some extra cash that could go in the new house kitty. I would have preferred to go home and relax.

We left Sampson's office and drove to the crappy little house where Ryan Tazo lived with his mom and grandmother. He was asleep when we arrived; his mother said he was working a night shift at the Denny's in Waikiki as a dishwasher. She woke him up and he came out to the living room where we were sitting, having resisted Denise Tazo's offers of something to eat or drink.

Ryan was about six-five, skinny as a palm tree, with a bushy dark blond afro. Denise was haole, but Ryan's dad was probably black; his skin was a *café au lait*, and his palms were noticeably lighter than the rest of his body. "I been straight, man," he said, after we'd introduced ourselves and asked what he'd been up to lately. "I work, I play video games, I stay out of trouble."

"I resent the fact that you suspect my son," Denise Tazo said. She was a heavyset bleached blonde in her early forties. "He's a good boy. He just got into a little trouble. But he's over that." She reached out and squeezed his hand, and he pulled away from her as soon as he could.

"Where were you Sunday night?" I asked.

"At work. You can check my time card. I clock in at eleven, and I didn't leave til my shift was over the next morning. Seven a.m."

I added the information to the file on my netbook, including his supervisor's name. "They watch you like a hawk there," he said. "There's always dishes to wash, and if you hang out too long smoking a cigarette or in the john, they start to pile up."

"You have a car?" I asked.

He shook his head. "I take the bus right now. But I work there long enough, I get a raise, and I can start saving up for a Camaro."

That seemed to let him out, assuming his time card proved what he said. It was unlikely that he'd have been able to sneak away from work, get a bus back up to Lopez Lane, and kill Zoë Greenfield without being noticed.

We stood up. "Thanks for your help. Good luck with the car."

We had a couple of other leads to follow, but none of them panned out. One guy with a rap sheet for breaking and entering was dead, and another was in Halawa State Prison. "All the good crooks are gone," Ray said, shaking his head. "What are we going to do?"

I dropped Ray off at headquarters, and drove home tired and cranky, switching out Jake Shimabukuro for Fiji and the upbeat tempo of "Stone Cold in Love with You." Once I opened the front door, I was attacked by Roby, the golden retriever Mike and I had adopted when his family was displaced by a fire and couldn't keep him. He was happy to see me, jumping up and down like a demented kangaroo, twirling around trying to grab his blonde plume of a tail. I clipped his leash on and we went for a walk.

Cruising around the neighborhood, I looked at each house we passed as a potential burglary target. The house next to ours had a column of glass squares next to the front door. Even though they had a burglar alarm, you could look through the glass and see if the system had been armed or not, and if not, all you had to do was knock out one of the glass squares, reach in and flip the lock.

The landscaping on the house across the street was overgrown, providing lots of cover for someone hiding there, waiting to attack the homeowner as he opened the front door. The garage door was open at the house on the corner, but there were no cars in the driveway and the house looked empty.

So many houses had no exterior lights, front doors without peepholes, or open windows. You wouldn't need to slam an aluminum chair into a sliding glass door to break into most of them.

At least our house was secure. We had a motion sensor light on the garage, a dog who barked when anyone got close, and a working burglar alarm. Because Mike was a fireman, he made sure there were no bushes close to the house that could catch fire during a dry season, so there wasn't anywhere convenient for a burglar to hide.

Walking around as evening fell, I saw lots of kids out playing in the street, and remembered the games I'd played – tag, it, Mother May I, kickball and so on. It was always the biggest thrill when one of my older brothers would come out and play, too.

I had a ton of cousins, on both sides of the family, and I always felt secure in the middle of my family. But my brothers were both finished having kids, and if Mike and I did have a child, he or she would be the youngest cousin. Could the two of us give a kid the kind of life both of us had enjoyed? Sure, we made enough money. But we both had demanding jobs that took a lot of time.

My mother had helped my father with his business, but she'd always been home when I came back from school, helping me with my homework, fixing dinner, keeping the household running. Mike's mom was a nurse, but she'd only worked half shifts while he was a kid. I didn't see either of us doing that.

By the time Roby had finished his sniff and pee survey of the neighborhood, and I'd depressed myself even further, Mike was home, with a bucket of fried chicken and biscuits. "That stuff is so bad for you," I said, as soon as I walked in and smelled the rich aroma.

Roby, the traitor, went right to Mike, sitting on his haunches next to Mike's place at the table. Mike pulled off a piece of chicken and fed it to him.

"I told you not to feed the dog people food," I said.

"Good evening to you, too. Who stuck a baseball bat up your ass?" He'd stripped down to a pair of shorts when he got home, and I was struck, as I often was, by how handsome he was. Six-four, with wavy dark hair, a black mustache, and eyes that sparkled when he wasn't crabby. His looks weren't perfect; his nose hooked down at the end, his eyebrows were bushy, and at 35, little tufts of hair were already growing out of his ears. But none of those mattered to me; when I looked at him all I saw was the man I loved.

I blew a breath out, and sat down next to him. "Sorry. Bad day. Home invasion that ended in a homicide—a lesbian mom with two little girls. At least the kids weren't home when it happened. But it made me think about how safe—or unsafe—we are up here." I didn't say I was thinking about kids, too; I'd save that for a quieter time.

"You can't let the job get to you," Mike said, gnawing on a chicken wing. "You know that."

"I know."

I reached for a piece of chicken but Mike swatted my hand away. "I thought this stuff is so bad for you."

"Yeah, but I'm hungry."

"Well, wash your hands first."

"Yes, Dad."

Welcome to life at our household. Mike and I battled frequently, each of us trying to get the upper hand. Maybe it was testosterone, or maybe sheer orneriness. Or maybe I'd picked Mike because I could repeat some power play with my father, try and change some old grievances.

We ate dinner, talked about our days, and watched some TV. But around eleven, when I took Roby out for a quick pee before bed, I remembered Zoë Greenfield's death as I looked at all the houses without outside lights, at how easy it would be to sneak up on any of us.

The only way to feel better, I knew, was to find the mokes, our homegrown name for tough guys, who had broken into Zoë's house, ransacked it and killed her. Then, maybe, I'd worry a bit less.

Only a bit, though.

The next morning, I retrieved the Honolulu *Star-Advertiser* from the driveway when I returned from walking Roby. I paged through, scanning articles with only the slightest interest, until I came to a brief article about a woman's death in a home invasion robbery. She wasn't named in the paper; our public information officer regularly withholds that information until given the go-ahead by the investigating officers.

The police blotter stories were compiled by Greg Oshiro, the reporter who covered law enforcement for the *Star-Advertiser*. Usually he was all over Ray and me when we had homicide cases, always hoping that there would be something sensational in the crime that would elevate his position at the paper. Like most newsgathering organizations, the *Star-Advertiser* was teetering on the brink of economic trouble, always threatening layoffs and cutbacks.

I wondered why Greg hadn't already called Ray and me about Zoë Greenfield's murder, looking for something he could make a story out of. A young mother had been cut down in her prime, and if he could get hold of pictures of the little girls then heart strings would be tugged all over the island. He could flesh the story out with statistics, especially the ones I'd seen the day before that showed crime escalating in the area around Lopez Lane, the rates rising on robbery, burglary and homicide.

I pulled up the *Star-Advertiser's* website on the netbook and copied the article into a file for the folder on Zoë Greenfield's murder.

When I got to headquarters, Ray and I sat down to brainstorm leads. Beyond Ryan Tazo and those two guys we'd eliminated the day before, our search through case histories had come up empty. Every moke with a record for that type of home invasion was either dead or in jail on other charges. I leaned back in my chair. "We must be doing something right. Putting the bad guys behind bars."

"There are always new ones." Ray was leaning toward the crime being drug-related; the frenzy of stab wounds in Zoë's body implied, to him at least, that the assailant had been high, or desperate for a fix. "How about if we expand our search area? Look at Waikiki, for example. Lots of mokes hang out there to prey on tourists."

"We could do that." I pulled up a few cases, and Ray did the same, and we started reading. "Hey, here's a familiar name," I said, about an hour later. "Judy Evangelista."

Judy was a tita, a tough girl, a sometime hooker, sometime pickpocket, and could usually be found hanging around Waikiki. We'd picked her up on an assault charge soon after Ray became my partner, and we discovered she was the kind of girl who knew the Honolulu underworld and worked it to her advantage. It was easy to consider that she might know of someone breaking into houses in Zoë's neighborhood.

We got into my Jeep, opened the flaps, and started cruising. It was sunny, with a scallop of cirrus clouds across the sky, and as we passed Ala Wai Beach Park there was a line of cars waiting to turn in, tourists heading out for sport-fishing or ready to lobster up on the sand. I had the "Island Warriors" CD of Jawaiian music playing, our home grown mix of ukulele and reggae rhythm, and it felt like a day we were going to make some progress.

We crossed the Ala Wai Canal into Waikiki and it felt like coming home. I had lived on Lili'uokalani Street, patrolled the neighborhood as a beat cop, and also, for a brief time, been assigned to the Waikiki station as a detective. I knew where the mokes and titas lurked, in the shadowy places tourists should avoid. Someone had scrawled HELP WANTED, TELEPATH. YOU KNOW WHERE TO APPLY on the side wall of a convenience store.

A couple of blocks later I swung onto Kalakaua Avenue and we started looking for Judy. We spotted her as we were entering the hotel district, near the recently renovated Royal Hawaiian. I was sure they appreciated having her hang around outside the hotel, in her low-riding jeans, midriff-baring white t-shirt, and multiple heavy stainless steel chains around her neck.

She was leaning against a palm tree, smoking a cigarette. "Hey, Judy," Ray called, leaning out the Jeep's window.

Her hair was a bottle blonde, and I could see the dark roots starting to show. I thought that the shark tattoo above her belly button was new. "Aren't you guys out of your native habitat?" she said. "You got nothing to do downtown, you gotta come over to Waikiki and harass innocent people?"

I slid the Jeep up next to a fire hydrant, put on my flashers, and Ray and I got out.

"Now, is that the way to greet a couple of old pals?" Ray asked. "We came all the way over here to see you."

She took a long drag from her cigarette. "I ain't been in trouble in ages."

I leaned back against the Jeep. "We're not looking to bust you, Judy. We're looking for information. You know anybody who breaks into houses?"

"What's in it for me?"

I always kept a few fifty-dollar bills in the back of my wallet for such occasions. I keep a log and periodically put in requests for reimbursement from the department's petty cash fund. I pulled one out and Judy frowned. "Houses where? Round here?"

"Over around the Kapalama Canal," I said. "Between there and the H1."

She took the fifty from my fingers, folded it, and stuck it into the pocket of her jeans. "I'll ask around. You still got the same cell number?"

"You have me in your favorites?" I asked. "I'm touched."

"Touch this." She grabbed her crotch.

"No thanks. You know I don't go there."

We got back into the Jeep, and I made a note for the folder of the fifty I'd given Judy.

The Department of Business, Economic Development and

Tourism was housed in one of the high-rise buildings near the Iolani Palace. Ray and I showed our ID to the receptionist, and asked to speak to Zoë's boss. She had to look Zoë up in a directory, and then work backwards to figure out who she reported to. Her phone kept ringing, though, and so it took her a few minutes. "She was in the energy office," she said finally. "That would be Mr. Nishimura. I'll call him."

Nishimura, a tall, stoop-shouldered Nisei, came out to the reception area a few minutes later. "This is about Zoë Greenfield?" he asked.

"It is. Can we speak with you somewhere private?"

He nodded, and led us back through a series of hallways to a small windowless office where there was just room enough for a pair of metal visitors' chairs. He sat behind his desk, which was piled with manila file folders and random office supplies, as well as a computer monitor that had to be at least ten years old.

"I read about Zoë's murder in the paper. Someone broke into her house?"

"On Saturday night," I said. "When was the last time you spoke to her?"

"It must have been Friday afternoon. She didn't come to work on Monday, and she didn't call in. She's always been a very conscientious employee. But she didn't return any phone calls and I didn't know what else to do." He motioned at the pile of folders on his desk. "We're running short handed here as it is. I just didn't have the time to go searching for her."

"What is it that you do here?" I asked. "Or rather, what did Zoë do?"

"As you saw out front, we're a division of the Department of Business, Economic Development and Tourism, which collects and analyzes economic development statistics. Our focus here is on energy policy and analysis. Did you know that Hawaii is the most oil-dependent of all the fifty states?"

We both shook our heads.

"Ninety percent of our energy needs are supplied by imported petroleum. Given the current political climate worldwide, it's important for us to do what we can to reduce that dependency. Zoë worked on alternative energy sources—administering grants, compiling statistics, making recommendations."

I remembered the boat trip Mike and I had taken on Levi Hirsh's boat, when Levi had been pointing out his investment in harnessing the ocean's waves. "Wind power, ocean power, that kind of thing?" I asked.

He nodded. "We have a mandate to supply 70% of Hawaii's energy demand with renewable resources by 2030. We're working with researchers at UH, and with private industry, to develop biomass, hydroelectric power, solar power, anything we can. Zoë reviewed budgets in the hundreds of millions of dollars."

"Do you know if she received any threats as a part of her work?" I asked.

"Threats?" Nishimura almost laughed. "Detective, we're accountants. Yes, we work with a lot of money—but there are so many checks and balances, so much bureaucracy, that one person couldn't do much to favor one group over another. There's some subtle influence peddling, of course; you're going to get that in any agency. But threats? No."

"How about in her personal life? Do you know if she was dating anyone?"

"Zoë worked for me, so we kept our relationship on a professional basis," he said. "But she might have talked to one of the other analysts, or one of the support staff." He picked up the phone. "I'll get my admin to ask around for you."

I held up my hand. "If you don't mind, we'd rather ask ourselves."

He put the receiver back down. "Of course. If there's anything we can do…"

"We'll need to look at her office as well."

Nishimura introduced us to his administrative assistant, a

Chinese woman in her mid-fifties, with the kind of no-nonsense attitude that reminded me of Juanita Lum, the admin for Lieutenant Kee in Vice. Though Kee was the guy with the gold braid on his shoulders, she was the one who ran the department.

"Zoë was a quiet girl," she said. Her name plate read Gladys Yuu. "She kept to herself. But then, most of these accountants are like that. More comfortable with numbers than people." She pursed her lips for a minute. "There's a girl in the statistics department. Miriam Rose. They had lunch together sometimes." Her face softened. "You don't think it was just a terrible accident—some burglary gone wrong?"

"We're looking into everything. So anything you know about her, or her life, might help us."

She thought for a minute. "Well, there is one thing. I didn't approve, but of course, it's not my place to say." She hesitated, then gave in to her impulse. "I'm not a nosy person, you understand, but I like to know what's going on in the department. It helps Mr. Nishimura to have someone like me around."

"I'm sure," I said. "When I was a kid, my mom used to help out in my dad's business. And she was always the one who kept track of him and the other guys."

She smiled. "Then you understand. One of Zoë's jobs was to monitor contracts and grants. Though she wasn't the friendliest person, she did get to know the people at the various companies." She lowered her voice. "I understand she got one of them to hire a friend of hers."

"What company would that be?"

"A Chinese firm. I have a card here." She opened her desk and pulled out a vinyl storage book for business cards. After flipping through a few pages, she drew one out of its plastic holder. The front of the card was in English, the back in Chinese ideograms.

The company name was Néng Yuán, which didn't tell me much, though the logo was a stylized wave. The president's name was Xiao Zenshen. "You know anything about them?" I asked.

Gladys turned to her computer and started typing. "They

have a grant from the state to explore wave power," she said. The boat trip with Levi Hirsch came to my mind again. It looked like I was going to be calling him. That was okay; he was dating Terri Clark Gonsalves, my best gal pal from high school, and Mike and I often double-dated with them.

Gladys looked up. "The rest of this is pretty scientific. I'm afraid I don't understand much of it. I can print it out for you, though."

She hit a couple of keys and the printer behind her desk came to life. "Do you know the name of the friend she got hired there?" I asked.

Gladys shook her head. "It was just something I overheard. But Miriam might know more."

We took the printout from Gladys, and she led us back through the maze of corridors and introduced us to Miriam Rose. She was a young Filipina, probably late twenties, in a white blouse with a floral print wrap skirt. Big round sunglasses were propped on her head, and she had a red silk rose pinned to the right shoulder of her blouse.

Gladys introduced us. I could see she wanted to stick around and hear what Miriam had to say, but I smiled and thanked her for her help, and said we'd be back to her if we needed anything further.

Miriam worked at a tiny cubicle, just big enough for a worktable and a rolling chair. The walls were plastered with photos of what looked like her family – middle-aged parents, Miriam, a younger sister and an even younger brother. She was a cat lover, too; there were pictures of a fat calico sunning on a white sofa, Miriam holding the cat, the cat playing with her brother and sister.

She smiled at Ray and I could tell from the way she held his hand a little longer than she held mine that he was the best one to take lead. "Is there someplace we can talk?" he asked her.

She led us down the hall to a small lunchroom that smelled of stale coffee. "Sorry," she said, lifting the glass pot off its warming stand. "Somebody always leaves the coffee to burn." She began cleaning the pot. "I was so upset when I heard about Zoë. We were friends—well, not out-of-work friends, or anything. Zoë was quiet. But we ate lunch together sometimes. We both like sushi, and we'd bring in different stuff for each other to try."

She filled the pot with water, ripped open a bag of coffee and poured it into the filter, then joined us at a round table.

"Did Zoë ever mention any problems she was having?" I asked. "Anyone threatening her, for example?"

"I got the feeling she was having problems with her ex," Miriam said. "She never came right out and said he was harassing her, but sometimes she'd get a call, and she'd be angry. I never asked about him, though."

And never knew that the ex was a woman, I figured. That's a big problem when you're investigating what happened to a person in the closet, whether gay or lesbian. They don't talk about their personal life at work, because they're always worried about using the wrong pronoun. So they say little or nothing, and then when you go to interview the co-workers, they're clueless.

Miriam didn't know anything else. She introduced us a couple of other co-workers, but none of them had anything to add. We handed cards around and asked them all to call if they thought of anything. Miriam took us back to Gladys, who showed us the cubicle where Zoë worked. There weren't any personal items there – not even snapshots of her daughters. It was sad.

Gladys promised to look through the things Zoë had been working on and let us know if there was anything that looked odd. "Miriam will help," she said.

We thanked them both, and Miriam led us back to the elevators. "I feel so bad for Zoë. I wish there was something I could do."

A scruffy guy with a t-shirt that read 'I said no to drugs, but they wouldn't listen' passed us as we walked back to where I'd parked the Jeep. It was clouding over, and a light breeze tossed the palm trees around us, skittering a paper cup down the street.

My stomach grumbled. "Lunch?" I asked.

"That sour coffee smell put me off my feed," Ray said. "But I guess I could eat."

We decided to get some lunch at a Zippy's down the street. It had stopped raining, but the sky was still full of heavy clouds. "I feel like trying something different," Ray said, as we stood in line.

"Mike loves the soup with *mandoo*—they're Korean dumplings, and the *kim chee* fried rice. He says it reminds him of stuff his grandmother made."

I preferred to stick with the old Hawaiian specialties my mother had made when I was a kid, stuff like *lau lau,* steamed packages of pork and fish, and *kalua* pig, baked in a traditional oven pit. Or chicken rolled in *mochiko* flour and fried, or sweet and sour spare ribs. But I'd been putting on a few pounds lately; I wasn't surfing nearly as much living with Mike up in Aiea Heights as I had when I lived on Waikiki. So I opted for the *somen* salad instead, skinny Japanese noodles like vermicelli over lettuce, eggs, *char siu* pork and imitation crab meat. I wasn't sure it was that much healthier, but it was a salad.

Ray decided not to experiment after all, and got a teriyaki burger with fries. The restaurant was crowded but we managed to squeeze into a side table. As we ate, I told Ray about Levi Hirsch and his interest in wave power. "I'm thinking maybe we call him and see what he knows about Néng Yuán before we go over there."

He agreed, so I flipped open my phone and found Levi's office number at Wave Power Technologies. The receptionist put me through to Levi, and he agreed we could stop by the office after lunch. "You're lucky you caught me here today. I'm heading to Idaho tomorrow."

"Idaho?" I asked. "You hungry for potatoes?"

"It's my daughter's spring break. We're going skiing in Squaw Valley. It'll be the first time Danny has seen snow."

Danny was Terri's son, and I was glad to see that things were moving forward between Levi and Terri well enough that the families were meshing.

When we got to his office, I showed him the paperwork Gladys Yuu had printed out for us and asked if he could interpret it. He put on a pair of horn-rimmed reading glasses and took a look at it.

"They're one of our competitors," he said, after reading through it. "There are lots of people looking for the magic ticket, and a bunch of different ways to approach harnessing wave power. Néng Yuán's approach is different from ours. I've heard that Dr. Zenshen really knows her stuff, but I don't understand all the tech stuff. I'm not even on the staff here; I'm just an angel investor and I help out where I can."

"Angel? Like with wings?" Ray asked.

Levi laughed. "It's a venture capital term. Angels rush in where mortals fear to tread. We get in on the ground floor with new businesses. Sometimes they pan out, sometimes they go bust. But if they make it big, the payoff can be huge."

"Huge enough to be a motive for murder?" I told him about Zoë Greenfield's death.

He frowned. "Can't say. Of course, there are millions of dollars floating around these days, even in tough economic times. Renewable energy is a buzz word, and there are foundation grants, corporate investments, and lots of greedy people trying to make a buck. I don't see how killing a mid-level government bureaucrat could benefit anybody, but I'll keep an ear to the ground for you."

The radio crackled as we were leaving Levi's office. Dispatch reported that a pawn shop in an industrial neighborhood out by the Aloha Stadium, just beyond Pearl Harbor, had responded to our bulletin about Zoë Greenfield's pendant.

After navigating the tourist-clogged streets of Waikiki, we picked up the H1 and headed *ewa*. We don't use directions like north, east, south and west on O'ahu; *makai* means towards the sea, while *mauka* is toward the mountains. Diamond Head is in the direction of the extinct volcano that towers over Waikiki, while *ewa* means the opposite way, toward the city of that name.

We pulled up a half hour later in front of Lucky Lou's. He ran a tourist trap operation out front, catching visitors on their way to Pearl Harbor with counterfeit Guccis and Cartiers, and rows of shiny gold chains that would turn your neck green about a day after you got home from your vacation. Around the back, there's another entrance for the pawn shop, and that's the one we took, scrambling to close the flaps on the Jeep and scurry inside as a light rain started to fall.

Lucky Lou was about three hundred pounds and balding, a crabby New Jersey transplant. "Hey, Lou," I said, making my way past racks of nearly new guitars, stereo equipment that would probably be warm to the touch, and cameras that troops from Schofield Barracks pawned to pay for working girls and their tender ministrations. "Let's see that pendant you got."

"I gotta tell you, it's expensive cooperating with the boys in blue," he said. "I gave out fifty bucks on this." He pulled a tray out of a glass-topped cabinet, and pawed through the earrings, chains and watches until he found the dragon pendant.

I unfolded the picture Anna Yang had drawn and compared the two. It was an excellent match, down to the chip in the dragon's hind claw. "Who brought this in?" I asked.

"Chinese lady, maybe fifty-something. Dressed nice. Said it had belonged to her grandmother, but her husband was out of work and they needed cash."

I looked at Ray. That didn't fit with our idea that Zoë

Greenfield's killer had been an ice addict. But it was a damn good lead, the first one we had. "You got information on her?" I asked.

He pulled out the pawn form, which listed her name and address. I copied it down. "If it turns out it's the wrong pendant, you'll get it back. Did she bring anything else in?"

Lou frowned. "Some crap. There wasn't much pawn value, so I bought it from her for the gold. But I don't know which pieces came from her—I just throw all that stuff into a box and eventually I sell it to a guy."

If the dragon pendant was a match, I figured that we could bring Anna Yang out to the pawnshop and have her look through Lou's box, though most likely we could make a case just from the pendant.

I looked at the information from the pawn slip the Chinese woman had left. "You know this address?" I asked Lou.

He shook his head. "The zip is 96817. That's Chinatown. May be some little alley."

I pulled up a mapping program on the netbook, but couldn't locate Yu Chun Street. So I called Mary Luo, a detective I knew who worked out of the Chinatown Substation, at the corner of Maunakea and North Hotel. She had been on bicycle detail there before getting her shield, so if anyone knew the back alleys she would.

"You know where Yu Chun Street is in Chinatown?" I asked.

"Spell it."

I did. Mary laughed. "I thought so. Yu Chun means silly or stupid in Chinese. Sounds like somebody gave you a fake address."

I thanked her, hung up, and turned back to Ray. "Curious. How did this woman get hold of Zoë Greenfield's pendant?" An idea flashed in my head. "Anna Yang said she's living next door to a Chinese woman who's like a grandmother to her. Maybe this was all a set-up—Anna killed Zoë and gave the pendant to grandma to pawn."

"We could interview the grandma and take a picture of her,

then show it to Lucky Lou," Ray said.

My phone rang. I looked at the display. "Well, what do you know. It's our reporter friend Greg Oshiro, grand pooh-bah of the fourth estate." I wasn't surprised to hear from him, but I did think it odd he'd waited so long to call.

Greg and I had worked well together for a couple of years, until I was dragged out of the closet. After that, Greg had turned as cold to me as a morning just before sunrise on Haleakala. It was Ray's contention that Greg was gay but closeted, leading him to envy me my freedom.

I doubted that, until a year before, when a guy Greg had slept with was murdered, and since then, he'd been carefully edging out of the closet and warming up to me. He'd come to our house a couple of times for parties, and while I wouldn't call us friends, our working relationship had improved.

"I need to talk to you about a case, Kimo," he said. He was breathless, as if he'd been running, though it was hard to imagine Greg, a slow, heavyset guy, moving too fast.

"Which one?"

"Zoë Greenfield."

"You know something about the case? Or you just looking for information?"

"I know something. I'm the father of her children."

Greg was agitated, but he had a doctor's appointment he couldn't cancel, so we agreed to meet at the Kope Bean coffee shop at the Central Pacific Bank just after three. "Poor guy," Ray said. "Were they friends, did he say?"

"He didn't get into much detail. And Anna Yang called him the sperm donor, so I'm not thinking they were best buddies."

"Still, it's got to be a shock."

"I wonder why he waited so long to call," I said. "I read about the murder in the paper this morning. If he knew Zoë Greenfield he should have been all over us for more information."

We went back out to the Jeep. "Should we interview the grandma?" I asked.

"Do we know her name?" Ray asked.

I looked back through the notes on my netbook. "Never got it. But I'm sure we'll be talking to Anna Yang again soon. Let's hold off on chasing down grandma until we know all the right questions to ask."

We returned to headquarters, where we sent the dragon pendant downstairs to be dusted for fingerprints, on the off chance that the thief might be in the system. I didn't hold much hope, though.

The ME's report came in. As expected, Zoë Greenfield had died from multiple stab wounds. The lesions were long and narrow, indicating a flat blade, and the width of the wounds suggested a double-edged blade. The characteristics of the gashes were similar enough that Doc Takayama established that the same or similar knife had been used for each of the cuts on Zoë's body.

I went back to our inventory of the kitchen. The evidence techs had identified and packaged every knife they found, though when they used the blue LED ultraviolet light none had traces of blood. But knives are often sold in sets, so there was a possibility that we could identify a weapon by figuring out which knife was missing.

No luck there. No two knives from the house on Lopez Lane matched each other. They looked like a typical collection of hand-me-downs and what was on sale at Sears or some other discount store. There was an 8" sushi knife, a santoku knife, a sort of narrow-bladed cleaver, a bread knife, and a couple of steak knives with serrated blades.

Zoë had been stabbed once in the fleshy place where her neck met her right shoulder, by a right-handed person of similar height. That was useful information, because it could help us build a case and establish a scenario once we had a suspect.

The knife had slid under her collarbone and then been withdrawn. Then she had turned or been turned, because the rest of the cuts were from the front. There were numerous shallow cuts on her hands, evidence that she had attempted to defend herself. The ultimate cause of her death was bleeding from several deep wounds in her lower chest, just below her rib cage.

It was always sad to read that kind of report, and then envision the process by which someone had died. It was all too easy to imagine Zoë's fear, her pain, her desperate attempt to protect herself.

But as a homicide detective, it's my job to put those emotions aside and concentrate on the facts. I scanned down the report, looking for additional information that might be useful.

"Listen to this," I said to Ray. "Her blood alcohol was .08."

He scooted his chair over to look at the report with me. "And that matters because …? She wasn't operating a motor vehicle at the time of her death."

I pulled out my notes from the scene. "No beer or wine bottles in the trash," I said. "There was a vodka bottle in the freezer, though no dirty glasses in the sink."

I flashed back to a time nearly two years before, when Mike and I had been estranged, when we were forced to work a case together. I picked up a water bottle he'd been drinking from, and discovered it was filled with vodka.

I shook that memory away. "I wonder if she did her drinking somewhere else."

"Perhaps with her assailant?"

"I think that's an interesting conjecture."

We looked at her stomach contents. There was ethanol present, the kind of alcohol in beer, wine and cocktails. Doc's tests couldn't tell exactly what kind of alcohol she'd had, but he could tell that her last meal had been sushi. The process of digesting food stops at death, so from the food there he could determine that she had eaten various types of seasoned raw fish and rice about six hours before her death.

That was a good lead. Since there was none of the residue you might expect in the trash if someone was preparing a meal at home, and no glassware used for drinking, we could assume that she had eaten out. "Any restaurant receipts in her purse?" Ray asked.

We looked at the reports from the evidence techs. There were several credit card receipts in a compartment of her wallet, but none from Sunday, and none from a sushi restaurant. "That would have been too easy," Ray said.

"We can still request a list of her charges from her credit card companies if we need to," I said. "See if she had a regular place she liked to go. Or we could just ask Anna Yang."

I started making a list of questions to ask Anna. We needed to know about Zoë's drinking habits, and if she had a favorite restaurant where she might have taken a date. If we couldn't get a good guess from Anna, we'd start at the closest restaurants and then radiate outward.

The next thing in the autopsy report was a surprise. Tests for acid phosphatase, an enzyme in semen, and P30, a semen-specific glycoprotein, revealed the presence of semen in her vaginal fluid. "Why would there be sperm in a lesbian's vagina?" I asked Ray. "Was she raped?"

Making the distinction between rape and consensual sex is often a tough call, particularly when the woman is dead and can't give us her side of the story. In that case, her corpse has to tell the tale.

A woman who is raped often scratches her assailant with her fingernails, and traces of the assailant's hair or blood can be found under her nails. Doc Takayama's report, though, showed no evidence of anything there.

He had looked for bruising that might indicate if the sex was consensual or not. Again, it's not a great indicator; the couple could simply have engaged in rough sex or playful fighting. In Zoë's case, though, there was no bruising other than what had occurred when she was assaulted and fell to the ground. There was no evidence in the vaginal area that might have indicated penetration without her consent.

Today's criminals watch the same TV shows the rest of the public does, and your average rapist often knows that his DNA can be found on the victim. Even so, the last statistic I read said that only fifteen to twenty percent of rapists use condoms to prevent the chance of leaving sperm behind.

In a corpse, sperm can live up to two weeks, but in a living woman, the vagina produces chemicals that destroy it. Since we'd found her body within hours after her death, the presence of viable sperm indicated that Zoë Greenfield had had consensual sex with a man within the past 72 hours. But it was tough to narrow the window any smaller. So she could have had sex Saturday night, and that might have had no connection with her Sunday dinner or the assault.

Investigating a homicide is like putting together a jigsaw puzzle with extra pieces. You find something that doesn't seem to fit—and sometimes it never does. But then again, sometimes that one awkward piece is the key to solving the whole puzzle.

"Did Anna Yang say anything about Zoë being bisexual?" Ray asked.

Because I'm openly gay, both in the department and in the

larger community, I hear things, and people tell me things, that a straight cop might not find out. But if Anna recognized me, she hadn't mentioned it, and she hadn't told me anything that she hadn't said in front of Ray.

"Nope. But at least in my experience, women's sexuality is more fluid than men. Women tend to fall in love with the person, rather than the parts. Look at Ellen Degeneres and Anne Heche. Or that woman, what's her name, Melissa Etheridge's ex, who went back to a man. Once a guy comes out, it's pretty unusual for him to go back to girls, but women seem to go back and forth more easily."

We looked through the autopsy report again, but there was nothing more to glean from it. We both sat back to consider.

"There are a lot of different ways this could have played out," I said.

Ray picked up his pen. "Well, let's start listing them. The most obvious answer is that she picked up a guy somewhere and things went sour." He leaned forward. "You used to date women, didn't you?"

"What does that have to do with this?"

"If you were to decide to start again," he said, "you might not be on your game, you know? Maybe you wouldn't read the girl's signals right, you wouldn't be able to tell if she was psycho or not."

"Trust me, I could tell if she was psycho."

"But maybe Zoë couldn't. Men and women are different, you know."

"Really?"

"If you could just listen for a minute, you might learn something." He sat back. "Say Zoë gets lonely, and she's thinking maybe she should see what it's like to be with a guy. You said women are more likely to go back and forth. She goes out to some singles bar, a place where they serve sushi, for example, and she picks a guy up."

"She brings him home," I continued. "They have sex. But in the middle of the night, she hears somebody in the living room, and it's the guy. He's looking for stuff to steal."

Ray got into it. "She confronts him, and he stabs her."

I shook my head. The story didn't add up. "If he's a casual trick, why didn't she make him use a condom? She wasn't stupid. She wouldn't want to catch anything from him."

"But what if she wanted another baby?"

"Then why not just get sperm from Greg Oshiro again? He's the father of the twins. And what about the knife? In your scenario, she discovers him trying to rip her off. But the robber would have to have heard her, and positioned himself to attack as Zoë entered the room."

"She was drunk, so she probably wasn't moving quietly," Ray said. "He heard her coming, and got the knife."

I tapped the case of the netbook, on the desk in front of me. "Why not just get out? Or why not just knock her out and run away? She didn't have much to steal. He must have seen that before they went to bed together."

I stood up and started pacing. "Suppose the guy was looking for her in that bar. He wanted her dead, for some reason. That would explain why he had the knife in hand when Zoë left the bedroom."

"It can't have been a casual meeting." Ray shook his head. "There would be no way to guarantee she'd be at a particular bar, that she wouldn't have the kids—too many factors."

"And we have to explain the broken sliding glass door. That implies intent, too. Unless our guy was so sharp that he knocked in the door after she was dead, to make it look like a break-in."

We went back and forth for an hour or more, trying out different theories, but we didn't have enough evidence to make any of them make sense. I called Anna Yang and left her a message, and then just before three, we headed to our meeting with Greg Oshiro. We saw him pacing back at forth at the corner of Richards and South King as we approached. The skies were gray and a cool breeze ruffled the tops of the palm trees. Traffic was heavy on South King, five lanes of tourist convertibles, delivery vans and the Waikiki Trolley moving along, so we couldn't cross until the light changed.

When we reached him, I could see that Greg was sweating heavily. He's at least fifty pounds overweight, most of it in his stomach, so it isn't unusual to see him perspiring in the Honolulu heat and humidity. But there was something more, as if he had a thousand watts of electricity flowing through his veins instead of blood.

"I took a couple of days off," he said as we reached him, not even bothering with hello. But that's Greg. "I didn't even know about Zoë until I checked in with the paper this morning." He looked accusingly at us. "Why didn't you call me right away?"

"Hold on, Greg," I said. "Calm down." There was a nice little park around the bandshell on the grounds of the Iolani Palace across the street, and I thought we'd be better off walking there. It didn't look like Greg needed caffeine.

The light had changed again, and we crossed and entered the park. In the background I heard bullhorns from some protest at the front of the palace. "Let's start from the beginning," I said. "You didn't write the police blotter in today's paper?"

He shook his head. "I told you. I took a couple of days off."

"Okay. And you know Zoë Greenfield how?"

He glared.

"Yes, you told me, you're the father of the two girls. But how did that all come about?"

We walked under the trees as Greg spoke. "I'm an only child, and I wanted to give my parents grandchildren," he said. "But I knew it wasn't feasible for me to do it on my own. I work crazy hours, I'm always digging around for a story. Then there was a robbery at this artists' collective where Anna used to have space, and I interviewed her about it. We got to talking, and she invited me to come back and see some of her work on exhibit the next week."

He was starting to calm down. "I loved her work, and I bought one of her paintings. The beach at Makapu'u Point, with Rabbit Island in the background. I just look at it and it relaxes me."

Ray and I just nodded, not wanting to interrupt his flow.

"A couple of months later, I ran into her at a party. She was with Zoë, and we got to talking. They were looking for a sperm donor, and Zoë was going to carry the kids. They wanted an Asian guy so that the kids would be mixed, representing both of them."

"How well did you know Zoë?" I asked.

He shrugged. "We hung out a couple of times before we all agreed to go through with the process. Artificial insemination. They made me sign an agreement that said I had no custody rights, but that didn't matter to me. I knew I couldn't commit to raising the girls. And they were happy to have me be a part of the girls' lives informally."

"What about your parents?" Ray asked. "Were they okay with all this?"

Greg nodded. "They know I'm gay and they know the kind of hours I work. The twins' first year, I'd just come over to the house on the weekends, kind of like babysitting. Sometimes my parents would come, too. Anna and Zoë got some time off that way. When the girls turned two, I started taking them to my house for the weekend, once a month. My parents made a big deal out of *Hina-Matsuri*, and started a collection of dolls for the girls."

I turned to Ray. "Hina-Matsuri is a Japanese tradition—Girls' Day. Drove my mother nuts that she had only boys. She used to give dolls to all my girl cousins."

"How about if you hold the cultural background 'til Greg finishes?"

"Hey, just saying. Greg?"

He pulled a handkerchief from his pocket and wiped his forehead. "Everything was going along fine. Then about three months ago, Anna moved out. Since then, everything's been up in the air. Zoë started making noises like she was going to cut Anna out of the parenting. And once Anna wasn't in the picture anymore, I knew I'd be next."

"Are you on the birth certificate?" I asked.

"Yes. But remember, I signed away my rights as part of the donation agreement. Even Anna didn't have any official standing, because she hadn't gone through with plans to adopt the twins. Zoë could have taken Sarah and Emily to the mainland, for example, and I'd get to see them once a year, if she let me."

"You must have been pretty angry about that," Ray said.

"Not angry enough to kill Zoë." Greg stopped underneath a palm tree and crossed his arms.

"Where were you Sunday night?" I asked.

"Come on, guys. You don't think I'm a suspect, do you?"

"Sunday night, Greg," I said.

He raised his upper lip into a snarl. "I was at home. Alone."

Ray's always the one who plays good cop to my bad one, especially around Greg, who still resents me because I can be out and proud and he keeps one foot in the closet. "What do you know about Zoë's drinking habits?" he asked, shifting the conversation away from any kind of direct accusation. "Beer? Wine? Mixed drinks?"

Greg turned to him. "Drinking?"

Ray nodded. Greg struggled to focus. "When we first started talking about the donation, I'd go over there so we could get to know each other. I'd bring a bottle of wine, and we'd all have a drink or two. Just to lubricate the situation, you know? I mean, it was awkward, at first. To them, I was just a dick on legs. After a while, we got to be friends, sort of. I mean, at least I was part of their lives."

He took in a deep breath. "Then things got tough between Anna and Zoë, and when I'd go over to pick up the girls, the wine helped us all ignore the problem." He looked at us. "Never enough for anybody to get drunk, or put the girls in danger, you know. Just social drinking."

"How about vodka?" I asked. "We found a bottle of vodka in the freezer."

"That was Anna's. I guess she didn't take it when she moved out. Zoë didn't like mixed drinks. Said she got drunk too fast on them. She didn't like to lose control." I could see the reporter in Greg starting to surface. "Are you saying Zoë was drunk when she was killed?"

"There weren't any wine bottles in the house or the garbage," I said. "Do you know, was she dating anyone new?"

"We weren't that close," he said. "Anna might know."

I told him we were waiting for a call back from Anna Yang, and he said, "I'm going over to her place in Chinatown now. I want to see the girls, and Anna and I are going to talk to them together about Zoë. I said I'd be over there at four, and she promised to be home, with Sarah and Emily."

"Isn't that convenient," I said. "Guess you'll be bringing her some visitors."

"I just got your message, Detective," Anna Yang said, when she opened the door to her apartment. She was wearing black sweat pants and a long sleeve t-shirt from the Honolulu Academy of Arts with a Buddhist painting on it. "I was going to call you."

"We'll save you the trouble," I said. "Can we come in?"

She stepped back to let us in. The apartment was small but charming, like the house where Zoë Greenfield had been killed. The walls were a light salmon, the overstuffed sofa a bright green scattered with silk throw pillows. In the background I heard the Putumayo Kids "Hawaiian Playground" CD playing.

The two girls were playing on the striped rug on the living room floor, and when they saw Greg behind us they jumped up and ran to him. They wore matching t-shirts, though one had white shorts while the other's was green. Both had pierced ears with tiny silver studs.

Greg and Anna hugged. "I'm so sorry about Zoë," he said. Then he dropped to the floor and the girls climbed onto him, crying, "Daddy!" It was sweet to see, and I wondered if I'd ever get such a welcome from something without fur. It unleashed the same longing I had felt seeing the little boy with his mother the day before.

Greg gathered the pair of two-year-olds into his arms, kissing their heads, and took them into another room. Anna turned off the music and Ray and I sat down with her, declining her offer of coffee or some other beverage. "Tell us about Zoë and alcohol," I asked.

She turned her head slightly in confusion. "Zoë didn't drink that much."

"The vodka in the freezer?"

"Mine. I never took it when I moved out." She looked from Ray to me. "What's this about?"

"There was alcohol in Zoë's blood," I said. "But we didn't find any empty bottles in the trash, or even a half-full wine bottle in the fridge."

"She drank wine sometimes," Anna said. "But I don't think I ever saw her drunk. She didn't like to lose control like that."

"Did she like sushi?" Ray asked.

"Oh, yeah. Pretty much anything Asian, you know. Sushi, sashimi, teriyaki, won ton soup, pad Thai, anything."

"Did she drink when she was eating sushi?"

"Yeah, she liked sake. Again, I think it's just because she was so into everything Asian." She blushed. "I guess she had a bad case of yellow fever."

Ray looked confused.

"Caucasians who are interested in Asian people and things," I said. "Ask Julie about it."

In the gay world, people have started using the acronym PAPI-- Philippine/Asian/Pacific Islander. Since I fall into that category myself, I wondered sometimes if Mike was a bit of a rice queen—did he like me because I was exotic? He took after his Italian father much more than his Korean mother. So while I looked very Eurasian, he looked more Italian than anything else, with just a slight epicanthic fold over his eyes.

Did he like me because he was fixated on his mother, maybe?

I shook it all off. It was stupid speculation; it's not like either of us was wholly one thing or the other. I'd known haole men who only were attracted to Asians, often the slim-hipped, smooth-skinned types like Thais or Filipinos, and vice versa. The whole dynamic was uncomfortable for me, with overtones of cultural imperialism.

I pulled myself back to the case. "Did you guys have a favorite place for sushi?"

"Zoë liked to try different restaurants." She gave us the names of five in the neighborhood where they had been, and one they had been meaning to try before they broke up. "Why would it matter where she went to dinner?" she asked. "Do you think someone followed her home from the restaurant?"

"That's a possibility." I paused, took a breath. "I'm afraid I need to ask you some questions that might be uncomfortable. The autopsy report on Zoë showed that there was semen in her vagina."

"She was raped?" Anna looked ready to cry.

"We don't know that. There wasn't any evidence of bruising or anything that might indicate the sex wasn't consensual." I gave her a minute to digest that. "Was Zoë bisexual?"

Anna played with the catch on her gold bracelet, then looked up. "About a year ago, she started talking about men. At first, she was just admiring guys we saw—you know, that one looks hot, and so on. Then she suggested trying a threesome." She did start crying then. "That hurt." She dabbed at her eyes with a tissue. "I loved her, and I didn't want to bring anyone else into the relationship, man or woman." She looked toward the bedroom. "It was enough we had Greg, you know?"

"I hate to pry," I said. "But do you know if Zoë was seeing anyone?"

She shook her head. "No. I thought her interest in men was just a phase, so I hung in there. But she pulled back from me, and started keeping little secrets. That's when I knew I had to move out."

Greg returned from the bedroom, one tiny girl in each arm. "Sarah and Emily are hungry. What are we doing for dinner?"

Ray and I looked at each other, then stood up. "We'll leave you to it," I said. "We'll be in touch again. In the meantime, we'll check out the restaurants you suggested. Can you direct us to the woman you said watches the girls when you're out?"

"Why do you want to talk to her?" Greg asked.

"Just tying up loose ends," I said. "You know how it is."

Anna crossed the room and took one of the girls from Greg. They looked like such a happy family there, mom and dad juggling the twins, and once again I considered whether Mike and I would ever be a part of something like that. We knew some lesbians; perhaps we could enter into some kind of co-parenting agreement, like the one Greg had with Anna and Zoë.

There was always surrogate parenting, or adoption. I knew gay men who were raising nieces or nephews, and a couple who were foster parents. There was a whole array of things we could do—if we both wanted it.

It wasn't something we'd talked about a lot. Mike was an only child, and he was spoiled in the way that only children often are—accustomed to doing what he wanted, going his own way. I was the youngest of three, and I had my hands full playing Uncle Kimo to seven nieces and nephews. But I couldn't deny that I'd felt something.

Anna carried one of the girls with her as she walked out of the apartment, and we followed. She knocked on the door next to hers, and a tiny, stooped old woman came out. Anna spoke to her briefly in Mandarin. I didn't catch much beyond *jing cha*, police; *gu*, dead; and Zoë.

"You have questions?" the old woman asked.

"Yes, Auntie, if you wouldn't mind." Anna took her daughter back to her own apartment, and we walked into her neighbor's. It was decorated in faded red and gold, and there were children's toys on the floor and the sofa.

Even though she looked nothing like the woman Lucky Lou said had pawned the dragon pendant, we asked her about her relationship with Anna and Zoë. She said she had known Anna a long time, since Anna first came to Hawai'i, and that she often took care of the girls for her.

I pulled out the picture of the dragon pendant that Anna had drawn. "Have you ever seen this pin?" I asked.

She peered at the drawing, held it up to the light, then shook her head. "No, but Anna drew this, didn't she?"

"She did." I took the page back from her. "Were you taking care of the girls on Sunday night?"

"Sunday? No. My grandson was here visiting. I took him next door to see Sarah and Emily. Anna was there with them."

We thanked for her help and walked back out to Hotel Street. "Doesn't sound like she was the woman who pawned the dragon pendant, and she corroborates Anna's alibi," I said.

I looked over at Ray. "Hello? Earth to Ray."

"Sorry. I was spaced. I can't stop thinking about that term you said, yellow fever." He turned to me. "I mean, what if Julie has it? And that means she's going to dump me for some Asian guy?"

"I've seen how Julie looks at you. She's not going to dump you for some Asian guy just because he can talk Japanese or Chinese to her." I smiled. "How about if we start canvassing these restaurants, and we arrange with Julie and Mike to meet us at the last place?"

We got on our cell phones and called. We arranged to meet up at seven at Simple Sushi, the only place on the list I'd heard good things about, and we started quizzing the staff at the other restaurants. At Tokyo House, one of the waiters recognized Zoë's picture when I turned my netbook screen toward him, and knew that she often came in with a Chinese woman, but hadn't seen her in a while.

No one at Sushi Siam, Aloha Sushi, Madame Wong's, or My Japan recognized the photo of Zoë. We established that the staff in each place had been on duty on Sunday night, so we wiped them off our list.

We finished more quickly than we had expected, so I dropped Ray off at his apartment and drove up to Aiea Heights. Mike was still at work, so I leashed up Roby and we went for a walk around the neighborhood.

A preteen boy was bouncing a rubber ball against the driveway of his house, so that it banged against the garage and ricocheted back toward him. A few houses farther on, a mother was shepherding four little kids into a minivan. Someone was playing John Keawe's "Play with me, Papa," a song I seemed to hear more and more. When Roby and I rounded the corner, a dad and a boy of six or seven were playing catch in the street. The night was cool, with a light breeze, and as we walked the sky darkened and stars started to come out.

By the time we'd circled back home, the families had all gone inside for dinner, and I was in full melancholy mode. Mike had just walked in, and was unloading his briefcase.

"You ever think about having kids?" I asked.

"Whoa. Where did that come from?"

"Just thinking." I told him about seeing the woman the day before with her son, then Greg Oshiro with his twins, then all the families in the neighborhood.

"A kid is a lifetime commitment," he said. "I'm not sure I'm ready for something like that."

I thought of the commitment we had to each other. Was that what he was saying he wasn't sure about? Was he worried about bringing a kid into a relationship that might end, leaving the kid adrift?

Look what had happened to Anna and Zoë. Not only had they broken up, but Zoë had changed her whole idea of who she was. Talk about an unstable environment.

Mike came over to me and wrapped his arms around me. "I know how you think," he said. "I love you. Our relationship is the rock I build everything else in my life on. Okay?"

I relaxed into his body. He's a couple of inches taller than I am, so my head's always against his shoulder. His smell was earthy: layers of sweat, the lavender soap we both used, and the slightest smell of smoke, which often lingers around a guy like Mike who spends his days among fire and ash.

We cleaned up and headed over to Simple Sushi, arriving in the parking lot just as Ray and Julie pulled in. Mike and Julie had met often during the time that Ray and I had been partners, and they got along well.

"So what's this about yellow fever?" Julie asked, as we walked toward the restaurant. "Ray has some idea in his head that I have it."

"You never heard the term?" I asked. I looked at Mike, and he shook his head. "You guys are clueless." I explained what it was as Mike opened the door for us.

We entered the restaurant through a *torii* gate, and the hostess seated us at a four-top in the back of the restaurant. The name might have been Simple Sushi, but the décor was anything but. The walls were papered with something that looked like the pattern from blue willow china. There were little brass lanterns on each table with a votive candle, chopsticks, and placemats with a map of Japan.

Before we looked at the menus, Julie reached over to Ray and pushed the edges of his eyes up diagonally with her index fingers. She considered, then shook her head and pulled back. "Nah, I think I'll stick with what I've got."

We all laughed. "Anybody want sake?" Ray asked.

"You hate sake," Julie said.

"Hey, I'm trying to go with the flow."

We all just wanted water. Mike has had problems with alcohol in the past, and though he's been fine for a long time, I always get a twinge when the chance comes to order a beverage. I know he's watching me so I try not to let it show.

We ordered a couple of sampler platters and a teriyaki chicken entrée to share. After the waiter had taken our order, Ray and I went up to the hostess to ask about Zoë Greenfield. When we showed the picture, she nodded her head. "Yeah, she in here just few days ago," she said. "They sit in back with chef, Shinichi. She like him."

Ray and I walked back to the counter at the rear of the restaurant. The real sushi connoisseurs like to sit where the chef is preparing his dishes, so they can talk to him about what's best that day.

Shinichi was a Japanese guy in his late twenties, with straight black hair cut at a weird angle, and a pink stripe on the side.

Clearly an island Japanese, not a tourist. And if he wasn't gay, you can take back that toaster they gave me when I came out.

"You remember this woman?" I asked, showing him the photo.

He recognized her. He recognized me, too, but that's another story. "Yeah, she was here Sunday night." He leaned in close and lowered his voice. "With a man."

"You noticed that?" I asked.

He nodded. "Yeah. She always used to come in with this Chinese chick. I thought they were partners. But then the last couple of times, it's been with a guy."

"Same guy every time?"

"Yeah. Tough-looking white guy, tattoos on his forearms. I guess when she went the other way, she really went the other way, if you know what I mean." He continued to chop and roll sushi as we talked.

"I know. Anything more about the guy? Age? Hair color?"

He put his lips together like he was thinking. "Maybe thirty-five or forty. Buzz-cut hair, like light brown. Looked like he worked out."

"You remember how they paid?" Ray asked. "Credit card?"

He shook his head. "The guy always paid. Cash. Pretty good tipper, too."

He wasn't sure exactly what time they'd been in, it had been a busy night, but the place closed at midnight and he knew they were gone before that.

"You find anything out?" Mike asked, when we returned to the table.

"Yeah. Don't know if it will help, though." We told him and Julie what the waiter had said.

"Sounds like she had a boyfriend," Julie said. "If the waiter said they've been in a few times."

"Maybe you could see if anyone she works with knew who

she was dating," Mike suggested.

"Been there, done that," I said. "Her coworker didn't even know she was a lesbian."

We shared the sushi and the teriyaki and tried to forget that it was murder that had brought us all together. Mike told us about the fire he was investigating, at a wind farm under construction in the Koolau mountains. "Neighbors don't like the place. They say it's going to spoil the view, make noise, frighten away the birds."

"You think it's arson?" Ray asked.

"Not sure yet. It looks like one of the generators the contractors were using might have short-circuited and started the fire. But it's not clear why that happened."

I was always fascinated to hear the details of Mike's cases; they were a lot like mine, in that they required deductive powers and lots of nose-to-the-grindstone footwork. But there was an extra layer of knowledge he needed, about fire and electricity and combustion. Sometimes the details made my head spin. I was always in awe of his ability to interpret the data and come up with conclusions.

When we got home, Mike and I relaxed on the couch with Roby. It had been a nice evening, and I wondered how things would change if we had a child to worry about. I saw the way my brothers' kids dominated everything that went on in their households. They needed to be fed and clothed and driven around, and even when the whole family was at home, they were always asking questions, banging things around, playing music too loud.

My sisters-in-law were often frazzled, even Liliha, who tried to make everything look effortless. Tatiana, the artsy one, was more haphazard in her parenting, but I had seen her put her painting ability on the sidelines while she focused on her kids. Even now, when her youngest daughter, Akipela, was seven years old and in school all day, Tatiana was swamped with laundry, PTA and chauffeuring duties.

Did Mike and I want to sacrifice everything in our lives that way? It wasn't all taking the kids surfing or playing video games with them. Were we too selfish to let ourselves in for years of diapers, homework and then dating dramas?

I wondered if the idea of kids was percolating through Mike's brain the way it was with mine. Neither of us brought it up again as we watched TV, but the idea stayed in the back of my mind.

On my way in to work Wednesday morning I plugged in my Bluetooth and dialed Anna Yang's apartment in Chinatown on my cell. When she answered, I heard at least one of the girls crying in the background. "I'll try and make this quick," I said. "Did Zoë have an email account?"

We thought maybe Zoë might have been corresponding with the guy she had dinner with, but I didn't see the need to pass that information on to Anna until it became relevant. "Yes. She has an account with IslandMail. Her user name is MissNumbered." She spelled it for me.

"Clever. Password?"

"I'm sorry, I don't know it."

"I have a friend who might be able to get into the account. Can you give me some clues? Maybe her birthday, the girls', that kind of thing?"

She listed a bunch of dates and a couple of Zoë's favorite words, and I pulled up in front of Harry Ho's house and added them to my computer file. I heard her turn to the girl who was crying. "Because I say so," she said.

I remembered that one from my own childhood. I guess Anna had heard the same thing, growing up in China, and it had imprinted on her the same way it sunk in to every American kid who grew up to be a parent. I hung up and sat in front of Harry's house for a minute.

Harry and Arleen live in the same neighborhood as Mike and me, though their house is a lot nicer than ours. They have a single-family, while ours is a duplex with the added pleasure of having Mike's parents sharing a wall. We have two bedrooms, while Harry and Arleen have three. We had a nicer bathroom, because Mike had remodeled it a year before he met me, but I knew it was just a matter of time before Harry's house surpassed ours in that regard, too.

Arleen had had the kitchen remodeled and expanded before they moved in, with sliding glass doors to the back yard, where they'd had a swimming pool put in as well. Our kitchen was small and dark, but since neither Mike or I cooked much, that didn't matter. I did want a pool, though.

In addition to being my best friend, aside from Mike of course, Harry's a computer genius with degrees from MIT and a bunch of patents in his name. Arleen was just walking out the front door, with Brandon in tow. Harry had met Arleen a couple of years before, when she was working for a man who'd been murdered, and Harry had helped me with some computer problems. Brandon was a toddler then, but he was growing up smart and confident.

Arleen was a sweet Japanese girl, just a couple of years younger than Harry and me. She had finished her associate's degree in computer science with Harry's tutelage, and now worked with him. She'd lost the baby fat she once had, and her black hair was styled into a sleek bob.

I watched Harry kiss them both goodbye. Once again I felt that little pang, wondering about parenthood.

When Arleen had Brandon in the car, backing down the driveway, Harry turned to me. "Hey, brah, howzit?" he asked.

"Pretty good. Think you can hack into an email account?"

"Brah, you insult me. Of course I can."

I could have tried to get a subpoena to IslandMail, and if I needed evidence that would stand up in a court case, I would. But for now I just wanted to figure out who Zoë was dating.

We went into Harry's home office, where computers, printers, scanners, and all kinds of other equipment were on tables that lined the room. He sat down at a monitor and keyboard and started typing. "Give me the user name."

"MissNumbered." I spelled it for him, just as Anna had spelled it for me. We worked our way through her birthday, their address, the kids' birthdays. None of them worked.

"Time to get creative," Harry said. "Know anything about her childhood? Address? Nickname?"

"She grew up on a commune, but she hated it," I said. "You know what, though? Try fallopian."

"You mean as in tubes?"

"Yeah, that was the name her parents gave her."

Harry made a face. "Yuk."

"She has a brother named Vas," I said. "As in vas deferens."

"At least they didn't call him Scrotum."

Harry typed fallopian into the password box, and immediately the screen clicked forward into Zoë Greenfield's email list.

She was still involved with the volunteer group she'd met Anna Yang through; there was a message from one of the organizers. A bunch of spam, too. Nigerians asking for help investing money, someone touting açai as a breakthrough drug, that kind of thing. She didn't seem to archive old messages, and there weren't any emails from guys confirming a date for Sunday evening.

We read through everything in her in box, and there was nothing useful. "Great, another dead end," I said.

"You doubt my skills, young grasshopper." Harry opened a new message and clicked into the "to" box. When he typed the letter 'a,' the web interface obligingly listed all the people Zoë had ever emailed whose addresses began with that letter.

"You want to take notes?" Harry asked.

"Yes, honorable master."

A lot of the addresses weren't useful; it was doubtful, for example, that Zoë had made plans to meet "support@amazon. com" for dinner on Sunday night. But I did harvest about fifty email addresses, from a to z.

"So what do I do with these?" I asked Harry, when I had added the last address to the list on my netbook. "Email them all and ask if they had dinner plans with Zoë Greenfield on Sunday night?"

"It's a possibility. But let's try something more subtle first. Give me a couple of hours to play around with these addresses and see what else I can dig up."

Under Harry's tutelage, I've been getting better at using the computer. I can Google, email, and place online orders as good as anyone, and I was increasingly comfortable with using my netbook as a tool for organizing case materials. But when you get into more sophisticated techniques, I bow at his feet.

When I finally got to headquarters, Ray was filling out paperwork. I explained that I had Harry on the case, and I sat down to help him. The brass hadn't yet moved into the computer generation, so we had to transfer my notes to the appropriate forms. We had to document everything we'd seen and done at the house on Lopez Lane, as well as our interviews with Ryan Tazo, the people at Zoë's office, the receptionist at the homeless shelter, and the waiters and other staff at the restaurants we'd visited, including Shinichi at Simple Sushi.

We worked until noon, and we were just about to break for lunch when my cell phone rang. From the display I could see it was Judy Evangelista, the Waikiki prostitute. "Yo, Judy," I said. "Wazzup?"

"Cut the crap, detective. I've got a name for you, but it's going to cost you."

"Judy, Judy," I said. "I just gave you fifty bucks yesterday."

"You want the name? It'll cost you another fifty."

I arranged to meet her back in an hour at the International Marketplace in Waikiki, an open-air market of stalls and carts that was a tourist favorite. It was also where Judy scored her regular fixes, so I figured it was convenient that we'd be giving her the cash to complete her next transaction.

We got there early, so we wandered under the banyan trees, looking at the tourist crap. They were playing the Matt Catingub Orchestra's cover of "Oh, Pretty Woman," and I liked the way they'd changed up Roy Orbison with an island beat.

Moms with babies in strollers navigated the crowd, kids carried shave ice that dripped on the ground, and a tourist with a heavy German accent was trying to negotiate for a koa bangle with a woman whose Chinese accent was equally as impenetrable. We picked up some gourmet hot dogs from Hank's Haute Dogs and sat at a table in the food court, next to a tiki-hut stand.

"You think Judy will have anything useful to give us?" Ray asked.

I shrugged. "This case just isn't adding up yet, so who knows? Maybe somebody hired this person Judy knows. Or maybe it's just a waste of time." I took a bite of the hot dog. "At least we get a good lunch out of it."

"My gut is telling me that somebody wanted her dead," Ray said.

"Yeah, but yesterday your gut was telling you it was drug-related, because of the number of times she got stabbed. I think maybe your gut is suffering from indigestion."

"As long as you keep thinking a couple of hot dogs are a good lunch, that's not unlikely."

We finished eating, threw our trash in a basket with the word "Mahalo" on the flap, and started looking for Judy. We found her a few minutes later at the Maui Divers store, looking at a ring with a giant Tahitian black pearl in the center and tiny diamonds wrapped around it.

"That's a little out of my price range, honey," I said, walking up to her.

"Everything about me is out of your price range." She nodded her head toward a banyan tree outside, and we followed her out there.

"This name, you didn't get it from me," she said.

"Of course not." I opened my wallet and pulled out another fifty, which I held folded in my fingers.

"I only know the guy as Freddie," she said. "Skinny ice head, they say he used to play football at UH til he wrecked his knee.

His dealer told me Freddie's suddenly flush with cash, and his knuckles are banged up, like he's been breaking into places." She took the bill from me. "He's a crazy motherfucker. Be careful with him."

"Judy. You care. I could almost kiss you."

"That'd be at least another fifty." She turned on her heel and walked away, but I caught a smile before she left.

If there's a bigger UH football fan in Hawaii than my brother Haoa, I'd be surprised. He was a linebacker when he was in college, and since then you'd think he bled green and white, the colors of the Rainbow Warriors. I wondered if he knew anything about Freddie.

"Kanapa'aka Landscaping," he said, when he answered his cell phone.

"Hey, brah, it's me. Can I ask you a question?"

"I'm just finishing up a meeting." He named a hotel a few blocks from the International Marketplace. "Can I call you back?"

"How about I meet you over there?"

"Give me ten, fifteen minutes."

Ray and I walked down Kalakaua Boulevard, taking our time. The sun had come out again, and it was a gorgeous spring day. You might wonder how I knew it was spring, because we don't have a lot of seasonal change in Hawaii. But there are little things—trees budding, new bedding plants at the big hotels, a kind of freshness in the air. It's not like we have crocuses pushing up through the snow or anything, but it's spring.

Haoa was just coming out the front door of the hotel as we walked up. He's the middle child, two years younger than Lui and eight years older than I am. He's the most Hawaiian-looking of the three of us—as tall as I am, but broader. He looked like a proper island businessman, in a polo shirt with his company logo and a pair of aviator-framed sunglasses on his head.

"You bidding on this job?" I asked.

"Yeah. They're not happy with the guy they've got doing it

now. And they shouldn't be. Look at these yellow leaves. And over there—weeds. A job like this, you've got to be on it every day." He looked at us. "So what's up, brah?"

"You ever hear of a UH football player named Freddie, who wrecked his knee?"

"Freddie Walsh. Tight end. Recruited from northern California, I think. Must be about twenty-eight, twenty-nine by now. Why do you ask?"

"His name came up in an investigation," I said.

Haoa frowned. "I heard he got hooked on pain pills after his knee blew out. Then I think it got worse. Ice."

Ice was what we called the smokeable form of crystal meth, a real scourge in the islands. "That's what we heard," I said. "Thanks. Now that we have a last name, we can run him down."

Back at headquarters, Ray ran Freddie Walsh through the system while I Googled him. He had been a promising player at Mendocino High in northern California, as Haoa remembered, recruited for the Rainbow Warriors—who used to be called the Rainbows, until someone in the college administration thought that was too gay. He'd played JV for a year, then started on the varsity team his sophomore year. He was a good player, though a better partier, and one night during his junior year he'd fallen from a dorm balcony and broken both his legs.

That was the end of his football career. Ray picked up his story from police records. Freddie had built up a record over the past few years, starting back when he was still at UH with a couple of arrests for public intoxication, disorderly conduct, and resisting arrest. Then he moved on to assault, possession, and possession with intent to distribute.

He hadn't been picked up for burglary yet, which is why he hadn't shown up on our earlier searches. "There's something just on the edge of my brain," I said to Ray, when we'd looked it all over. "I just can't put my finger on it yet."

"What kind of thing?"

I shook my head. "I don't know. Let's go look for him. Maybe it'll come to me while we drive." We got his latest address, an apartment building a few blocks off the UH campus, and got into the Jeep. There was an accident on University Avenue, a Kawasaki motorcycle that had broadsided a Toyota Camry, so it took us forever to get up there. The building was a nondescript two-story on a side street, the kind of place that a bunch of undergrads share. We climbed the outside stairs and walked down the catwalk to apartment 2D.

Along the way, we passed several open doors. College kids were hanging out, playing music or video games. One or two were even studying. The aroma of *pakalolo*, home grown Hawaiian dope, floated around us. The door to 2D was open, too, and a Hawaiian kid in his late teens was sprawled on the sofa. I knocked on the door and stuck my head in.

"HPD," I said, flashing my badge. "Looking for Freddie Walsh."

The kid looked up from an anatomy textbook. His eyes were red and his speech was slurred. The future of medicine. "We kicked him out. Like two weeks ago. He was just too crazy."

"You know where he went?"

He shrugged. "Dude had serious problems, you know? Anger management, for one." He nodded across the room, where there was a fist-sized hole in the wall. "Landlord says we've got to fix that."

"Focus," I said. "He have any friends he might be crashing with?"

"Maybe this older chick named Zoë he knew from home," the kid said. "I remember him talking about her. Nobody else would have anything to do with him."

Mendocino. Zoë Greenfield had grown up on a commune in Mendocino. Had she known Freddie Walsh then? "You have any recent pictures of Freddie?" I asked. All we had been able to find were photos of him as a Rainbow Warrior, and then mug shots. None of those were going to be all that close to what he actually looked like.

"Facebook."

"Under whose name?" Ray asked. "His?"

The kid got up reluctantly, and pulled a laptop computer out of a pile of junk on the kitchen table. "There's some shots of him at a party in my album," he said.

Ray looked at me while the kid booted up the computer. "Aren't you and Mike on Facebook yet?"

I shook my head. "I don't have time for that crap."

"Yeah, well, you still live where you grew up. I use it to keep up with my old crowd from Philly."

By then the kid had his computer up and showed us a slide show of party pictures, kids hanging out on the catwalk, drinking, mooning the camera. The kind of stuff potential employers would love to see. I handed the kid my card and asked him to email me the photos, and we waited there until I saw the email show on my netbook.

It was already the end of our shift. We had no leads on how to find Freddie Walsh, though he was looking like a good suspect in Zoë Greenfield's murder. Perhaps he knew a middle-aged Chinese woman who had pawned Zoë's jewelry and given him the cash; savvy pawn brokers like Lucky Lou were suspicious of ice heads pawning jewelry, after all.

We spent the next hour going from room to room in the building, asking if anyone knew Freddie Walsh or where he might be. Some of the kids were downright hostile, others too busy studying to be polite. The few who would talk to us had nothing new to contribute.

By the end of our shift we were both discouraged. "Maybe Harry will come up with an email connection between Freddie Walsh and Zoë Greenfield," I said.

"We still have to find him in order to arrest him."

"We'll go back to Judy. She said she knew Freddie's dealer. We find the dealer, we find the ice head."

We drove down to Waikiki but couldn't find Judy at any of her regular hangouts. We'd already put in an hour of overtime without making progress, so we hung up our shields for the night.

Haoa and Tatiana had invited Mike and me for a barbecue that night. Mike loved going over there; he often joined Haoa on Sunday afternoons and Monday nights to watch football on Haoa's big screen TV. Because he had no siblings, and his only cousins were far away, he liked being part of my big family. That was fine with me, because I liked them, too.

Plus, Tatiana is an amazing cook. My mother can prepare a good meal, but Tatiana combines her artistic nature, her Russian heritage, and the fresh fish, meat and produce of the islands to create meals that rival any restaurant. Between my brother's skill at the barbecue and hers in the kitchen, eating there is always a great time.

My niece Ashley answered the door. She's the oldest kid, and at sixteen she was blooming into a great beauty. She was five ten, with her mom's ash-blonde hair and blue eyes, as well as the high cheekbones from the Russian side of the family. From us, she got her deeply tanned skin and a slight epicanthic fold above her eyes. Haoa had been complaining about boys buzzing around for the last two years, and I could tell it was only going to get worse.

She kissed us both on the cheek, hardly stepping up on tiptoe to do so, and then said, "You are such a tease!"

It wasn't until I saw the Bluetooth earpiece that I realized she wasn't talking to us. "They're all in the back yard," she said. "No, I don't say that to all the boys. Only the cute ones."

I looked at Mike and we both laughed. We walked through the house, passing thirteen-year-old Alec, sprawled on the living room floor playing a video game. He was going to be as tall as his dad soon, but it looked like his arms and legs were waiting for the rest of him to catch up. I remembered poses like that myself, one leg on the sofa (when my mother wasn't watching), the rest of me on the carpet, one arm crooked behind my head, though I was usually reading a book, not playing a game.

I waved hello to him, and heard his two younger sisters, Ailina and Akipela, squabbling somewhere upstairs. I wasn't about to intervene.

The night was just cool enough to make you want to stand next to the barbecue, and that's where I found Haoa and Tatiana, talking with Tico Robles, Tatiana's best friend. Tico owned a hair salon, with Tatiana as a silent partner. He was about fifty, Puerto Rican, the kind of very dramatic gay man who made me uncomfortable before I came out of the closet.

Next to him was a handsome young guy in jeans and a white shirt, which showed off his biceps and his deep tan. "Tico's got himself a young boyfriend," Mike whispered to me as we walked through the sliding doors.

When Tico saw us, he said, "My favorite defenders of law and order!" and rushed over to hug and kiss us. Then he said, "I have someone I want you to meet." He looked shy, which is unusual for him, but I assumed it was because his boyfriend was so much younger. "This is Alfredo. My son."

"Close your mouths before the flies get in," Tatiana said, laughing at Mike's and my surprise.

Why did it seem like every gay man I knew was turning out to have kids? First Greg Oshiro, then Tico Robles. The next thing I knew Gunter would be cradling a buzz-cut blond baby in his arms.

"You didn't know I was married back in Puerto Rico," Tico said. "Just for a little while. But long enough to make a beautiful baby."

Alfredo blushed. He shook hands with both of us, and Haoa delivered a couple of rum punches in big plastic globes. "You both look like you could use a drink," he said, laughing.

"My son has finally come to visit me," Tico said, putting his arm proudly around Alfredo's shoulders. "After all these years."

Tatiana brought out a tray of appetizers, tiny pastry tarts filled with cheese, chopped meat, and green vegetables. We learned that Alfredo had graduated from the University of Puerto Rico with a major in Spanish, hoping to become a teacher, and decided to visit his father before embarking on his career. We nibbled, we talked, and eventually Haoa said, "I'm going to put the steaks on. Kimo, you want to help me?"

The lively beat of Times Five playing "School's Out" was on the CD as he slapped the big hunks of meat on the grill and a sweet smell rose from the charcoal. "I called around to see what I could find out about Freddie Walsh."

In the light of a tiki torch, I could see him frowning. "I feel bad for the guy. He was in the hospital for a week after he broke his legs, and then a month in rehab. In the end, he missed so much school that he flunked out. He didn't want to go back to the mainland, so he moved around. A couple of the alumni tried to do right for him, but he pissed away everything anybody tried to give him."

He placed the last steak down, then took a swig of his punch. "He's in trouble, isn't he? That's why you're looking for him."

I didn't want to reveal details of the case when I didn't know how Freddie Walsh could be connected so all I said was, "Just want to talk to him."

Haoa considered for a minute. "I think he might be at the homeless shelter on North Vineyard. An old teammate I called does some volunteer work there, said he saw him."

"Thanks. We'll check it out."

We went back to the lounge chairs where Mike, Tatiana, Tico and Alfredo were relaxing. The pool lights were on, blue shadows moving restlessly as the trees around us swayed in the light breeze. Haoa's back yard is a showplace of his landscaping skills and Tatiana's knack for using color. Purple and white orchids hung in the boughs of a big kiawe tree, and the hibiscus hedges were full of red blossoms as big as dinner plates. In one corner, fragrant plumeria blossoms bent branches like the arms of a beautiful hula dancer.

Sitting down across from Alfredo, I tried to figure out if, like his father, he was gay. I knew a number of older gay men who had kids the old-fashioned way, often as a result of a straight marriage, and in many cases the kids were gay, too. But from the way Alfredo talked, he was straight; at least he said he had a girlfriend back home.

Well, I dated girls for a long time myself, so that's no real indicator.

The steaks were great, served with baked potatoes and grilled asparagus. Even Mike, who's not the biggest vegetable fan, asked for second helpings of the caramelized stalks.

When Tatiana brought out a massive chocolate cake, decorated with tiny flowers made of icing, all four kids came out to join us, and as always, the world revolved around them. Ashley was full of stories about high school, cheerleading and prom, which her brother snorted at. Alec bragged about playing basketball at Punahou, the private school where my brothers and I had all gone, talking stink about Farrington High, where Mike had gone. That got him a cuff on the head from his dad.

Ailina, the quiet one in the middle, was nine years old, a round, brown girl with dark hair in a ponytail. She didn't have much to say, but I could see she was watching everything. Akipela, the baby, was playing a princess in the second grade play.

"Typecasting," Haoa said, and Tatiana punched him in the arm.

By the time Mike and I got home, we were both feeling sleepy. We let Roby out for a quick run in the back yard, then stumbled into bed.

"I like your family," Mike said, just before we dozed off.

"They're your family, too, now," I said. But I couldn't help wondering if he was trying to tell me that he wanted our family to grow.

I woke to find Mike sitting up in bed next to me tapping at his phone. "Just answering an email." He yawned, and put the phone down. "Weird about Tico having a son, huh?"

"It was a surprise. But I'm glad Alfredo is getting to know his father."

"Not always a good thing," Mike said. "Look at my dad and me."

"You argue with your father because you're too much like him," I said. "Besides, relations between fathers and sons are tough. I think I'm lucky that my father has almost always been supportive of me."

"You think that's because you're the baby?"

"Hardly a baby at thirty-five," I said. "But you're right, maybe it's because I'm the third son, and by the time I came along my parents had already gotten worn down by Lui and Haoa. But when I wanted to go surf after college, my dad was the one who stood up for me."

"I think my life would have been easier if my dad hadn't always been pushing me to be a doctor," he said.

I shook my head. "No, it wouldn't. I know you. You function best when you have someone to push against. Your father, me. If no one ever pressured you, you'd never do anything."

"Oh yeah?" He flipped over so that he was on top of me, his hands pressing my arms down. "You like it just as much as I do when we fight."

"I like it even better when we make up." I wrapped my leg around his, and he leaned down and kissed me. Then his phone rang. He groaned and let me go, rolling over to grab it. "All right, I'm on it," he said, then hung up. "Fire at a house on Round Top Drive that looks like arson. We'll continue this conversation later."

I stayed in bed with Roby snuggled up next to me, thinking of my brothers. Because they were so much older than I was, they'd taken the pressure off me in many areas—both were married and successful by the time I graduated from college, which freed me up to take time off to surf. I think maybe my father liked that in me, too—that I had a chance to chase my dreams, when at my age he'd had to knuckle down and support his growing family.

Thinking of fathers and sons reminded me of Jimmy Ah Wong, who I'd adopted in a way, guiding him through the pitfalls of adolescence and coming out. I'd met Jimmy when he was sixteen, after he'd been victimized by a sexual predator and gotten roped into a case I was investigating.

When his father discovered he was gay, he kicked Jimmy out of the house. Jimmy had lived on the streets for a while, until I found him a place to live with my godparents, and he had finished his GED and then gotten in to UH.

There were the kids I mentored at the gay teen center on Waikiki, too. A couple of them had been real success stories, graduating from high school, getting jobs, and establishing real relationships. Maybe they would be all the kids I'd ever have.

But soon enough my furry child was crawling all over me like I was an obstruction in the roadway, trying to lick my face, and I knew I had to get up and walk him. Once outside, I saw the neighbor across the street shepherding her kids into the family minivan, and then a block away a baby was squalling like a fire alert siren, and I was glad I only had a dog to worry about.

I just didn't know how Mike would feel about the same questions.

Lieutenant Sampson called us in soon after Ray and I got to headquarters. This morning's extra-large polo shirt was tan, over black slacks. "How are things going with your home invasion murder case?" he asked.

I looked at Ray, and he looked back at me. "We've got a lot of different directions going, and nothing's adding up yet," I said.

I described our fruitless search for similar break-ins, and the dragon pendant that had showed up at Lucky Lou's pawn shop. "An older Chinese woman pawned it, and that doesn't fit the idea of a break-in by local mokes or ice addicts."

"She could be an intermediary," Sampson suggested. "Did Lou recognize her?"

"Nope. But we can check other pawn shops, see if she gets around."

"Good. Go on."

"We got a lead late yesterday on a moke who's been breaking into houses," I said. "We're going to keep looking for him today. We got a tip that he might be staying at the homeless shelter on North Vineyard."

"Sounds like you're making progress," Sampson said.

"Maybe, maybe not. The way the victim was stabbed doesn't fit the profile of a random assault." I explained the unusual circumstance of Zoë Greenfield's wounds. "It looks like her assailant was waiting for her with the knife."

"Don't forget the semen," Ray said.

Sampson's eyebrows raised.

"Yeah. She was a lesbian, or so we've been told. She had recently broken up with a long-time partner. But she had unprotected sex with a man within seventy-two hours before she was killed. She could have picked up a guy, brought him home, and things went wrong."

"Are you looking into the victim's life?" Sampson asked.

Ray took over. "Her stomach contents indicated her last meal was sushi, so we got a list of her favorite sushi places from her ex. We canvassed them last night and found she had dinner a few hours before she was killed with a Caucasian male in his late twenties or early thirties, with tattoos on his forearms."

"What about the partner?" Sampson asked. "She have any motive?"

"Not sure yet," I said. "They had twin girls, and Greenfield was the birth mother. So there could have been custody issues. And there's the birth father, too, Greg Oshiro, the crime reporter for the *Star-Advertiser*."

"Oshiro?"

I nodded. "There was some talk, apparently, that she might be taking the kids to the mainland. He wasn't happy about that."

"We've got Kimo's friend looking into her emails, too," Ray said. "See if there's anything there might lead us to someone interesting."

"You've got your hands full, I see. Keep me in the loop."

He picked up his phone, which meant we were dismissed. As we walked back to our desks, Thanh Nguyen, the fingerprint tech, stepped out of the elevator.

He was a wiry guy in his early sixties, and word around the building was that he'd been in the South Vietnamese army. "I did some work on that dragon pendant you sent down," he said, as we met at my desk. "A couple of the prints on it match the pawnbroker. But there was a pretty decent thumbprint that doesn't match anyone in our files, so I ran a couple of other tests."

"What kind of tests?"

"I've been reading about new work from England that extrapolates information about the subject from the sweat in their fingerprints. Our prints contain a mixture of skin cells, sweat secretions and other stuff we pick up. Metabolites – breakdown parts of substances people consume – end up in our pores, and they get transferred along with our fingerprints."

"Cool," Ray said. I nodded in agreement.

"I got the department to authorize some research and thought your case would be a good test. I used gold nanoparticles to give me some idea of the profile of the person behind the print. Based on what I found, I can say that the print belongs to a woman, and there was a good chance she was a heavy coffee drinker, based on the secretions in the print."

"Great, let's stake out every Kope Bean in town and take comparison prints," Ray grumbled.

Thanh held up his hands. "Hey, just trying to help."

"It's interesting stuff," I said. "Anything else?"

He shook his head. "The print tested negative for tobacco or any controlled substances, so that's all I've got."

We thanked him, and after he left we decided to go look for Freddie Walsh. Since it was Ray's turn to drive, we climbed up into the Highlander, pulling into traffic behind a woman in a blue convertible who appeared to be applying makeup and talking on her cell phone at the same time she was driving.

"Makes you wish for the old days when you were on patrol, doesn't it?" I asked. "If we were in a squad car we could light her up and pull her over."

"Nothing is going to make me wish for those days," Ray said. "You know how bad the snow and ice get in Philly in the winter?"

"Nope, and I don't want to." We rocked along to a classic Bruce Springsteen CD until we arrived at the homeless shelter on North Vineyard. We parked behind a pickup truck with a bumper sticker that read "Talk is cheap until you hire a lawyer."

The homeless shelter was a former church, a one-story building with a gothic arched roof and a makeshift addition out back. The receptionist told us Walsh was in the back courtyard, and there were five guys there, each one sitting by himself. A skinny moke with ropy upper arms sipping coffee in the shade of an anemic palm tree matched the description we had. "Mr. Walsh?" I asked, showing him my badge. "HPD. Can we ask you a few questions?"

Freddie was a tough-looking haole with a brown buzz cut and tribal tattoos on his biceps. I noted that and wondered if Shinichi, the waiter at Simple Sushi, had gotten his body parts wrong; he had said the man with Zoë Greenfield the night she died had tattoos on his forearms.

"What's this about?" Walsh asked.

"Mind if we sit?" I motioned to the two other chairs at the wire table.

"It's a free country."

I thought I'd try the direct approach. "You know a woman named Zoë Greenfield?"

That wasn't what he was expecting, and it threw him. "Zoë? Yeah. We grew up together in that rat hole commune."

"Really? What was your name back then?"

He laughed. "I was lucky. My parents were big fans of Queen, so they called me Freddie, after Freddie Mercury. Zoë wasn't so lucky. You know her parents called her Fallopian? And her brother Vas? That family was like a living anatomy lesson."

"You been in touch with her lately?"

He looked suspicious. "Why?"

"How about if I ask the questions, and you answer them? That work for you?"

"Maybe a month ago," he said. "She took me to dinner."

"That all?" Ray asked. "She take you to bed, too?"

Freddie laughed. "Zoë's a dyke, man."

"Well, let's just say she's flexible," I said.

"Look, I don't know what Zoë's been saying about me, but whatever it is, it's not true. I sure as hell didn't bang her."

"You ever go to her house?"

He looked suspicious once more. "I'm not saying anything more. I want an attorney."

Ray and I laughed. "You're not under arrest, Freddie," I said. "We're just asking some questions. But it makes us wonder, you know? What have you got to hide that you need an attorney for? Maybe we should bring you downtown, set you up in an interview room. Ask around among the other detectives, see if any of them have any questions for you."

Freddie sneered and started clenching his fists. "Yeah, I went to her house once," he said after a while. "But I didn't take anything, and I sure as hell didn't have sex with her."

"When was that?"

He frowned. Long-term memory looked like it wasn't his strong point. "At least a couple of months ago. Like I said, last time I saw her was like a month ago. We had sushi."

"Simple Sushi?"

He looked confused, but then it sunk in. "Oh, the restaurant. Yeah, I think that was it."

"Where were you on Sunday night?" I asked.

"Why?"

"Remember the deal, Freddie? I ask the questions and you answer them?"

He slammed his hand on the table, and it rocked. "God dammit, what the hell do you want?"

A couple of other guys in the courtyard looked our way, and two of them got up and left quickly.

"I want to know where you were on Sunday night."

"I was in custody, all right? In Wahiawa. But I was totally innocent. Just in the wrong place at the wrong time. They didn't even press charges."

He had been at a bar in Mililani late Sunday afternoon, minding his own business, he said, when an airman at Hickam started talking stink. So he'd taken a swing at the guy. Turns out the airman had a bunch of friends in the bar. There had been a brawl, and a half dozen of them had spent the night in holding cells at the station in Wahiawa.

I called Wahiawa on my cell and talked to the duty sergeant, who checked the records and verified Freddie's alibi. When I snapped my phone shut, I said, "Somebody killed Zoë Greenfield on Sunday night."

I watched Freddie's response, and noted surprise, and what looked like grief, too.

"Jesus. She's dead? Man, I liked her. She was one of the few people who knew the kind of crap we went through as kids."

"You knew her," I said. "She ever say she was worried about anything?"

I waited. I could see Freddie trying to access brain cells. "She was worried about something," he said. "Something at work." He shook his head. "I wasn't paying attention, you know? It was some kind of accounting shit."

We established that Freddie was going to be staying at the shelter for a while. He was trying to get into a training program, he said, selling insurance. A UH alum was pulling some strings for him. "I used to play ball there," he boasted. "Til I busted my legs."

The way he said it, you'd think he'd been hit by one linebacker too many, instead of taking a drunken fall. But I wasn't going to push him on it.

When we got back to the Jeep, I plugged in my Bluetooth and called Harry to see if he was making any progress on Zoë's emails.

"I'm tracking the addresses, but it's a slow process. Why don't you come over in an hour or so and I'll show you what I've got?"

"Sounds like a plan, man," I said.

"What do you think about Freddie?" I asked Ray as we drove back into town.

"I don't know. He looks like he's telling the truth. But if he is, then we've got nothing."

"Well, maybe Harry dug up something in her email."

Neither Ray nor I said much as I drove, both of us trying to figure out where to go next. We grabbed some takeout lunch and made our way up to Aiea Heights.

Arleen let us in and sent us back to Harry's office. He was hunched over a computer, punching keys. "Give me a minute," he said. "Bastard."

"Excuse me?" Ray asked, but I knew Harry well enough to know that he was talking to the computer. Arleen brought us a pair of folding chairs and we sat down while Harry typed and cursed.

Finally he turned his chair around. "I have good news and bad news."

I leaned up against the pressed-wood console that held the printer. "Let's start with the good. We could use a dose of good news."

"I got into her email account, as you saw. She was very methodical, saved all her incoming and outgoing messages and archived them in folders."

"That is good. Anything interesting in them?"

"Well, that's part of the bad news. There is stuff there, but it's all very cryptic. She never comes right out and says what's going on."

Ray crossed his arms over his chest. "Give us a hint. Or an example."

"She uses a lot of initials. 'I talked to M today. Her numbers don't add up either.' But I haven't figured out who M is or what the numbers are."

"M is for Miriam," I put in. "Her friend at work."

"Then there's a friend, a guy called W," Harry continued. "They have dinner together. There's another guy named F."

"F is for Freddie," I said. "But who's W? Maybe Miriam knows."

I pulled out my phone and called the Office of Business and Economic Development. When Miriam came on the line I asked, "Did Zoe ever mention a male friend whose name begins with a W?"

"Oh, yeah, she did. But what was it? Willy, Wiley, Wyatt. That's it, Wyatt. I don't know his last name. She met him online, and she really liked him. He moved here from the mainland, and she was trying to help him get settled."

"Help him get a job, you mean? At Néng Yuán?"

"Gladys told you that, didn't she? She's always nosing around in everyone's business."

"She didn't know his name. You think it was this Wyatt?"

"Yes. Do you think that's who killed her?"

"We're just asking questions right now, Miriam. Thanks for your help."

I hung up and turned to Harry. "See what a good team we make? We turn your bad news into a lead."

"You find anything else, Harry?" Ray asked. "Bad or good."

"I figured out she used an online backup server," he said. "It looks like she backed up all her files at least once a week. The problem is I haven't been able to crack the system yet, because they generate a random number key as a password, and those are a bitch to break. If you lose the security code, you're supposed to go back to the computer you used to set up the account. There's some kind of buried key there."

He looked at us. "I don't suppose you have access to her

computer?"

"Stolen."

"Probably already cannibalized for parts." Harry sighed. "I can do it, but it's going to take some time. And Arleen's mom has a big party planned for Sunday, so we'll be tied up all weekend helping out." He laughed. "I wish I could get out of it, but Arleen has already spelled out the consequences if I try."

It was early afternoon, so we had enough time to drive all the way back across the island to Néng Yuán's office in Hawai'i Kai, in a modern two-story building with a hipped roof, big windows, and underground parking. We showed the receptionist our IDs and said we were there to see Wyatt. She was a beautiful young Chinese girl, with long black hair and porcelain skin, and she didn't speak much English. I handed her my card, which had my office and cell phone numbers on it, and by pointing to the card and repeating Wyatt's name, we got the message through, and she buzzed someone.

The guy who came out to the reception area was a haole in his mid-thirties. He had short brown hair that could use a trim, and he wore a long-sleeved plaid shirt, so we couldn't see if he had any tattoos.

"I'm Wyatt Collins," he said. "You're looking for me?"

"Can we talk someplace?" I asked.

"I could use a cigarette. Let's go outside."

The building backed on a canal. A forty-foot powerboat called the Wave Walker was tied up there, but I couldn't tell if it was better or worse than Levi's. I don't know much about boats except that they cost a lot more to run than a guy on a cop's salary can afford.

From the butts stamped out on the concrete lanai beneath a round table with an umbrella, I figured it was a common smoking area. "Do you know a woman named Zoë Greenfield?" I asked, as Wyatt was lighting his cigarette.

He stopped, with the unlit cigarette in his mouth, and the

match went out. "Zoë? Is she all right? I've been calling her all week and she hasn't answered."

He looked right at me, which was interesting. Often, if someone's lying, his gaze will flicker away for a minute, indicating he has no faith in what he's saying. But Wyatt Collins appeared genuinely worried.

"When was the last time you saw her?" I asked.

His gaze flickered back and forth from me to Ray. "I'm not sure."

"How about Sunday? Sunday ring a bell?"

His eyelids fluttered a couple of times. He lit his cigarette, stalling for time, and looked out at the canal, where a small powerboat was heading out to sea. Finally he said, "Yeah. We had dinner."

"And sex?" I asked.

"Listen, man, tell me what's going on? What's Zoë saying?"

"Zoë's not saying anything. She's dead."

Both Ray and I watched him. He showed all the signs of surprise—raised eyebrows, widened eyes, open mouth. He even stepped backward, as if he could get away from the news.

"What happened?"

"That's what we're trying to find out," I said. "Tell us about Sunday night."

He took a deep drag on his cigarette. "It was Anna's week for the girls. I spent the weekend at Zoë's place. And yeah, we had sex on Saturday night. But I left her after dinner on Sunday and went back to my own place. She said she had some work she wanted to get done before Monday morning."

"Where did you have dinner?"

He thought for a minute. "Sushi place she liked." He grimaced. "Back home in Tennessee, they call that stuff bait, but she liked it. She liked anything Chinese, anything Japanese."

"And you went back to her house after dinner?" I asked.

He shook his head. "No, like I told you. I went back to my place. I don't have a car yet, so she dropped me off after dinner."

"You don't have a car?" I asked. "How do you get around?"

"The bus. There's a stop right outside the office, takes me into the city. I have an apartment about a mile away from Zoë's. Sometimes I walk over there, sometimes she picks me up."

"How did you two hook up?" Ray asked.

"I read this article she published in an accounting journal and I emailed her. We got to be friends online, and things went on from there."

"So you're an accountant?" I asked. Another boat came by, this one revving its engines, and we had to wait until it passed.

"Not really. Accounting clerk, more like."

"She helped you get this job?"

He looked back and forth between us. "She put in a word for me. No law against that."

We went back over Sunday a couple of times, in different ways, but his answers were always the same. He'd spent the weekend with her, had sex on Saturday night, dinner on Sunday, then gone home. He didn't know what happened after that.

He had no alibi for Sunday night, since he lived alone. Eventually he said, "Listen, I've got to get back to work. They don't like you to take your break too long."

We got his cell phone number and said we'd be back in touch.

"What do you think?" Ray asked, as we drove back to headquarters.

"I believe him. Which means we still have nothing."

It was nearly the end of our shift by then, and after we reported our lack of progress to Lieutenant Sampson, we decided to call it a day. I drove home, where I spent some time hanging out with Roby, brushing his golden coat and pulling off enough hair to knit a sweater with.

While I was walking him, I plugged in my Bluetooth headset

and called my mother to check in on her. "I'm walking your granddog," I said when she asked how I was. "I may have to put the phone down in order to pick up his poop."

My brother Lui's daughter Malia was twelve, and getting ready for her first boy-girl dance – escorted by her cousin Alec, who was thirteen. "Liliha and I picked Malia up when she got out of school and we went shopping for a dress," she said. "When Alec finished basketball practice we made him come over so we could teach them both to dance."

"Alec must have loved that." I remembered my mother teaching me to dance at around the same age and how embarrassed I had been. "You still have those same slow dance records?"

"It's all on CD now," my mother said. Roby stopped to sniff a hibiscus hedge and it looked like he was preparing to squat. "And Liliha had a video for them. It was silly—footsteps dancing across the screen. But they seemed to like it."

I watched Roby do his business. "How'd they do?" I asked, as I stooped to scoop.

"It was so sweet. They both go to Hawaiian school, you know, so they both can do some hula. They were okay on their own, but Alec kept stepping on Malia's toes."

There was a wistfulness in her voice. "Alec, he is so much like Haoa. And Malia, you can see Lui in her face. I wish you had children, Kimo."

"Come on, Mom, you've got your hands full with the grandchildren you already have."

"But they grow up. Even Akipela, she's not a baby anymore."

"In case you haven't noticed, Mom, neither Mike or I has the right plumbing for kids." Roby saw another dog and took off at a gallop, and I struggled to rein him in.

My mother made a little noise. "You can adopt. Or hire a woman, what do they call them?"

"A prostitute?"

"A surrogate." Roby was doing a dance with a white Lab, and

I struggled to keep the leashes from tangling while listening to my mother. "Don't you think about it sometimes?" she asked.

"Sure," I said, pulling Roby away. "But you know, Mom, having a kid is a lifetime commitment. I'm not sure Mike or I are ready for that."

"You're never ready. But then the baby comes and you figure it out."

"Thanks for the advice, Mom. Right now, I've got my hands full with Roby. Kiss Dad for me, all right?"

I was saying goodbye to her as we turned the corner toward our house, and Roby saw Mike getting out of his truck, and took off again. This time I just gave up and let him go. Sometimes you have to do that, with kids and with dogs. But I wasn't sure that was a lesson my mother understood.

Mike brought home take-out barbecue with him, and we sat at the kitchen table, him slipping Roby bits of pork when he thought I wasn't looking. My mom's words were still in my head, but I wasn't sure how to start the conversation I knew we had to have at some point.

Finally I said, "Do you think Roby is the only kid we'll ever have?"

Mike looked up. "Whoa. Where did that come from?"

I shrugged. "A bunch of things. This case. Talking to my mom tonight."

"Let me guess. She wants more grandchildren."

I broke off a piece of cornbread and fed it to Roby. "Yeah. Don't your parents feel the same way?"

"You know my dad. He thinks I'm still a big kid myself. And I don't think they're as liberated as your folks. They probably can't conceive of me having kids."

"Can't conceive," I said, laughing.

"You know what I mean."

"I do. But do you feel like we're missing out on something by not being parents?"

He pushed his empty plate away from him. "I like being part of your family, and hanging out with your nieces and nephews. But I also like being able to walk away from them."

"Me, too. But my mom says it's different when it's your own kid."

"It shouldn't be about what your parents want, or mine. Do you want to have a kid?"

I started to say something, then stopped. "I don't know. I mean, I see so many bad parents, and so many kids in trouble.

Could we do any better?"

Mike stood up and picked up his plate. "I do think about having kids, sometimes," he said. "But it wouldn't be easy for us. And we'd have to really want a kid to go through everything— adopting or finding a surrogate or some lesbian who needs a baby daddy. I don't think I feel strongly enough to go through all that—no less raise a kid. Do you?"

I had to say I wasn't sure. We talked around the topic as we cleaned up the dinner dishes. Then it was time for us to head down to Waikiki for the gay teen youth group I mentored. Mike came with me when he was free; we thought it was good for the kids to see a successful partnership, even if we did bicker sometimes.

My friend Cathy Selkirk, who ran a drop-in program for gay teens out of a church on Waikiki, had asked me to put the group together right after I came out of the closet. Working with them had been therapeutic for me, and I hoped I'd helped them deal with the problems they faced. I had lost a few in the four years I'd been working with them, but had had some success stories, too. Jimmy Ah Wang was studying at UH, and two kids, Frankie and Pua, had graduated from high school and started taking courses at Honolulu Community College.

I shared the mentoring duties with Fred, the cute, brainless bartender at the Rod and Reel Club; he took the kids bowling and to the movies, and I taught them self-defense and talked about feelings and self-empowerment.

We met in a big room at the church where dance and yoga classes were held during the day; there were mirrors on the walls and a bunch of mats we could pull out to sit on. When Mike and I walked in that evening, there were already a half-dozen kids there, including two who were new.

Pua was a tough girl, the kind who wouldn't be caught dead in a dress, while Frankie was chubby and feminine, with his sleek black hair pulled into a ponytail. They were sitting on mats already, so we said hi to them, then focused on the new kids, introducing ourselves and asking a couple of questions. Dakota was thirteen, a recent transplant from the mainland, who lived with his mom on the back side of Waikiki. He was haole and slim-hipped and had black hair that cascaded down his back. Naiuli was fifteen, Samoan, with the build of a sumo wrestler.

Zoë Greenfield's murder had me thinking about knife attacks, which I knew were more common on the streets than HPD would like to admit. So I decided we'd talk about how to defend yourself from an assailant with a knife that night.

"Your first choice when someone threatens you with a knife should be to run away," I said. "You can't outrun a bullet, but you have a chance to outrun someone who's holding a knife, especially if you can get to a more populated area."

I did a slow motion jog for a couple of steps, and the kids laughed. "But if you can't get away, then you have to consider the kind of knife." I had brought a rubber knife with me, for demonstration purposes. "Who can give me some examples of knives you've seen on the street? Naiuli? How about you?"

He frowned, but said, "Ice picks. Steak knives. Switchblades."

"Some knives have blades on both sides," Frankie said. "And they can be short or long."

I nodded. "There's a lot of variety out there. Once you know what kind of knife, you have to think about where your assailant is in relation to your body."

Mike stood up with the rubber knife. "He or she could be a few feet away. Or close up, in front of you." Mike stepped up, holding the knife toward my stomach. "On your side, or behind you." Mike moved around as I spoke, indicating not just position of his body, but how the assailant could be holding the knife.

"The key is to move quickly, and to act as soon as possible," I said. "Look for a time when your attacker's attention is slightly distracted, such as when he is talking or giving orders. Stay as far from the hand holding the knife as you can, and if possible, use something to defend yourself, like a book or a backpack."

Mike came at me with the rubber knife, and I jumped out of his way. "See how I'm trying to stay out of range," I said, talking to them but focused on Mike. "If you can't get away from your attacker, try to get hold of the hand he's holding the knife in."

I reached out and grabbed Mike's wrist. Though he fought against me, I was able to keep him from getting the knife close to me. "See what I'm doing? I've got my open hand pressing against the back of Mike's hand, and I'm pushing his hand away from me. Once I've got the knife out of the way, I can kick or punch or scratch with my other hand."

We went through a couple of scenarios, and then I said, "Let's get you guys trying this out. Pua and Frankie, come on up."

Pua stood up awkwardly, and I realized she was pregnant—probably about three or four months along and just starting to show. That threw me for a loop; I'd always believed she was a lesbian. But I covered, and got her and Frankie to act out the scenario I thought had happened to Zoë Greenfield—Frankie coming up behind Pua and putting the knife at her neck. Then I walked them through how to get out of it. It made me wish I'd known Zoë before her death, and been able to show her the same kind of move.

I shook that off, and we tried a couple more exercises. After an hour we called it quits. As the kids were getting up to go I walked over to Pua. "So…" I said.

"Yeah, I'm pregnant."

"How do you feel about that?"

"I'm almost finished with my certificate in diesel mechanics technology," she said. "I'm going to have the baby, then go into my internship program. My auntie runs a day care program so I can leave the baby with her while I work."

Mike and Frankie joined us. "So, Pua," Mike said. "You're playing for the other team now?"

"I wanted a baby," she said, crossing her arms over her stomach. "There was this guy in my program and I thought we could make a pretty baby together. So I pretended to be straight for him."

I looked at Mike. Neither of us seemed to know what to say.

"Pua's going to be an awesome mom," Frankie said. "And she said I can be the godfather."

"What about you?" I asked him. "You in the same program as Pua?"

"Are you kidding? These hands are not touching car engines. I'm getting my AS in Audio Engineering Technology. I already have a part-time job with this computer company, processing audio files for computer games."

"Wow. I'm proud of you guys," I said.

Frankie put his arm in Pua's. "Come on, Mommy. You have to take your vitamins. We want the baby to be healthy!"

Pua smiled and squeezed up next to Frankie. "See you soon, guys," she said.

Mike and I didn't talk about Pua until we were back in the Jeep on our way home. "So easy for her," he said. "She just picked a guy and went to bed with him."

"She's just a kid herself. It's crazy." I shook my head. "I mean, what was she thinking? She has no idea what she's getting herself into."

"She'll grow up quick," Mike said. "It's what our parents did, right? And their parents before them?"

"I just never thought we'd have to talk about stuff like birth control and parenting in a gay teen group," I said, as we swung onto the H1 toward home. I turned on the CD player, and Israel Kamakawiwo'ole's sweet tenor filled the space, singing his mashup of "Aho Wela" and "Twinkle Twinkle Little Star." Mike and I both sat back and listened to the music.

When we got home, we played with Roby for a bit, then ended up in bed, watching TV. "Straight people have it easier," Mike said, when the program was over. "For them, making a baby together is an expression of the love they feel for each other. But no matter how much I love you, or how many times we have sex, we're never getting a baby without bringing a third party in. I'm just not ready to change what we have forever."

I leaned over and kissed him. "We do have a pretty good thing going."

"That we do." He pushed me back to the bed, and climbed on top of me, and we made love. I felt a momentary pang when I was cleaning up, thinking about the sperm I was washing away, wondering if I was denying some biological imperative—or maybe Mike and I were part of nature's grand plan to avoid overpopulation.

It was too much to think about, so I just went to sleep.

The next morning, Greg Oshiro called my cell when I was on my way into work. "I have some information for you about the guy Zoë was seeing," he said.

That was Greg. No hello, how are you, sorry for calling so early.

"Wyatt Collins."

"You know about him?"

"We talked to him yesterday afternoon." I turned from Houghtailing onto North King, and blew my horn at a clueless tourist who thought it was okay to stop in the middle of the street to take a picture.

"Did he tell you about his criminal record?"

I darted around the tourist, then had to stop short for an SUV with a turn signal on, who didn't want to bother getting into the median lane. "You dug something up?" I asked. "When can we meet? I want to see everything you've got."

"The Kope Bean downtown at eight-thirty," he said, then disconnected.

I didn't even bother to park; I called Ray and arranged to meet him outside headquarters. We got to the coffee shop before Greg and staked out a corner table. Once he showed up and got his coffee, he plunked down in the big chair we'd saved for him.

"After we talked on Tuesday night, I started calling anyone I knew who might have known Zoë. I remembered this lesbian I'd met at their house once, and she gave me the guy's name. Wyatt Collins."

"We'll need to talk to her, too," I said.

He nodded. "It's all here." He held up a couple of photocopies. "He's 38, divorced, no kids. He just got out of ten years in a state prison in Tennessee, for armed robbery."

I looked at Ray. "You got copies of his record?"

Greg shook his head. "There's a woman in Tennessee who posts all the parolees in the state on a website. I can't get anything on his record without official authorization."

"We can do that," I said.

"Collins was paroled last November. It looks like he moved to Honolulu about two months ago. Here's the address I found for him."

He handed Ray a piece of paper. "I knew he was bad news," he continued. "I met him once, when I went over to see the girls. Skinny redneck with a chipped tooth and tattoos up and down his arms. Zoë just introduced him as a friend, another accountant. But he didn't look like any accounting geek I ever met."

He took a sip of his coffee. "That's all I've got, but I'm going to keep on it."

"How are the girls?" Ray asked. "Did Anna tell them yet?"

"Yeah, we told them together. They're so little though, it's hard to know if it's sunk in. Anna said she needed some time on her own, so they're with my parents right now." He smiled. "They love those girls. It makes me so happy to see them all together. You know, like all the aggravation is worth it."

We went back to headquarters and set out to learn as much as we could about Wyatt Collins. Ray worked on getting copies of his police records, and I started looking into his personal life. I found the street address where he had lived as a kid, in a small town in eastern Tennessee, and used a reverse directory to get phone numbers of every house on the street.

The first person I reached was his next door neighbor, Rebecca Czick, which she pronounced Chizzik. "I'm not surprised he's in trouble," she said, after I'd introduced myself as a police detective. "Honolulu, you said? That's in Hawai'i?"

"Yes, it is, ma'am."

"That Wyatt, he was always trouble," she said, and there was a slight southern twang in her voice. "He was a nasty little bully, used to beat up other kids on the corner and in the school yard. But he started getting in serious trouble when he turned twelve."

"What happened then, ma'am?"

"He started smoking cigarettes. He was real proud of it, used to sit on the porch smoking. And then I caught him in a shed in his family's back yard when he was thirteen, drinking moonshine whiskey and making out with this trampy girl who was twenty if she was a day."

I started taking notes. "He was smoking marijuana when he was fifteen. I used to smell it coming across my yard. No matter how much I complained to his parents they didn't do a thing about him. And then a year later the sheriff caught him with cocaine."

That meant he had a juvenile record. It had probably been sealed, but I scrawled a note and passed it to Ray.

"He went to prison when he was nineteen, and I thank God every day he got out of this neighborhood," she said. "I used to just live in fear of what he might do. I could have been murdered in my bed."

That reminded me of Zoë Greenfield, who had been in bed when the events that led to her murder began.

"Thank you very much for your help, ma'am," I said. "Is there anyone else in town that I should talk to?"

She gave me a couple of names and phone numbers. "Most of the old timers, they've passed on," she said. "Wyatt's parents went to Jesus while he was in prison. And the young people, they don't stay in town, with no work for them."

I worked my way down the list of neighbor houses, and then spoke to the two women Mrs. Czick had given me. They didn't have as much specific information as she did, but they agreed that Wyatt had been a very bad boy. A woman named Mary Elizabeth Kraun told me that a girl had accused Wyatt of raping her when he was seventeen.

"Of course, she was no better than he was," Mrs. Kraun said.

"So no one believed her. She liked the bad boys, anyway."

I left a message for Ellen Toyama, the woman who had given Wyatt's name to Greg. When I hung up, Ray swiveled his chair around to face me.

"Wyatt has an impressive record," he said. "He went to prison at nineteen for his role as the getaway driver in a bungled bank robbery, and served six years. But almost as soon as he was released, he robbed a 7-Eleven and went back to prison."

"What the hell did Zoë see in him?" I asked. "He sounds like a loser from the word go."

"When he was in prison the second time, he passed his GED and got an associate's degree in accounting. That must be how he came to be reading accounting journals, and came across Zoë."

"I wonder how many other women he was corresponding with from prison," I said. "If we subpoena her bank records you think we'll find that she was sending him money?"

We went in to see Lieutenant Sampson and give him an update. His polo shirt was white, and there was a loose thread on his sleeve, but I resisted the impulse to pull it off. There's only so far you can go with your boss.

"So you think this guy is a solid suspect?" Sampson asked, when we'd laid it out for him. "What's his motive?"

I looked at Ray. "Not sure yet."

"The woman likes him enough to get him a job. He's trying to go straight. I'm not saying he didn't kill her—but you've got to have something more than what you've got if you want to charge him."

"We'll talk to him again," I said. "See what he says when we tell him we know about his record."

"Give it 'til Monday," Sampson said. "It doesn't sound like he's going anywhere, and my overtime budget for this month is shot."

Ray was disappointed; I could see he'd been hoping to pick up some extra cash for his new house fund. But there's always special duty assignments; he could spend a few hours as a security guard for the Aloha Stadium flea market, if no one else had signed up for the job already.

I went home, walked the dog, and read until Mike got home. We went to dinner, then ended up back on the sofa watching TV. I couldn't help wondering how our lives would change if we had a baby to look after.

Saturday morning we woke up early and went for a long run around our neighborhood. I did our week's grocery shopping while Mike repaired a shutter that had come loose. I remembered when I was a kid, our Saturdays were filled with running errands and visiting family. How many hours had my mother spent buying us new shoes, fixing meals, sewing buttons back on, or doing the million other chores that went with having a family?

At three, Mike and I went to see Lui's oldest son Jeffrey in a junior surf competition at Makapu'u Point. It was a gorgeous afternoon, the kind the tourist office brags about, endless sunshine and blue skies, with just a few wisps of clouds decorating the sky. An offshore breeze churned the water, and Jeffrey's first wave was a strong one. He had a great take off from the peak, followed by a backhand bottom turn.

"Damn, that was nice," I said.

"He's got the surfing gene," Lui bragged.

Jeffrey rode the rail a bit, managed a decent forehand snap, and finished with a bottom turn that showed excellent control.

The key to success in a competition is to use the most powerful part of the wave, and demonstrate as much skill with it as you can. If you play it safe, you get a low score—so I've always believed you go big or you go home. Jeffrey was strong, agile and fearless. He had his father's slimmer build, and the height my brothers and I share—he was nearly six feet tall, with none of his cousin Alec's gangliness.

In a contest, you can get anywhere from a point-five to a ten for your ride. The surfer who rides his or her wave with the most speed, control, and power in the most critical section gets the best score; getting to your feet and riding the wave, without doing anything more, gets you a .5. Every move you manage, every bit of difficulty in the wave itself, adds to the score.

Jeffrey's maneuvers brought him a nine-point-five, which I thought was pretty damn good. I couldn't have done that well when I was just turning sixteen.

The whole family—my parents, and both my brothers and their wives and kids—had turned out to watch and cheer Jeffrey, even my Aunt Pua and a couple of my cousins. Aunt Pua is my mother's youngest sister, and as different from her as two siblings can be. My mother is organized and no-nonsense; she raised us with an iron hand. Aunt Pua is an aromatherapist in Hawaii Kai, a faded flower child whose kids were allowed to run wild.

Her youngest son, Ben, was a championship surfer, but he was out of the country at a surf match somewhere. Her daughter Selena, from her second husband, was there, with her own two sons, who both wanted to be surfers. Selena reminded me of Zoë Greenfield in a way; though they looked nothing alike, they both had rebelled against flaky parents by becoming straight-laced worker bees, though Selena was an engineer rather than an accountant.

Jeffrey wasn't the best surfer in the competition; a kid a year older than he was scored a couple of perfect tens, and my nephew had to settle for second place. But it was a great performance, and lots of fun to watch.

I couldn't help thinking, though, of my conversation with my mother Thursday night. What would a kid with my genes be like? Would he look more Japanese, like Lui, or be big and Hawaiian like Haoa? Would the haole genes that dominated in me follow through to my son?

Would he like to surf? To read? Would he be gay, too?

Or would the combination of my sperm and a woman's egg result in a girl? How in the world could Mike and I raise a daughter, in a house full of testosterone? I could just imagine Mike and me sitting down to a tea party with our little daughter, her eyebrows raising at our clumsiness.

First, Mike and I had to be on the same page about procreating. I'd seen too many kids on the street who were the children of ill-advised couplings, teen moms who just wanted someone to love, babies born in attempts to save failing marriages, children brought into households without financial stability. I sure as hell wasn't going to commit to bringing a child into my world until I knew that Mike and I both could manage.

Sunday we met Gunter for brunch in Waikiki. The beautiful weather had moved on, as it often does, and a cold front had come in. Not too cold, you understand, just enough so that we had to bring out the long-sleeved shirts and sit indoors to eat. Bruddah Norm was singing "We are Hawaiian" on the loudspeakers.

As if the universe was conspiring to keep the idea of child-rearing in the air, Gunter was full of news of a mutual friend who had just discovered that he was a father. "Can you just imagine?" Gunter said, after we'd ordered. "Out of the blue, this girl he slept with in college calls him up and tells him he has a kid."

We were drinking mimosas at a window table, and the restaurant buzzed around us, a combination of gay men and vacationing tourists. When a man passed us wearing a t-shirt that read "I'm shy, but I have a big dick," I saw Gunter try to catch his eye. Fake flower leis hung from the ceilings, and the walls were hung with reproductions of *hapa-haole* music covers, the ones from the twenties and thirties with a beautiful island girl strumming a ukulele.

"Is he sure it's his?" Mike asked.

"She wants him to have his blood tested," Gunter said. "The kid is twelve or thirteen, and he has some kind of a blood disease. He needs a transfusion from a close relative who matches him, and no one in her family will work."

"Wow," I said. "What a way to find out."

"Yeah. He's flying to Chicago tomorrow for the testing."

The waiter, a slim-hipped blond with a flirty manner that I was sure brought in big tips, delivered our platters. Gunter was having an egg-white omelet with a side of steamed vegetables. "A boy's got to watch his figure," he said. "Now you two, you can get fat together and no one will mind."

"I'll mind if Kimo gets fat." Mike poked my stomach. "We both need to do some more exercise."

"Speak for yourself, big boy," I said.

Neither of us were heavy—but settled domesticity, regular meals together, and a lack of physical activity were definitely adding a couple of pounds. But I still ordered a plate of chocolate chip pancakes with a side of bacon, and Mike had a sausage, onion and pepper scramble with home fries.

"So, Kimo," Gunter said, a sly grin on his face. "You ever worry you'll get a phone call like that?"

Mike looked over at me. He knew that I'd slept with a lot of girls before coming out. And I knew that he'd never been with a woman, despite staying in the closet for years before he met me.

I shrugged. "I was always pretty careful. Haoa got a girl pregnant when he was in high school, and that made my folks hyper-conscious. From the time I was fourteen or so, my father was leaving condoms in my room."

"You never told me that about Haoa," Mike said. "What happened?"

"The girl had an abortion. She was sweet, but kind of lost. Beautiful voice, though. Eventually she moved to Vegas to become a singer."

"Wow," Mike said. "That experience must have been tough for your brother."

"This is Haoa we're talking about. He's not exactly Mr. Sensitive now, and he sure as hell wasn't when he was seventeen."

"Still. You see how he loves his kids. I wonder if he ever thinks about that one."

"Somebody wants to be a daddy," Gunter said.

"We've been talking," Mike said.

I was surprised he'd bring it up again—and with Gunter there. It was too public a space, and I hadn't figured out where I stood on the issue.

"You thinking turkey baster, or doing it the old fashioned way?" Gunter asked.

Trust Gunter to get right to the nitty gritty. "We're not even at that stage yet," I said.

The waiter kept stopping by to see how we were doing and flirt with Gunter, so there was no way we could have a serious conversation. The subject seemed to hang in the air the rest of the day, though neither Mike nor I addressed it. I didn't even want to talk about Zoë Greenfield's murder, because every time I thought of her I remembered those two little girls and wondered what was going to happen to them.

Mike and I went for another run in the afternoon, working off that big brunch, and everywhere where we ran we saw families and kids. Sometimes they were having fun, but other times babies were crying or parents were yelling.

That was life, for sure. But was it going to be our life?

Monday morning, Ray and I drove back out to Hawai'i Kai to talk to Wyatt Collins again. He wasn't happy to see us. "Look, I told you everything the other day," he said. "I didn't kill Zoë."

The Chinese receptionist, the one with the limited English, seemed to know enough to understand what Wyatt had said. "Let's go outside," I said.

"No. If you don't have a warrant for my arrest, then I don't have to talk to you."

"Actually, we can take you down to the station," I said. "We can hold you for twenty-four hours without charging you. But then, you probably already know that, don't you?"

In the background I saw the receptionist on the phone, speaking to someone. "This is harassment," Wyatt said.

"Your employers here know about you?" I asked. "Or did Zoë fudge the facts a little?"

An elegant young Chinese woman stepped through the door from the main office into the reception area. "I'm Dr. Zenshen," she said, with a heavy accent. "How can we help you gentlemen today?"

She was probably in her early thirties, slim and pretty, in a well-tailored gray business suit. She wore funky glasses with multicolored frames, and her black hair hung loosely to her shoulders.

I showed her my ID. "We have some questions for Mr. Collins," I said. "About a personal matter."

She looked to Wyatt, who stood with his feet apart, his arms crossed in a posture of defiance. "Why don't you use our conference room." She opened the door back into the office, and motioned us to follow her.

Wyatt recognized that he didn't have any choice, and followed her sullenly, Ray and me behind him. "Please let me know if I can help you in any way," she said, opening the door to a large room that faced the waterway behind the building.

She closed the door as she left, and Wyatt turned to look at us.

"Why won't you leave me alone?" he asked, the southern twang in his voice getting stronger. "I told you everything I know."

"Well, that's not really true," I said, taking a seat across from Wyatt at the round conference table. Ray sat next to me. "You didn't tell us about your record."

"Not relevant."

"We'll be the judge of what's relevant and what's not," I said. "Let's start with how you met Zoë. You started corresponding with her when you were in prison?"

"It's not like what you're thinking. I wanted to turn my life around. I never did so well in school, because the teachers hated me. They thought I was some low-class loser who deserved to fail. But I got my GED and the teachers in prison said that I had a brain, and a head for numbers."

I nodded and smiled. "Go on."

"So I got my associate's degree in accounting. I had a 4.0, man. I was good. But nobody would give me a job when I got out because of my record."

"It's tough, I agree," I said.

"So I was emailing back and forth with Zoë all that time. We got to be friends, you know? There weren't a lot of people in her life she could depend on. She invited me to come out here, said she could help me get a job."

"That was nice of her."

"She was a good person. But everybody around her was taking advantage of her. That ex-girlfriend, Anna. She was always whining to Zoë about money. And that loser guy, Greg. He wanted more time with the girls, and Zoë had to fight to keep her time with them."

He blew out a breath. "She was having a lot of problems at work, too. Her boss is a fool and his secretary is a bitch. She was always making problems for Zoë. We started talking about moving to the mainland, to get away from all of them. We could go to California, she said. She could get a job there easy, and I'd help out with the girls until we could find something for me."

"Anna and Greg probably wouldn't like that," I said.

"You should have seen Anna when Zoë told her. She went ballistic. I swear, I've seen tough guys, but I was scared of her."

"Did she tell Greg, too?" I asked.

"I think so. I only met the guy once, so I can't say for sure."

He looked at us. "Come on, guys, I need this job. Especially without Zoë around, I'm on my own here. I lose this, I'm going back to Tennessee, and I'm up shit creek."

"We're not looking to hang you out to dry, Wyatt," I said. "But if we find you left anything else out, or we find some evidence that you killed Zoë Greenfield, we'll be back."

"Then I'll never see you again," Wyatt said, standing up.

"He's a sharp guy," Ray said, as we walked back through the underground garage to his Highlander. "He shifted suspicion very neatly away from him and onto Anna and Greg."

"Yeah, a nice long time in prison gives you lots of practice talking to cops and guards. I'm not willing to wipe him off the suspect list, but I can't see his motive. I mean, Zoë helped him find a job, she trusted him, she was ready to move things forward. He's not going to get many chances like that. And he seems smart enough to recognize that."

"But he's got a violent past," Ray said. "Suppose they had an argument Sunday night and he snapped. Then he tried to cover it up by making it look like a home invasion."

"I wonder if he used a knife in any of his past crimes?" I opened my netbook and made notes about our interview with Wyatt. As Ray drove, I flipped through the files and found Wyatt's arrest record for the convenience store robbery that had sent him to prison the second time. The weapon there was a knife; he'd held it to the clerk's neck while the guy pulled the cash out of the drawer.

Accidentally or on purpose, Wyatt's hand had slipped, and the clerk's neck had been cut, though not fatally. That had added extra time to Wyatt's sentence. It also showed us that he liked knives.

My cell rang. "You guys want to stop by here?" Harry asked. "I've pulled up a couple of emails I want to show you."

We were already on the H1, so it was easy to turn mauka at the Punahou Street exit and climb the hill to Harry's house.

"Hey, brah, howzit?" I asked, when he met us at the front door.

"Don't ask. Brandon has decided he doesn't want to go to school any more. Every morning it's a major battle, and every afternoon we have to fight with him to get him to do his homework."

"What's behind it?" I asked. "Something going wrong at school?"

"He flunked a test last week," Harry said, sitting back down at his computer. "So he decided that he's stupid and he doesn't need to go to school any more. He says he wants to be a motorcycle mechanic instead. We're working on it, but it's an uphill struggle."

"Better you than me, brah. So what have you got?"

He showed us some printouts of emails that supported what Wyatt had said—Zoë had been emailing people about jobs in California. A couple of messages were obviously to college friends and business acquaintances, and at least two emails attached copies of her resume and cover letters for accounting jobs, one in San Francisco and the other in Silicon Valley.

"Anything in there between Zoë and Anna, or Zoë and Greg?" I asked. "To prove that they knew she was considering moving?"

Harry looked up. "You think one of them might have killed her?"

"I don't know. But neither Greg nor Anna had a strong legal claim on those kids. If Zoë took them to the mainland, I don't think either could have convinced the courts to intervene."

"And remember, Greg told us the other day that his parents love the girls," Ray added.

"He did really want to have them," I agreed. "And he seems to love them a lot."

"Anna too," Ray said. "I saw her with them when we went to her apartment. You don't want to get in the way of a mom with her kids."

"Even though she wasn't the biological mom," I put in.

Harry hunted through Zoë's email box, finding messages to both Anna and Greg. The message to Anna read, "I am tired of your constant begging and harassment. If you don't ease up I am going to take the girls and you will never see them again."

"That must have made Anna crazy," I said.

The message to Greg was pretty strong as well. "Remember, you don't have any legal standing in whatever Anna and I do," Zoë wrote. "I believe that the girls need to know their father, so I don't intend to shut you out. But I have to do what is best for me and them."

I called Anna's cell, hoping to catch her, but the number she had given me was disconnected. "That's weird. Why would she change numbers now?"

"Maybe because she's fleeing from the police," Harry suggested.

"Thanks, brah. Any luck on getting into that online backup you said Zoë had?"

"I'm working on it. Gonna take at least another day or two, by the time I run through all the possible password combinations."

"Let's go past Anna's apartment anyway," I said to Ray as we left Harry's. "See if we can get a lead on where she is."

There was no answer at her door, but the old lady next door

stuck her head out when she heard us banging. "She's gone. Moved out yesterday."

"She had the girls with her?" I asked.

The woman shook her head. "I didn't see them." She still had a key to the apartment door, and she let us in. The furniture was all there, and the kids' toys and clothes, but all Anna Yang's clothes were gone.

"That moves Anna up on the suspect list," I said to Ray as we left the building. "Where do you think she went?"

"She doesn't have any family here, does she?"

I shook my head. "She told us that neighbor was like her adopted grandmother. Any other family she has is back in China."

"Could she be running scared? Maybe she knows more about why Zoë was killed than she let on, and she's gone into hiding."

"Or she's worried we'll get on to her, and she's on the run."

"All possibilities," Ray said.

On our way back to headquarters, I called Greg. He said his parents still had the girls, and he was running down a story. He promised to get back to me later in the day, when he had a couple of minutes to talk.

We made one more stop, at the FBI office on Ala Moana. Francisco Salinas had worked with us in the past, and he owed both of us a couple of favors. He was a tall dark-haired haole with a military-short hair cut and navy suit and white shirt, the Cuban-American edition of standard FBI guy.

"I hope you're not bringing me more trouble," he said, as he led us back to his office. "I've got enough on my plate as it is."

"Just need a small favor," I said.

We got to his office and he raised his eyebrows.

"Really. Just a quick record check. You can get into the INS database, can't you?"

He walked into his office and got behind his desk. "What's this about?"

I explained about Anna Yang. "She moved out of her apartment yesterday and shut off her cell phone. We just want to know if she left the country."

He typed for a few minutes, swore once, and then typed again. "What was the name again?"

"Anna Yang."

"There are a lot of them. Got a social security number?"

"Address." I gave it to him.

"No matches," he said, after a couple of minutes. "Any other identifiers?"

We went back over what we knew of Anna. "Let me check expired student visas." Salinas typed again. "OK, here she is. She entered the country on a F-1 visa eight years ago. She was allowed to stay in the US for as long as it took for her to complete her course of study. You said she went to UH?"

"Yup."

He typed some more. "I swear, if I had a dollar for every different password I have, I could retire." He pulled an address book out of his jacket pocket and paged through it. He typed something in, then said, "OK. She graduated from UH in 2001 with an MFA in painting. That means she should have left within 60 days after graduation."

He jumped back to his previous screen. "There's no record that she ever left the country, or applied for any other paperwork. We've been cracking down since 9/11, of course, but it looks like she managed to slip through the cracks. Now that she's out of status, she's subject to immediate deportation."

"What about if she has kids who were born in the US?" I asked.

"She's not the birth mother," Ray said.

"But she's the only one they've got now."

"Hard to say," Salinas said. "She'd have to go before an immigration judge and plead her case. But the father's a U.S.

citizen?"

"Yeah."

"Then I don't see much chance for her."

He agreed to put an alert out for all border guards, in case Anna tried to leave the country. Beyond that, there wasn't much he could do to help. Which meant we were on our own, as usual.

We got back to headquarters around noon and brought Lieutenant Sampson up to date. "The partner and Greg Oshiro both have motives," Sampson said. "You need to talk to both of them again."

"Anna Yang is in the wind," Ray said. "But she's a mother. She's going to check on those girls sooner or later. We're talking to Greg later, and we'll make sure Greg knows we're looking for her."

"It's been a week. Your trail is getting colder every day. I want to see some results soon."

His phone rang, and he glared at it. As he picked up the receiver and barked into it, he motioned us to leave.

Back at our desks, Ray and I looked at each. "Where do we go from here?" he asked. "Any ideas? We have to try and run Anna Yang to ground."

"We never heard back from Ellen Toyama, the girl who gave Greg Wyatt's name." I called and left another message for her, then turned back to Ray. "If she doesn't call back by tomorrow we'll track her down."

"You know any lesbians?" Ray asked. "I mean, I watched *The L Word*. In LA, they're all sleeping with each other. Why not here?"

"That's a TV show. But I can give it a try." I called my friend Sandra Guarino, an attorney with a prominent downtown law firm who's also the most connected lesbian in the islands.

"Kimo. You never call. Cathy and I were just talking about you the other day."

"Then you could have picked up the phone." Cathy was her partner, the tiny half-Japanese woman who'd recruited me for the gay teen group. "Listen, do you have a few minutes? I need to talk to you about something."

"You're in luck," she said. "My lunch date just cancelled a few minutes ago and nothing else has had a chance to take over the time. How about the Little Village, one o'clock?"

While I was on the phone, Ray had been Googling Anna Yang. He found a website for her murals, including an email link. "I already emailed her," he said, when I swiveled over to his desk. "We'll see if she gets in touch."

Her work was beautiful, more photos of murals like the ones in the house on Lopez Lane and the apartment in Chinatown. Fortunately, there were a couple of client testimonials, and we were able to track down full names and phone numbers for three of them.

We left messages at two of the numbers, but got the lady of the house on the third call. "Mrs. Buchanan?" I gave her my name and said I wanted to ask about Anna Yang.

"I can't recommend her highly enough. The mural she did for my daughter's room is just lovely."

"I'm afraid I'm not calling for a recommendation. Do you think I could come over and talk to you for a few minutes?"

She lived in a high-rise just a few minutes from downtown, and Ray and I got there about half-past noon. The doorman buzzed us up, and an elegant haole woman in her forties opened the apartment door to us.

The first thing we saw was the magnificent view of Honolulu harbor. "Please come in," Renata Buchanan said. "I hope Anna isn't in any trouble."

"We're just trying to learn about her," I said, as she led us into the living room. We sat on a half-round white couch. "Can you tell us what she was like to work with?"

"A real perfectionist. She knew exactly what she wanted to do, and she was determined to get it done right. The hardware store sent over the wrong color blue—and you should have heard her tell them, in no uncertain terms, what was wrong, and what she expected them to do to fix it."

"Would you say she had a temper?" Ray asked.

Renata shifted uncomfortably on a plush chair. "Well, when you put it that way..." She hesitated. "I did see her get very angry a couple of times, when things weren't going right. She accidentally put a brush with paint on it into a different color, and she got very upset."

She leaned forward. "She isn't in any trouble, is she?" She hesitated again. "I never asked her for her papers. I didn't think it was my responsibility. She was just an independent contractor, after all. Not like an employee. She spoke with an accent, of course, but so many people do. That doesn't mean someone is illegal."

"We're not from Immigration," I said. "And Anna's not in any trouble right now. We're just trying to learn about her."

Renata relaxed. "She was devoted to her children, I know that," she said. "She loves those girls. You should see her face light up when she talks about them."

We thanked Renata Buchanan for her time. "Well, we know she has a temper," I said. "She has a motive, too."

"And she has the upper body strength to wield a knife," Ray added.

I dropped him back at headquarters and drove over to the Little Village, a Chinese restaurant favored by attorneys since the tables were far enough apart to have private conversations. I parked behind an SUV with a bumper sticker that read, "Your kid's an honors student but you're a moron."

I walked in the restaurant a few minutes before Sandra and snagged us a table under the trellis, ordering us both water and hot tea. She was talking when she walked in, the picture of the corporate lawyer, in a dark suit and sensible pumps. It took me a minute to notice the wireless earpiece and realize she was on the phone. Only the pink pin on her lapel in the shape of the Greek *lambda* indicated she was anything beyond the norm.

"So how's that handsome fireman of yours?" she asked, after she'd finished her call, kissed my cheek and sat down.

"Still as handsome as ever. Though if I could train him not to leave his underwear on the living room floor, our house would be more peaceful."

"You sound just like a woman," she said. "Don't you drop your shorts on the floor too? Leave the toilet seat up? And all those other stereotypical man things?"

"Spoken like a true lesbian," I said. "Some of us have manners, you know."

The waiter brought us a dish of cucumber pickles with our water and tea. I ordered the clams in lemon grass sauce, and Sandra had the steamed *basa*, catfish fillets in ginger and green onions. "So what's new in the world of homicide?" she asked. "I know you didn't call me just to chat."

"Sandra. I'm hurt."

"I refer to our previous conversation. You're a man."

"Did you or Cathy know Zoë Greenfield and Anna Yang?"

She pursed her lips. "Let me think for a minute. Neither of them are someone I know well, that's for sure." She pulled out her Blackberry and started scrolling through it. "Greenfield. Yup. Accountant, right? Works for the state?"

"I'm impressed," I said. "You have every lesbian in Hawai'i in there?"

"Almost. A girl's gotta network, you know."

"Did you know her personally?"

Sandra shook her head. "What was the other name again?"

"Anna Yang. She's an artist. Paints murals in peoples' houses."

She frowned. "Don't know how she got past me. I haven't heard of her."

The waiter brought our platters, my clams balanced on each other and smelling sweet and tart at the same time. "Which one of them is in trouble?" Sandra asked, cutting off a piece of her fillet.

"Zoë Greenfield's dead, and Anna Yang's in the wind." As we

ate, I gave her the basics of the case.

"What can I do to help?"

"Ask around. See if any of your friends knows anything about Zoë, or why someone might have killed her. And if you can get a handle on Anna's whereabouts, we need to talk to her."

"Sounds like she could use an attorney."

"Not quite yet. But if she overstayed her visa, she's in trouble for sure."

"I have an idea you might not have checked yet." She pushed her plate away while I was still working on my clams and pressed a couple of keys on her Blackberry. She placed the phone down on the table and stared into space. "Lucy, it's Sandra Guarino," she said after a minute. She laughed and made some small talk, then said, "I need a quick favor. Can you check your database for a woman named Anna Yang?"

She laughed again. "No, not one of those." She looked at me. "What's the guy's name?"

I looked at her, and then it clicked. "Greg Oshiro."

She repeated the name to Lucy, whoever she was. "You're going to need to write this down," she said to me.

I pulled out my pad and pen. "Great. That's what I thought. June 21, you said, 2010?"

I wrote the date down. She thanked Lucy and promised that they'd get together.

"Let me guess," I said, when she was finished. "Greg Oshiro and Anna Yang are married."

"Two points for the boy in blue," she said, even though I was wearing an aloha shirt in shades of green and white. "Lucy works in the Department of Health."

I knew that was the department that issued marriage licenses; I'd gone down for the license with Haoa and Tatiana when they applied. "So why doesn't INS know about that?" I asked. "Marriage is Anna's ticket to citizenship."

"Did they all live together?" she asked. "Zoë, Anna and this guy?"

I shook my head. "Not that I know." I told her about the house on Lopez Lane, and Anna's apartment in Chinatown.

Sandra shrugged. "Maybe it's just a backup plan," she said. "ICE is cracking down on marriages between citizens and foreign nationals. If they weren't living together, it could have been construed as immigration fraud."

She insisted on paying for lunch. "Call it a chit you owe me. You and Mike have to come over to the house for dinner sometime."

As we were walking out, I said, "You guys ever think about kids?"

She stopped and looked at me. "Are you and Mike thinking about it?"

I shrugged. "Everywhere I look these days, gay men and lesbians are having kids, or adopting, or showing up with kids from some previous relationship. It's like it's in the air or something." We stepped out into the sunshine.

"We've talked about it," Sandra said. "But Cathy's so busy with the teen center, and she doesn't have the chance to write as much as she should." Cathy was a poet with an MFA. I'd read a couple of her poems in the past, and though I'm no expert, I'd been moved by them.

"I love my career and my volunteer work. Neither of us think it would be fair to bring a child into the mix right now." She paused. "Cathy had fibroids a few years ago," she said, lowering her voice. "So if we decide to have children, I'd be the birth mom. We have some time to make the decision, though, so the jury's still out."

She looked at me. "How would you feel about being the sperm donor?"

I can't say I hadn't thought about it. When I discovered, a year before, that Greg had donated sperm and fathered two kids, I had wondered if anyone would ever ask me. Sandra and Cathy were my closest lesbian friends, so they'd been the obvious choice.

"Anna told me that they picked Greg Oshiro because Zoë was going to be the birth mom, and they wanted kids who were mixed race," I said.

Sandra looked at me like I was on a witness stand avoiding one of her questions. And I was. "It was great to see you," I said, kissing her cheek. "I promise we'll have dinner soon."

She laughed. "Think about it." Then her Blackberry buzzed and she was a corporate attorney once again, walking off down the street speaking into the air about an upcoming deposition.

When I got back to headquarters, Greg Oshiro was at Ray's desk talking to him. "Good, you're back," Ray said. "Greg just got here." He stood up. "Let's go into an interview room so we can talk."

Greg and I followed him down the hall. "What have you found out?" Greg asked, as soon as we were all in the room.

"How about if we ask a couple of questions first," I said. "That's the way we generally work it around here, you know."

Greg frowned. But he put down his notebook and pen.

"Let's talk about marriage first," I said. "Like you and Anna Yang, exchanging vows."

He looked down at the table, twiddling his pen back and forth in his fingers. Finally, he looked up. "Yeah, we got married. A couple of months before the twins were born."

"Why?" Ray asked. "For her citizenship?"

Greg looked at him. "I thought she had a green card. She worked all over the place."

Ray shook his head. "She had a student visa, which expired when she finished her degree. Nothing after that."

"Shit. I didn't know that. It's not like we were trying to scam ICE or anything."

"Then why did you get married?"

He looked embarrassed. "We were protecting ourselves," he said. "You know, in case something happened with Zoë."

"And something did," I said.

He glared at me. "It was nothing like that. It's just that Anna had no rights to the girls, and I was worried that the two of them might gang up on me and shut me out. I mean, for the longest time, they kept calling me the sperm donor, not even the dad."

Greg had started to sweat, and he reached into his pocket and found a handkerchief to wipe his forehead.

"You see how it looks," I said, playing the bad cop once more. "You and Anna thinking for so long about ganging up on Zoë. Then she ends up dead. And who benefits? Well, you and Anna get to keep the kids here in Hawai'i, for one thing."

Greg's eyes narrowed.

"Yeah, Greg, we know that Zoë was threatening to move the kids to the mainland with her new boyfriend. That must have made you and Anna both pretty angry."

"I didn't kill Zoë," he said. "If you're accusing me, then you should be reading me my rights and letting me call an attorney."

"Nobody's accusing you of anything yet," I said. "We're just asking questions. And you know we don't have to Mirandize you until we take you into custody and you're no longer free to leave. Right now we're just talking."

Ray jumped in. "Kimo gets a little over excited, Greg. You know that. We're just trying to figure out what's going on. And you want to help us find out who killed Zoë, don't you?"

I said, "We know you love the girls. Your parents love them, too. You want them to stay in Hawai'i. You've got to admit, you've got a motive."

He looked from me to Ray, and then back at me again. I could see he was struggling to keep his voice calm. "I didn't kill Zoë. Hell, I haven't even been in a fight since junior high. But Anna had a temper. I saw her and Zoë argue sometimes. If you're looking for a personal motive, Anna's the one with the most to gain."

Nice, I thought. Throw your wife under the bus.

But then, there was the possibility that Anna Yang, Zoë's life partner for nearly seven years, had turned around and killed her. That was even worse than throwing suspicion on someone.

Greg asked a couple of questions about Zoë's death, but I had to tell him that we couldn't say much as long as he was a possible suspect. He didn't like that, but he knew the way things worked.

Ray and I stayed in the interview room after he left. "What do you think?" I asked.

"I think you shook him up," he said. "Beyond that, I don't know. A week ago, if you'd asked me if Greg Oshiro could kill somebody, I'd have laughed. But parenting is a powerful thing, especially if he thought those girls were in danger."

"Taking them to the mainland's not putting them in danger."

"Taking them to the mainland with an ex-con, though?" Ray said. "You love your nephews and nieces. How'd you feel if one of your brothers died, and your sister-in-law was dating some guy with a rap sheet?"

"Crazy." I nodded. But crazy enough to kill? I didn't know that. But how many of us would?

We gave up at the end of our shift. I was in a bad mood, and knew that if I didn't do something to shake myself up, I'd make Mike miserable too. So I went home, took Roby for a quick walk, put on shorts and a T-shirt, and threw my short board into the back of the Jeep.

I drove down to Makapu'u Point, parked alongside the road, and pulled on my rash guard. The wind was calm and the swell direction was just right for a good point break to the left. It was about an hour before dark, and the early evening sky was flecked with clouds and painted in a hundred different shades of blue, so many different ones that there weren't names for half of them.

I nodded to a couple of other surfers, then plunged into the cool water and duck dived through the incoming waves. I sat on my board and felt myself finally relaxing.

When I was single and lived in Waikiki, I surfed nearly every day. It was as important to me as breathing. But love does strange things to you. It became more important to me to live with Mike up in Aiea Heights than it was to be able to walk to the beach. As a result, I didn't get into the water as much as I wanted.

Sitting there on my board, I tried to empty my brain of Zoë Greenfield's murder, and all the questions about kids that had come up in its wake. Surfing is great for that; you have to focus on the waves, the wind, and the other surfers, and there isn't room for anything else.

I caught a strong wave, jumped onto my board, and immediately turned to ride the lip. I kept my balance, did a bottom turn, and rode the wave into the shore. Not a world class ride, but it felt great.

I kept on surfing for an hour, until my muscles had that old familiar ache and my brain felt clear. When I got back up to my car, I found Mike had called my cell. "Where are you?" he asked, when I called back.

"Makapu'u Point. I had to surf for a while."

"What are we doing for dinner?"

I said I'd pick up a pizza on my way home. "I'll walk the dog," he said.

We finished the call with mutual promises of love. And by the time I got home, pizza in hand, I was feeling relaxed and happy.

That all changed the next morning.

Ray and I went back to Chinatown, asking around the neighborhood for Anna Yang without much success. It was about 9:30 when the radio crackled. "All available units," the dispatcher said. "Student with a gun at Chinatown Christian Academy." She read off the street address. "Approach with extreme caution."

We were only about five blocks away. While I looked for a parking spot, Ray unholstered his gun and popped the magazine, making sure he had ammunition.

I was carrying mine in a belt holster, and I pulled it out and handed it to him, grip first. "Check mine, will you?"

"Don't suppose you have a vest, do you?" Ray asked, sliding the magazine out.

I shook my head. "Who knew we'd need them?"

I snagged a parking spot on River Street, about two blocks from the school, and we took off, both of us fastening our radios to our shoulders. By the time we got there, cop cars were arriving from every direction, and the scene was controlled chaos. We checked in with a lieutenant who was managing the situation, and he said there was a kid holed up in the cafeteria with a gun. We were told to stay close and wait for instructions. Then I saw Lieutenant Sampson's daughter, Kitty, who had become a uniformed officer a few months before, and headed toward her.

"Howzit, Kitty?" I asked. "You know anything about what's going on?"

I first met Kitty when she was a senior at UH. Since then, she'd graduated, gone through the police academy, and finished her probationary period.

"Just that there's a kid holed up inside, and there's been some shooting."

"You know what kind of gun he has?" Ray asked.

She shrugged. "Just got here myself."

We heard a series of rapid-fire bursts that sounded like they'd come from a semi-automatic shotgun. We all looked toward the source of the sound, a single-story building at the back of the school grounds. The shots were followed almost immediately by screaming and crying.

The one-story building had a flat roof and a series of louvered windows, and looked out on a small patch of worn grass shaded by a big kukui tree. The three of us ducked down and made our way toward the end of the building, where I could see a couple of other cops hunkered down.

"Where's the SWAT team when you need them?" Ray asked as we reached the other cops.

"On their way," one said. "ETA ten minutes."

A cop named Gary Saunders, whom I'd known for years, came hurrying across from the main building, accompanied by a short, rotund man in a clerical collar. "Reverend Hannaford is the principal of the school," Gary said. "My daughter goes to school here and she's inside."

Another cop asked, "Who's the kid?"

"His name is Randy Tsutsui," Hannaford said. "He's fifteen. Discipline problem. His father committed suicide about a year ago, and since then he's been acting out. He's been suspended twice already for insubordination, mouthing off to teachers, and bullying younger kids. I called his mother and she's on her way."

There was another staccato burst of gunfire. "I don't think we have ten minutes," I said.

A dark-haired girl in a plaid skirt and white blouse came running out of the building, tears streaming down her face. She was about ten; she was followed by a blonde girl a few years older, dressed the same way, who was crying, too. Only she was bleeding as well.

Ray and I looked at each other and nodded. We took off toward the two girls, who were perhaps ten feet from the building by then. I grabbed the older girl, Ray the younger, and we carried them onward. I didn't even think about the kid inside, or the possibility that he would be shooting at us through all those louvered windows. I just knew that we had to get those girls out of the way as soon as possible.

The older girl was Laura Mercado, the younger one Janice Chee. A pair of EMTs raced up as soon as we had the girls safe and started checking them out. I stood there and held Laura's hand, as the EMT examined her arm, where a bullet had grazed her. He spoke quietly and with authority, and between that and my hand-holding Laura stopped crying.

Ray didn't have as much luck with Janice. She was crying so much, and so loud, that the EMT working on her had to give her a sedative in order to get her calm enough so she could be bandaged.

I sat cross-legged on the skimpy grass, holding Laura's hand. "Mrs. Nguyen heard someone shooting," she said between hiccups. "She went out in the hall to see what was going on."

She sniffled, and blew her nose. "But as soon as she went out we heard more shooting. Janice and I like Mrs. Nguyen a lot so we went to look outside. Mrs. Nguyen was lying on the floor and there was a lot blood."

Around us I heard other cop cars arriving and lots of confused orders being given over the radio as the brass tried to figure out what was going on and coordinate everyone. The rotating blue lights of a dozen cop cars bounced off the school windows in crazy patterns.

Laura nodded toward the other little girl. "Janice was scared and started crying so I took her hand and we ran down the hall. Randy kept shooting at us."

"Did you see what kind of gun he had?"

"Shotgun, but one that goes really fast. My dad has one but he says we can never touch it."

I keyed the mike on my radio and relayed the news. The school building was almost ominously quiet—no shooting, but no crying or screaming either.

Gary Saunders came over. "Do you know Penny Saunders?" he asked, kneeling next to Laura.

She nodded. "She's in my class with Mrs. Nyugen. She's inside."

The look on Gary's face was one I hope I never see again.

A lieutenant from the hostage negotiation team stepped out of the crowd, holding a loudspeaker in his hand. "Randy Tsutsui!" he called. "This is Lieutenant Starrett from HPD. Put down your weapon and come outside."

There was no response from inside the building. Starrett had just raised the megaphone again when a tall, gawky girl with blonde hair stepped out the door. "Penny!" Saunders called.

She held up her hand. "Randy wants to come out," she said, in a quavering voice.

She turned back and opened the door, and a teenager in a blood-spattered T-shirt and pair of camouflage pants stepped out, with his hands up. There was no gun in sight.

In what I thought was admirable restraint, Gary Saunders walked slowly across the twenty feet that separated us from the door.

"It's okay, Randy. That's my dad," Penny said to the boy.

Carefully, Gary unhooked the handcuffs from his belt and held them up. Randy looked down at the pavement as Gary hooked the cuffs on him. He motioned his daughter over to us, and took Randy toward his squad car.

Within a minute the building was swarming with cops and EMTs. A cop emerged a moment later holding a semi-automatic shotgun, and he was followed quickly by a series of stretchers, carrying kids in blood-stained clothes.

It seemed like every ambulance on the island was there, and once they'd quieted down both girls were bundled up and taken to the Queen's Medical Center.

My old partner from Waikiki, Akoni Hapa'ele, came by as we were waving goodbye to the girls. He's a big guy, built like my brother Haoa, tall and broad. I could see from his face that he was shaken up by what he'd seen. "You know what happened in there?" I asked.

"Sad story," Akoni said. "The kid's father used to go shooting wild pigs in the hills. Last year he killed himself with that shotgun. The kid cleaned it up and held onto it. He started having problems in school after that, and he had it in for two of his teachers. He went to the English teacher's classroom first, walked inside and shot him. Then he went down the hall to the math teacher's and shot her in the hallway. A couple of kids from her class ran away, but the rest were stuck in the classroom with him. Gary Saunders' daughter talked him into giving up."

"How many kids got hurt?" Ray asked.

"A half-dozen." Akoni had always said he didn't want kids—he called them hostages to fortune. But his wife Mealoha had given him a son the year before, and I had seen him transformed when he was around the baby, into a combination of fierce and gentle. "One of the boys has a chest wound, but the others are just banged up." He shook his head. "It boggles the mind."

I agreed with him. We walked over to the main school building, where a makeshift triage area had been set up. Kitty, Lidia Portuondo, and a few other female cops were in one of the classrooms, trying to calm down a bunch of kids who had not been hurt.

Ray and I stayed around the school most of the day, helping with crowd control and matching up kids with frantic parents. It was hot in the bright sun, and there was little shade or breeze. The worst part was the having to tell a young mother, in a faded t-shirt and jeans, that her daughter's name was on the list of those taken to the hospital. Her mouth gaped open and her whole body sagged. Ray and I had to help her over to Lidia, who volunteered to drive her there.

By the time we left, I was soaked in sweat, my hair plastered down to my scalp. Laura Mercado's blood had dried on my aloha shirt, I smelled like a visit to the morgue, and I felt bone-weary. I dropped Ray back at headquarters to pick up his car, and drove home on autopilot.

Roby came bouncing up to me as I opened the door, and I sank to the flagstone in front of the doorway and hugged him for a long time. We were sitting there, him licking my face, when Mike pulled up in the driveway. "Don't tell me you were at that school shooting," he said, jumping out of the car. "You look like you've been through Hell."

Roby abandoned me for a minute to welcome Mike home, then rushed back to me. I nodded. "I feel like it. Remember we were talking about maybe having kids some day? Not on your life."

He took my hand and pulled me up and into a bear hug. I rested my head on his shoulder and sniffled. "Come on," he said. "You need a long, hot bath."

He led me inside, parked me at the kitchen table, then pulled a Fire Rock Pale Ale out of the fridge, popped the cap, and handed it to me. "Drink this."

A minute later I heard the water running in the oversized Roman tub in the bathroom. Mike had remodeled the room a year or so before he met me, and the tub had been his big indulgence. He liked to take baths, and at six-four, he needed a lot of space. Roby sat at my feet on the kitchen tile, resting his big golden head on my thigh, and I stroked his fur as I drank the beer. When Mike returned he said, "Come on. The bath's ready."

I was almost catatonic. He gently unbuttoned my shirt and slipped it off, tossing it into the laundry basket. He removed my holster from my pants, and put the gun on top of the bureau. Carefully he took off the rest of my clothes, kissing my cheek and the top of my head now and then. Then he led me into the bathroom.

I stepped into the warm water, then sunk down below the surface, closing my eyes and letting the water wash over me. When I came back up, I saw Mike, naked, ready to step into the water with me. I moved over to make room, and he joined me, careful not to splash the tile floor.

We turned toward each other, and I rested my head on his shoulder. "It's okay, baby," he said. "I'm right here."

Somewhere in there he lathered me up with lavender soap, then bundled me into a fluffy terrycloth robe. He led me into bed, and then brought me dinner on a wooden tray, elbow macaroni with butter and cheese, my comfort food. I remembered being home sick from school, and my mother would make that for me and bring it to me in my favorite bowl, a gray porcelain one with a handle in the shape of an elephant's head.

I wondered what ever happened to that bowl, if my mother was still using it when she took care of her grandchildren. And then I burst into the tears I had been holding back all day. Mike got into bed next to me, and Roby jumped up with us, and when I stopped crying we lay there together and watched TV for a while.

Our phone rang off and on that night. Everybody I knew was shaken up by what had happened at Chinatown Christian Academy. You couldn't turn on the TV without seeing the police moving around the school, and the story took up most of the front page of the *Star-Advertiser*. My family was horrified, and my sister-in-law Liliha was one of many parents who planned to go to Punahou to demand an audience with the principal about security measures.

Harry and Arleen had considered sending Brandon to Chinatown Christian, and they were filled with relief that they had decided against it. The only person I didn't hear from was Terri, and that was because she was skiing in Idaho with her son Danny, and with Levi and his daughter.

The mood at headquarters was somber the next morning. Everybody wanted to talk about Randy Tsutsui, about why he had done what he had. Theories abounded. He had been an abused child. He had been bullied. No, he was a bully himself. Why had he been allowed to keep the gun his father committed suicide with? Had there been any warning signs that he was unbalanced?

No one had any answers, but everyone had a theory. We were listening to Gary Saunders bluster about something when my cell rang. "Detective? My name is Ellen Toyama. You called me?"

I explained that we were investigating Zoë Greenfield's murder, and she said, "Fo' real? Like on TV?"

"Yeah, we're for real," I said. "Can we talk to you?"

"I'm on my way to work?" The way she raised her voice at the end of the sentence made it sound like a question, one I didn't have an answer for.

"Where do you work?"

"At the Old Navy in Ala Moana Mall?"

"If we come over there, you think you can take a break and

talk to us?"

"My boss loves *Hawai'i Five-O*," she said. "I'm sure she'd let me take break."

Finally, a sentence that didn't sound like a question.

I told her we'd be there in a half hour or so. Ray and I were glad to get out of the station and the gloom that pervaded it after the events of the day before.

We parked at the far end of the mall, near Sears, and waited until a tour bus had disgorged a horde of tourists heading for the Hilo Hattie store next door before we could go inside, where Hapa was singing "Lei Pikake" over the sound system. Ellen Toyama was an elf of a girl, only about five feet tall, with short dark hair and a perpetual smile. I wondered if Zoë had known any women who weren't Asian.

Ellen got permission from her boss to take a break, and we walked out into the center of the mall. We bypassed a convention of moms and strollers to find a quiet corner. "You knew Zoë Greenfield?" I asked.

She nodded. "We met at this girls night out party?" she said. "Like a year ago?" She pulled a package of gum from her pocket and offered us sticks. Ray took one.

"She was quiet, you know? But I was going through this thing, where I was sort of figuring out my own identity? And she was going through this thing, too, because she had met this guy on line?"

"Wyatt Collins," I said.

She nodded. "At first, she was just like being a friend, you know? And then as she got to know him, she was sort of reconsidering?"

I found Ellen's habit of making every statement sound like a question irritating, you know? But I kept my mouth shut.

"So we used to talk about it?" Ellen said, chewing her gum. "She was really, like conflicted? At least at first? Because, I mean, she had this girlfriend, and this family? But this guy, it was almost like he was hypnotizing her or something?"

"What do you mean, hypnotizing?" Ray asked. "Like in person?"

Oh, God. He was catching it, too. I'd have to ask for a new partner.

Ellen shook her head. "It wasn't anything bad like that," she said, definite for a moment. "But it was like his emails? She said they were like things she could have written herself? Like he could see into her soul?"

Zoë Greenfield didn't seem like the kind of woman who talked about her soul a lot. But still waters run deep, I guess.

Ellen went back over the same ground again, about the almost mystical connection between Zoë and Wyatt, but that was about all she could say. By the time we finished with her I was ready to bury myself in talk radio, where at least they had definite opinions, even if most of the time they were crazy.

We walked over to the Foodland after we'd finished with Ellen, bought a couple of bottles of cold water, and then strolled through the mall, thinking out loud. I said, "Wyatt has the violent background, and according to Ellen it was like he'd hypnotized her. He could have asked her to do something, and if she refused, he went off on her."

"Like, if you believe Ellen?" Ray said.

"I have a gun," I said. "And I'm not afraid to use it if you don't stop talking like that."

Ray laughed. "Then there's Anna Yang. She could still have a thing for Zoë, be the spurned lover, in danger of losing her kids. That's a big motive."

"Same for Greg Oshiro," I said. "He wanted those kids, and he said how much his parents loved them. He could have been protecting his position."

"And there's the marriage between him and Anna," Ray said. "They could have been planning something together."

We'd just about finished our water, and run through our ideas, when Harry called. "I finally broke into that online storage, brah. You want to come over and see what she had there?"

"Sure. We're at Ala Moana. Be there in a few."

"Hey, if you're at the mall, can you do me a favor? We're trying to bribe Brandon into going to school without so much complaining, and he loves these little anime toys from Shirokiya. They come out with a new one every month, and he's about two months behind. Can you stop by and pick up the latest two?"

"Sure. Got any dry cleaning you want me to pick up, too? Prescriptions at the pharmacy?"

He ignored the jibe and told me the two toys he wanted, and hung up the phone. We detoured past the big Japanese department store and then drove up to Aiea Heights.

"Zoë had these spreadsheets," Harry said, when we were sitting in his office looking at the computer monitor. "I don't know exactly what they are, but she gave them names that have nothing to do with their content, and had them hidden away in a folder with a weird name, which makes me suspicious."

I know about as much about spreadsheets as I do about fertilizer or national politics—which come to think of it, are pretty similar. "Weird name?" I asked.

"The names on the files and the folder don't match the contents. There are rows and rows of statistics there, and she called one file 'flowergirl' and another one 'winnebago.' And they're in a folder called 'plaid.'"

I looked at Ray and he shrugged. "What is it that you said she did for a living?" Harry asked.

"She worked for the Department of Business, Economic Development and Tourism," I said. "Monitoring energy statistics or something like that."

"Well, it looks like she took her work home with her," Harry said. "I'm just guessing here, but I think we're looking at two different sets of books being compared."

"Which means what?" Ray asked.

"Well, let's say you have a restaurant, and you do a lot of cash business," Harry said. "You have one set of books that show everything you take in, and everything you spend. Then you have a second set, where you wipe out all the cash receipts, anything that's not easily traceable. That's the set you show the tax man."

"But Zoë worked for a government agency," I said. "I don't understand."

"You said energy statistics?" Harry asked.

I nodded. He turned to the computer, opened up a new browser window, and started typing. "Okay, here's the department website. Look at all these different initiatives they have. Energy data, energy efficiency, renewable energy. Suppose somebody was fudging data, and Zoë figured it out. Hence the two different sets of books."

"Who was fudging?" Ray asked.

Harry shook his head. "That's beyond me. And remember, I'm just guessing here. You need somebody who knows what this data means to tell you what's going on."

He copied the data onto a flash drive, then handed it to me. "You can keep that," he said. "I went to a trade show last week and I picked up a half dozen of them."

Back at the station, we opened up Excel and looked at the data once again. But it was still impenetrable. "Who do you think we can get to look at this?" I asked. "Nishimura, Zoë's boss?"

"If there's something screwy going on at her office, don't you think he's part of it? If not, why keep it so secret? Why not have just gone to him?"

"Maybe she did," I said. "And maybe that's why she's dead."

I switched over to Word and looked through my notes, paging back to the day we'd gone to Zoë's office. "She had a friend there, remember? Miriam Rose. Maybe we can ask her."

I called Miriam and asked if we could talk to her. "Sure. I'm at work until five."

"How about after that," I said. "Maybe we can buy you a cup

of coffee after you get off."

She was curious, but agreed to meet us at a Kope Bean near her office at five. Sampson gave us a bunch of paperwork to fill out about the school shooting the day before, and that took up most of the rest of the day.

Ray and I were sitting at a table in the corner of the Kope Bean when Miriam walked in. That fabric rose pin was obviously her signature; she was wearing it on her shoulder, with a bamboo-print blouse and a skirt that would have been too short on my teenaged niece Ashley.

I got up and got her a latte while Ray opened up my netbook and showed her the files Harry had copied. They were playing cowboy music through the sound system, Willie Nelson wailing about wide open spaces, and I found myself singing along. I could use some of that cowboy quiet, I thought, just me and the stars and my cayuse, whatever the hell that was.

Miriam alternated between sipping her latte and scrolling through the spreadsheets. "It's hard to tell which company these belong to."

"But they're definitely work data?" I asked.

"Oh, absolutely. See this sheet? It represents kilowatt hours." She clicked a tab at the bottom of the screen. "And this one? These are dollar figures. State subsidies for alternative energy, I think. But I'd have to compare them to some other figures to see if I can figure out which company they belong to."

I looked over her shoulder. "Why do you think Zoë had this on her personal backup?"

She looked at me like I was dumb. And when it comes to computers, and statistics, I agreed with her. "Because there are two different versions of everything. She was onto something. Somebody cheating. I just don't know who."

She pulled her own flash drive out of her shoulder bag and copied the data from the one Harry had given us. "I'll try and figure this out tomorrow."

"Be careful. If this relates to Zoë's death it could be dangerous."

"People kill, detective," she said. "Numbers don't."

The next morning, the squad room was still quiet when I showed up to work. It's not often that we get a crime that shakes up a lot of cops, but the shooting at Chinatown Christian Academy had certainly done that.

Each of us who were at the scene had to meet with the department shrink, to deal with any post-traumatic stress. Ray's appointment was at ten and mine was at two, which pretty much killed the day and kept us stuck at our desks. We passed the time verifying Wyatt's arrest record and calling more of Anna's clients.

While Ray was upstairs with the shrink, I dug into Greg Oshiro's background. Though I'd known him casually for years, and gotten friendlier with him in the past twelve months or so, I still didn't know much about where he was from and what had shaped him.

From an interview I found which he'd done with some high school journalism students, I discovered that he had been born in Japan. His Oshiro grandparents were farm laborers in Sacramento, and his father was born there in 1940. The following year, his parents took him back to Japan to visit family, and they were stuck there when Pearl Harbor was attacked in December, 1941.

That technically made his father a *kibei*, someone born in the US but raised in Japan. He married a Japanese woman, and then Greg was born in a small town on the island of Hokkaido in 1970. Soon after that, his father exercised his US citizenship to return to the States with his wife and infant son.

"My parents gave up everything they had in Japan so that I could grow up in the US," Greg said in the interview. They had chosen not to have any other children, he said, to be sure that Greg had every advantage they could afford. His father worked as a landscaper, his mother in a factory sewing aloha shirts. He got a scholarship to UH, where he majored in journalism. He started at the *Advertiser* as an intern, and had worked there ever since.

I already knew that he was devoted to his parents, and that a big reason why he had donated his sperm to Zoë and Anna was to give them grandchildren. On a whim, I ran his name through the police database, and was surprised when I got a single hit. I was gaping at the screen when Ray returned from his interview.

"Greg Oshiro has a juvenile record," I said, turning my monitor around to face him. "What do you know?"

The record had been sealed, but we were still able to nose around enough to discover that he had assaulted a fellow student in high school. "What do you think that means?" I asked.

Ray shrugged. "Could be it was an accident. Some cafeteria beef that got out of hand."

"Or it could be that he has a temper," I said. "You see how short he gets sometimes. I can see him flying off the handle."

Ray frowned. "It's not like they were arguing and he just reached out and clocked her or something. Whoever killed Zoë Greenfield snuck up behind her with a knife."

"But there were a lot of cuts. That says passion."

We made a note to ask Greg about the conviction the next time we saw him. We kept looking for information on him and Anna, not finding much, and ducked out for a quick lunch. By the time we returned, it was time for my two o'clock appointment.

I went upstairs to a small conference room where the shrink was seeing cops. She was younger than I expected, a pretty haole woman in her mid-thirties, in a light gray business suit with a pale pink blouse. "I'm Dr. Lewis," she said, rising from her chair to shake my hand. "You're…"

She looked down at her roster. "Detective Kanapa'aka," I said. Her grip was firm and her gaze direct. I liked her.

"Have a seat," she said, and she sat down across from me. The room was a nice one, with four comfortable chairs clustered around a small round table. "Let's start with how you ended up at

Chinatown Christian on Tuesday."

I explained that we'd been canvassing in Chinatown for a murder case, and that we'd responded to the call.

"What was it like when you got there?"

"Confusion. Nobody knew exactly what was going on. Just that there was a kid in the cafeteria with a gun."

"Tough situation. What do you typically do when you're faced with so much uncertainty?"

"I think you take anything like that incrementally," I said. "My partner and I found a patrol officer we knew. Then another officer we knew came over with the principal of the school, and he filled in some of the blanks."

She nodded, then looked back down at her papers. "Tell me about Laura Mercado."

"My partner and I were positioned at the corner of the cafeteria building with the school principal and a couple of other cops when a girl stumbled out of the cafeteria, crying. An older girl followed her, and we could see she was bleeding."

I paused, remembering the scene. "My partner and I looked at each other and we kind of nodded. Then we started to run toward the girls. I grabbed Laura and hustled her away from the front of the building, and Ray picked up the other girl, Janice."

"Why you?" she asked. "There were a lot of other cops there, weren't there?"

"There were. I can't say what the other cops were thinking. But Ray and I, we've been working together for almost three years. I understand how he thinks, and he gets me. We both knew we had to get those girls out of the way."

"You didn't know whether Randy Tsutsui could shoot at you once you broke cover."

"Yes. But we know those girls were at risk. We thought we could get them out of harm's way, and that's what we did."

She nodded. "Instinct is a powerful thing, isn't it?" she asked.

"A lot of good cops operate that way. They know what has to be done, and they do it."

"You also have to evaluate the risks," I said. "If there was gunfire coming out of the building at the time the girls came out, I'm not sure we would have risked it."

"Your partner is Detective Donne, correct?"

"Yes."

"And he's married?"

"He is. His wife is finishing her PhD at UH."

"And you? You have a partner, don't you?"

I nodded. "He's an arson investigator." I paused. "I know where you're going, doctor. Were we really evaluating the risks? What if Ray had been killed? What would that do to Julie? That kind of thing." I took a deep breath. "My partner, Mike, and Julie Donne, they understand the risks of the job. Mike even more, because he runs into fires, and he's known men and women who died on the job."

She looked at me.

"They also know who we are. Mike knows me better than anyone else, ever, in my life. If anything happened to me, yeah, he'd be – I can't even describe it. But he'd know that I was doing what I felt I had to do. I can't speak for Julie as much, but I think she'd feel the same way." I smiled. "They wouldn't love us as much if we weren't the guys we are."

"Did you talk to Detective Donne about his conversation with me?" she asked.

I shook my head. "We're investigating a murder, like I told you. I'd just found a new piece of information when Ray came back from meeting with you, and we jumped into that."

"Interesting," she said. "Because his story is very close to yours."

"That's because it's the truth," I said, probably too tartly.

She smiled. "You'd be surprised at how often partners see

things differently."

"Anything else?" I asked. "Because like I said, we are investigating a homicide, and I'd like to get back downstairs."

"Just a few more questions. You and Detective Donne ever talk about kids?"

I frowned. "In what way?"

"Having them. You were partnered with Detective Hapa'ele when you were in Waikiki, weren't you?"

"Yes."

"I spoke to him yesterday. He has a lot of conflicted ideas about children."

I laughed. "You could say that. Or you could say that all that talk about kids being hostages to fortune turned to crap the minute his son was born."

"So? You want to have kids?"

"Neither Mike or I has the right plumbing for that."

She just looked at me.

"Okay, so that was flip. But it's true. Ray and Julie, if they decide they want kids, they just stop trying not to have them. But if Mike and I decide we want a child—and I'm not saying we ever would—it's a lot bigger deal."

"But doable."

"Yes." I knew I wasn't getting out of there until I satisfied the good doctor, so I said, "I have two older brothers, seven nieces and nephews between them. Mike and I love being uncles. Mike and I have been talking about having kids, but when you factor in all the difficulties, and the jobs Mike and I have, it doesn't look very possible." I closed my mouth, licked my lips. "For now, I can satisfy my parenting impulses with my nieces and nephews, and with helping kids out who need the help."

She wrote on her pad. "Do you think that contributed to your willingness to rescue those girls on Tuesday? That idea that you won't have kids of your own, but you'll help kids when you can?"

"We're getting into your territory now. If a couple of teachers had come stumbling out of that cafeteria on Tuesday, I think Ray and I would have done the same thing for them. Serving and protecting with aloha, you know. That's what it says downstairs."

"I know." She stood up and stuck her hand out once more. "Thanks for your time, Detective. I enjoyed speaking with you."

I stood up. "You know, I enjoyed our conversation too. Thanks."

It was just before three when Miriam called. "I looked at the data you gave me," she said in a low voice that made me think she was calling from her cubicle and didn't want anyone to overhear. "I have to get home right after work, though, to babysit my little brother. Maybe we can meet tomorrow?"

"How about if we come over to your house?" I asked. "Would that be okay?"

"I live with my folks, way up in the Ko'olaus. Nuuanu Pali Drive."

"Not a problem. What time is good for you?"

She gave me the street address and her cell phone number, and I agreed to meet her up there at seven. "My folks are going out to dinner, so that'll give me time to get Bobby fed and stuck in front of the TV."

Our shift was over, and we decided to head home for a while, then meet up again at headquarters, because it was convenient to the highway entrance. "We'll take the Jeep," I said. "There are some wicked turns on the Pali."

"Hey, the Highlander can turn on a dime. But you want to drive, more power to you."

I went home, had a light dinner, and spent some time playing with Roby. Then I left a note for Mike, turned around and went back downtown. We didn't have to worry about taking the turns on the Pali too fast, though, because there was a major backup starting just after the Dowsett Avenue interchange. I tuned in to the radio news and heard that a car had gone off the road at the

Nuuanu Pali Drive exit.

I looked over at Ray. "That's Miriam's exit. See if you can raise her on your cell."

He dialed. "No answer. Let me see if I can get her plate number." He spent a few minutes getting the plate, then connecting to the traffic department. Then he hung up. "It's her car."

"Shit."

We were both quiet for a while, considering what had happened, as we crept forward up the highway. It took us another half hour to get up to the site where the car had run off. Miriam was driving a Mini Cooper convertible, and it looked like she'd swerved off the highway at the exit and smashed into a tree.

We pulled off the road just ahead of the exit, joining a line of police and ME vehicles. Since Hawai'i is the only state in the union without a state police or highway patrol, the sheriff's department handles accident investigation on the highways. Nick Jameson, a tall, skinny haole in a dark blue uniform with the six-pointed star on his left breast, had been the first on the scene.

"She wasn't wearing her seat belt," he said, after we'd introduced ourselves. "Stupid move, with the top down. Looks like she catapulted out of the vehicle. ME's guys say she was dead on impact." He paused. "You say you're investigating her?"

"Not her specifically." I had to talk over the traffic on the highway just behind us. "One of her co-workers was murdered last week, and we were on our way up here to meet her at her house and talk about the crime."

"You think she might have been involved?"

I shrugged. "Don't know. Her getting killed certainly throws a monkey wrench into our case."

"Any indication this wasn't an accident?" Ray asked.

"Let's take a look." Nick pulled out a high-intensity flashlight and the three of us started walking the area. Darkness was falling fast and the wooded area just off the highway was spooky, headlights chasing across the tree trunks like restless ghosts.

"It looks like she was turning, there," Nick said, pointing at the exit ramp. "And then she either swerved, or lost control of the vehicle, and smashed into the tree."

Steam was still rising from the Mini's crumpled hood. The tiny car had accordioned together, and though the air bag had deployed, it hadn't been enough to keep Miriam Rose in her seat. "Can we look in the car?" I asked.

"Sure. You got gloves? We'll have to take the vehicle in and make sure it wasn't tampered with. Don't want stray prints."

Ray's the one who's always prepared. He handed me a pair of gloves and put a pair on himself. Nick shone his flashlight as we looked through the car. "Where's her purse?" I asked.

I remembered when she had met us at the Kope Bean the day before. She'd been carrying a tapestry bag with roses on it. But we couldn't find the bag, or a laptop. "I'm sure she would have had that little drive with her," I said to Ray. "But where is it?"

The ME's team were preparing to move Miriam's body. Before they did, we asked them if they'd found her purse, or the flash drive. The answer was no.

We widened the search. Nick had already cordoned off the area where Miriam's body had lain, and we scanned every inch. Then we moved outward, in concentric circles. I moved aside some underbrush and startled a white cat there. It turned to run, but Ray scooped it up.

"Hey, what's up, kitty?" he asked, keeping it snug in his arm and stroking its fur with the other hand. "What are you doing way out here?"

I walked over. "It have a tag?"

"It's a she," Ray said. The cat had stopped struggling. He felt around her furry neck. "Yeah, there's a collar here. Shine that flashlight over here. Just don't get it in her eyes or she'll spook."

I focused the light at his hand, which was showing a heart-shaped metal tag. "Hillside Avenue," I said. "That's down in

Manoa. How'd you get all the way up here, kitty?"

"She looks healthy and well-fed," Ray said. "Not like she's been living wild for a while."

There was a phone number on her tag. "Somebody's probably missing her," I said. "We might as well call and let them know she's all right."

I found my cell and dialed the number on the tag. The woman who answered sounded impossibly old, and didn't speak much English. It took a while before she put a kid on the phone. "Hello?"

I couldn't tell if it was a boy or a girl. "Hi, I'm a police officer, and I found a cat with this phone number on its tag."

"How?" the kid asked.

"How did I find it? In the woods, off the Pali Highway."

"No," the kid said. "Her name is Hao. It means white in Chinese."

"Oh. That makes sense. This cat's white. How long has she been missing?"

"I just saw her this morning," the kid said. "Hold on." He started speaking to the old woman in Chinese. Then he came back to the phone. "My grandmother says she put Hao out this afternoon. How did she get all the way up there?"

"Don't know," I said. "We'll get her back to you a little later, okay?"

"Okay." He – or she—I still couldn't tell—hung up.

We put Hao in the back of the Jeep, with the flaps rolled down and the car locked. "Don't scratch up the car, okay?" I asked her.

We looked around the area more, but couldn't find Miriam's purse, laptop, or the flash drive. By eight o'clock it was full dark and I knew we weren't going to find anything else. When we got back to the Jeep, Hao was curled up on the driver's seat, sound asleep.

Ray lifted her onto his lap, and she purred a couple of times, then went back to sleep. We drove down to Manoa, and found the address on Hillside Avenue. It was a small, well-kept house with a beat-up old Toyota sedan in the driveway. I rang the bell, while Ray carried Hao in his arms.

A middle-aged Chinese woman came to the door. She looked uncertain for a moment, until she saw the white cat. "You found Hao!" she said. The cat jumped out of Ray's arms and ran through the open door.

The woman invited us in. "Where did you say you found her?" she asked, after we'd introduced ourselves.

"Way up the Pali Highway," I said. "Any idea how she got up there?"

The woman looked baffled. "My mother let her out around three," she said. "When my son came home from school."

"There's no way she could have gotten up there on her own so quickly," I said. "Anybody in your household drive up that way?"

She shook her head. "I work in Ewa Beach. My mother doesn't drive. Hao must have jumped into a neighbor's car."

We left it at that. I dropped Ray back at headquarters and headed home for the second time that day. Mike was sprawled on the couch with Roby when I got home, though the big goof jumped off him and raced to the door when I walked in.

I rubbed behind his floppy golden ears and wondered again how the white cat had gotten all the way up to Nuuanu Pali Drive. But Roby didn't have any ideas, so I settled for joining him and Mike on the couch.

THE CAT IS THE KEY

I met Ray outside headquarters the next morning, and he drove us back up to the crash scene to look at it in daylight, playing an old CD from his Philly days of Southside Johnny and the Asbury Jukes with a rocking horn section.

There was a stiff breeze blowing, with an earthy scent. We took the Nuuanu Pali Drive exit, pulling off the road a few hundred yards beyond where Miriam's car had crashed. The area where her body had landed was still roped off with yellow crime scene tape, and the tree her car had hit was bowed in. But the car had been taken away the night before, and the area was quiet and peaceful, roofed over with tall trees that filtered the sunlight.

We spent a good hour combing the area and we were just about to call it quits when we found what looked like fresh tire tracks, a few hundred feet down Nuuanu Pali Road from the accident. The soil there was light and loosely packed, and we could see where a car, a sedan mostly likely, had pulled off the road and parked.

"We were all parked up by the highway," Ray said.

"Could be hikers. People go up the trail all the time. There's a waterfall at the top."

There was a faint whiff of engine oil in the area. I knelt down and sniffed. "I think these tracks are pretty fresh."

"The cat," Ray said.

"Excuse me? You think the cat drove up here and parked?"

"No, idiot. I think somebody drove the cat up here."

"Go on."

He started walking around the area. "We had this case back in Philly. This woman was mad because her boyfriend was breaking up with her. He had this little Doberman puppy, and she went to his house and got the puppy from the back yard."

He shook his head. "She hid in the shrubbery by his driveway, and when he drove in, she threw the puppy in front of his car."

"Jesus."

"He swerved to avoid hitting the dog, and ran right into the front of the house."

"I get you. Maybe someone drove up here with the cat, and threw the cat in front of her car as she was exiting the highway."

"We know she loved cats," he said. "All those cat photos in her cubicle. And that would explain how a cat from Manoa ended up here."

I wondered what would happen if someone threw a puppy in front of my Jeep. I couldn't even consider someone tossing Roby in front of me; he was just too big and squirmy. But a puppy? A cute little golden retriever puppy? I'd have swerved, too.

It took an hour for a crime scene tech with a plaster cast kit to get up there. There was an unusual wear pattern, like the car the tire came from needed an alignment, so there was a good possibility that if we had a suspect in mind, we could use the tire to connect him or her to Miriam's accident.

We stopped on the way down to Miriam's office for coffee and malasadas, and thus fortified, went up to the Department of Business, Economic Development and Tourism. Gladys Yuu met us at the receptionist's desk. "Good morning, detectives," she said. She looked tired, with dark circles under her eyes, and she was clutching a Kope Bean travel coffee mug like the caffeine was feeding into her system through it. "How can we help you this morning?"

"We're here about Miriam Rose," I said.

"Miriam? She's not in yet. I don't know where she is."

"Can we speak to you inside?" I asked.

She led us back to her desk, outside Nishimura's office. "I'm afraid Miriam was in car accident last night," I said. "She didn't survive."

Gladys frowned. "I always told that girl to wear her seatbelts.

But she said she was a good driver." She made a spitting noise. "I'm not surprised something happened to her. And that tiny car! What kind of protection does a little car like that give you in an accident?"

"May we look around her cubicle?" I asked.

Gladys looked suspicious. "Why? Wasn't this just a traffic accident?"

"We're investigating. We haven't made any determination yet."

"What are you looking for?"

"She didn't have her purse with her," I said. "We found that strange. Thought maybe she left it behind in a desk drawer."

"It probably flew out of the car."

Ray and I stood there and looked at her. "Well, come on then." She led us through the maze of hallways to Miriam's cubicle, then stood there, hands on hips.

"We can find our way out," I said. "Thanks."

"Whatever is here is state property. Aside from her personal belongings. I think I should stay while you search."

"If you want." Ray handed me a pair of rubber gloves, and Gladys watched us in a combination of fear and horror as we searched through Miriam's desk, her drawers, and the cubbyholes attached to the cubicle divider. We didn't find her purse, or her flash drive. But all those photos of her and her cat made me think that Ray was on to something with his theory that someone might have thrown the cat in front of Miriam's car.

"What time did Miriam leave yesterday?" I asked Gladys.

"I don't know. We don't clock in and out."

I looked at her. I was sure she knew exactly who came in late and who left early. She must have felt something in my gaze, because she said, "My mother's aide had an emergency yesterday afternoon, so I left early to get home and take over for her. I assume Miriam left at five. That's when we usually close down."

We stopped for lunch at Zippy's. While we waited in line we

were both quiet, thinking, but by the time we sat down with our food we both started to talk at once, then stopped. "I guess that shrink was right," I said. "She said you and I were in sync."

"Really? Because we both went after those kids?"

"Yeah. She seemed to think I did it because I know that I can't have kids of my own."

"You have something wrong?"

I shook my head. "You know what I mean."

"She wanted to know how I felt about Julie getting her PhD. Like I might be resenting her for not wanting to drop everything and have a couple of babies."

"When does she finish?" I asked.

"She's taking her last two classes this semester. She's been fiddling around with proposals for her dissertation. It's going to be something about how the geography of the islands has influenced their development patterns."

"Better her than me," I said. "Kids?"

"Funny you should ask." He looked down at the table, then back up at me, with a wide grin. "She just took one of those pregnancy tests last week. And, well, it looks like I'm going to be a dad in around eight months."

"Wow! Congratulations, brah. You happy about it?"

He laughed. "Are you kidding? I'm over the moon. But the women in Julie's family have some history of trouble, so we've been trying to keep things quiet. You know, don't want to jinx anything too soon."

"You tell Dr. Lewis?"

He shook his head. "She had enough to analyze me on."

We went back to our two cases. Though the Sheriff's office was the official investigative body on Miriam's crash, we knew that her death had to be connected to Zoë's, and to the data we had asked her to analyze.

"You think she asked the wrong person for help?" Ray

suggested, as we ate.

"Could be. I mean, I thought we were clear to her about staying quiet, but it turns out she wasn't the most sensible girl in the world."

"You mean the seat belt thing?"

I nodded, and took a bite of my sandwich. When I finished chewing, I said, "I mean, who's stupid enough to drive a convertible with the top down and no seat belts?"

"Half the tourists on O'ahu?"

"Yeah, but she wasn't a tourist." I shook my head. "And Gladys knew that she didn't wear the seat belts. I'll bet everybody who knew her knew that."

"Making it easy for someone to figure she'd get thrown out of the car if she crashed. And anybody who saw her cubicle knew she was into cats."

"So where does that leave us? I suppose we should get a list of the people who work in that department and see what we turn up."

Ray crumpled his paper coffee cup. "And we still need to know what's in that database. Think Harry should take another shot at it?"

I pursed my lips. "He already said he couldn't get much into it. We need somebody who'll know what's there. Too bad Levi Hirsch is skiing. He could probably get someone to read the data."

I stared up at the posters on the restaurant wall, trying to think of anyone else I knew. I focused on one advertising a surf competition. And then I remembered seeing my nephew Jeffrey surf, and that my cousin Selena had been there.

Selena had a lot in common with Zoë Greenfield, I realized. Both of them came from flaky family backgrounds. Zoë had grown up in the commune with Sunshine and Colorado, while Selena's mom was my Aunt Pua, who had always been a goofball.

Aunt Pua had three kids, each from different fathers. Not that any of the men had been in the picture for long. My cousin Ben's dad had been her third husband. They'd gotten married in Vegas, and then divorced six months later.

Aunt Pua had been an astrologer, had sold tie-dyed t-shirts at the Aloha Stadium flea market, wholesaled herbal tea, and who knows what else. She'd finally settled into a career that suited her, as an aromatherapist in Hawai'i Kai.

Selena, on the other hand, had always been a quiet, studious girl. She was a couple of years older than me, and while the rest of our cousins were outdoor kids, surfing, swimming, and hiking, Selena was a reader. She had big round glasses and frizzy hair, and whenever there was a family party you could find her in the corner, reading. I liked to read, too, and our best conversations had been ones about books, particularly once I was a teenager and she was in college.

She majored in engineering at UH, and went to work for a consulting firm after graduation. I just couldn't remember her married name, or where she worked.

So I called my mother. "I'm still shaken up from that school shooting," she said, when we'd gone through the ritual greetings, asking after her health and my father's. "Every time I see something terrible on the news I worry that you're there and you're going to get hurt."

"Oh, come on, Mom. You've got Lui and Haoa. I'm just the spare."

"Kimo! How can you say something like that!" She laughed. "So what do you want? You never call me unless you need something."

It was my turn to feign horror. "How can you say that, Mom? I called you last week when I was walking Roby. And I saw you on Saturday when we watched Jeffrey surf."

"Lui calls me every day."

"It's not a competition, Mom. What's Selena's last name? And do you have her phone number?"

"Her last name is Mitchell. Hold on and I'll get you her number."

"You don't know it by heart? I'm surprised."

"Don't start with me. I'm your mother."

"So you say."

"No one else would have put up with you. Here it is." She read the number off to me. "What do you want with Selena?"

"I need a little help. Thanks. Kiss Dad for me. Love you."

I hung up before she could probe any further. Selena's receptionist put me through to her, and she said, "I was just thinking of you, Kimo. It was nice to see you last weekend. We should get together more."

"That would be nice," I said. "You have any time this afternoon?"

She laughed. "Is this in a professional capacity?"

"I have a couple of spreadsheets I need some help with. I'm thinking maybe an engineer can make some sense out of them."

"I could use a break from load factors," she said. "When can you come over?"

Selena worked in one of the high-rise buildings near the Iolani Palace, just a couple of blocks from headquarters. Ray and I walked over there after lunch. The receptionist was a young haole woman with an asymmetrical haircut and glossy makeup that made her look like a fashion model.

She buzzed Selena. "Ms. Mitchell will be right out," she said, then punched a button to take an incoming call. I was fascinated to see how she managed the multi-line phone with the tips of her fingers, protecting the finish on her long, manicured nails.

Selena appeared a couple of minutes later, looked at Ray and me, and shook her head. As she led us back to her office, she said, "Even gay guys can't resist Marisa," she said.

"I've never seen anyone with nails like that who can actually work," I said.

"If you can call what she does work. I call it decoration." She motioned Ray and me to chairs across from her desk and sat down facing us.

Her office was organized for efficiency, much like Selena herself. The credenza, file cabinet, phone and computer were all within easy reach, and she had a slanted table alongside one wall with plans laid out on it. She could swivel her chair over with a minimum of effort.

"Let's see what you've got," she said. I handed her the flash drive and explained what I thought we had. She popped the drive in and started hitting keys. It was a lot like watching Harry work—that same sense of complete concentration on the task at hand. After a couple of minutes she looked up at us.

"Harry was right, in part. The first couple of spreadsheets here are engineering data." She shifted the monitor so we could see it, and Ray and I both leaned forward. "This sheet represents kilowatt hours generated by some kind of power project."

She clicked a tab at the bottom of the screen. "Now this sheet represents the same time period, but the numbers are much lower."

"What does that mean?"

"It means that the first sheet here is bullshit," she said. "Somebody is trying to make a bad project look good."

She opened a new window and pulled up a different spreadsheet. "These numbers here are dollar figures. It looks like the first sheet is what they would have submitted to whoever was funding them—notice how the figures are in black? That means they're making money."

Most of the numbers on the next sheet were in red. "I'm betting that these are the real numbers," she said. "They're bleeding money. If they let these numbers get out, they'd be out of business fast."

"Can you figure out anything about the company?" I asked. "Aren't there hidden thingies that tell you who created the sheet, or where they worked?"

Selena hit a couple of keys. "The file was created by Zoë Greenfield," she said. "She works for the Department of Business, Economic Development and Tourism."

"Worked," I said. "As in past tense. She's the woman whose murder we're investigating."

Selena jerked back from her keyboard, as if Zoë's dead body might pop out if she got too close.

"Nothing about which company she was investigating?" Ray asked.

Selena shook her head. "I don't know enough about alternative energy projects to speculate. Nobody at her office can tell you anything?"

"We had a contact," I said. "We gave her the spreadsheet, and she told me she'd figured something out. Then her car ran off the Pali Highway."

Selena closed the windows on her computer and popped the drive out. "Sorry, Kimo. I can't tell you anything more about this."

Friday evening I was fiddling around on my netbook and checked my email. There was a message from Terri. "We had lots of fun skiing in Squaw Valley," I read. "Danny fell in love with snow. I'll tell you all about the trip when I see you. Danny has a kite entered in the Ko'olau Kite Fest tomorrow—any chance you guys can come up and cheer him on? He'd love to see you."

I flashed back to the last time I'd seen Terri, when Levi had taken us out on his boat to show off his investment in Wave Power Technologies. Now that Levi was back from Squaw Valley, maybe he could tell us which company the spreadsheet represented. I emailed her back that we would be there. "Tell Levi I have some questions for him," I added at the end. "Love you."

On Saturday afternoon Mike and I met them up on a grassy slope in the Ko'olau mountains for the kite-flying festival. I hoped to pull Levi aside for a few minutes to ask him about the mysterious spreadsheets we'd found in Zoë Greenfield's online storage.

Kites are a real Japanese obsession, and March is the month for many kite flying festivals in cities like Nagasaki. For the kids, there were two competitions, a demonstration of kite making, and even a candy drop, sending them scrambling as candy fell from the skies, released from special kites. But we got there an hour before Danny's competition, and after establishing that Levi, Terry and Danny hadn't arrived yet, Mike and I were drawn to the fighting kites.

From nosing around, we learned that the tradition had come from India, where special lines coated with ground glass were used to try and slice your competitors out of the air. The Nagasaki fighting kite was different from the traditional Japanese kites I'd seen as a kid. It was square, light, and flown diagonally, as opposed to the traditional Japanese form.

It was fascinating to watch the kites battle each other in the sky to the beat of fat, barrel-like Japanese *taiko* drums. The crowd cheered when one kite cut another's string, and I wished all our violent and destructive impulses could take place in a way like that, with no one getting hurt or killed.

We strolled around, watching a Japanese kite master showing off his works, until I spotted Terri across from us. We called and waved and she came over to us.

I marveled again at how much better she looked than she had almost four years before, when she was married to a cop who had gotten in trouble, and the worry had started to etch lines on her oval face, on skin that had been clear and fresh ever since we had met as kids at Punahou.

Her brown hair was pulled back into a ponytail, and she wore khaki Capri pants and a dark green T-shirt from Squaw Valley. "Danny will be so glad you came," she said, kissing my cheek and then leaning up to do the same to Mike. "He and Levi are getting their kite ready for the competition."

"How was the skiing?" I asked. "Not too cold for you?"

"Levi and Danny did most of the skiing. I'm too much of an island girl. I spent most of the time by the fire in the lodge. But Danny took to it. And of course he loves Ilana."

Ilana was Levi's daughter from his previous marriage, a beautiful twenty-something I'd only met once or twice. She was getting her MBA at Harvard. "I'm surprised she could get away for skiing," I said.

"She had work to do every night," Terri said. "It was wonderful to see her huddled up with Levi. I didn't understand half of what they talked about, but he loved getting into her course work with her. You know he went to Harvard, too."

"I didn't know that," I said. "I assumed he'd gone somewhere in the northwest."

It didn't surprise me. Levi was a high-powered guy, and had a high-powered, Ivy League sort of vibe—Brooks Brothers clothes, a nose for good wine, and a sharp intelligence.

He joined us at the start of the competition. "Danny's kite is made of mulberry bark paper from Japan," he said. "We painted his dad's name on it. He says he wants to let it go when the competition is over, so it can go up to heaven and his dad can see it."

My eyes stung when he said that. Evan Gonsalves had been a good guy, and a good cop. We'd been friends mostly because he was married to Terri, but I liked him, and knew that he loved his son. It was good to know that his son still remembered him.

There were prizes for biggest and smallest kite, funniest kite and ugliest kite. In the competition, there were prizes for the highest flight, the angle of flight, and the sound that their hummers made in flight. Danny didn't win anything, but he looked like he had a lot of fun. When the competition was over, the four of us took him off to the side of the site, where the hill was steep and looked out over the Pacific.

"You ready to let it go, sport?" Levi asked, kneeling down to Danny's level.

Danny nodded.

"Well, let's give it a good run, okay?" He took Danny's hand in his and they ran across the grass, the kite gaining altitude behind them. Eventually Levi let go, and Danny kept running, the kite soaring behind him. "Let it go whenever you want," Levi called.

We watched as Danny released his grasp on the kite string, and the wind currents made the kite soar and dip. Danny stopped running and waved as the kite climbed higher and higher, and then took a turn out over the mountain. Mike and I hung back as Terri and Levi caught up with Danny, each taking one of his hands, all three of them watching the kite soar to heaven.

Terri took Danny off after that to get a shave ice, and I pulled Levi aside. "Can I get together with you on Monday?" I asked. "I've got this spreadsheet that relates to power companies somehow, and I need some help interpreting it."

"Sure," Levi said. We made a plan to meet up at his office late on Monday morning. We all went out for an early dinner, and then Mike and I went home and walked Roby.

"You still thinking about having kids?" Mike asked, as Roby sniffed around a succulent hinahina plant, blossoming with white flowers.

"Seems like everyone we know has them, huh?" Roby began licking the grass and I said, "Roby, that's gross," and jerked on his leash.

Mike appeared to be waiting for me to answer his question. "I had lunch with Sandra Guarino on Monday."

"What does that... oh."

"Yeah. Oh. She asked me if I'd consider being their sperm donor. Not now, but sometime in the future."

"What did you say?"

"I avoided the question. That's not something you can answer off the cuff."

"Who would be the mom?"

"Sandra. Cathy has some female problem."

"I used to work with this female fire captain," Mike said. "She was a ball-buster—tougher than most of the guys. Then she had a baby. She was still tough afterwards—but man, you should have seen her with her daughter. A totally different woman."

"You think Sandra would turn out that way?"

"Wouldn't be surprised." Mike picked up a stick from the ground and started twirling it in his hands. "Did she say how she wanted you to donate?"

"What do you mean?" I looked at him and then I knew. "I'm not interested in doing that anymore." I grimaced. "Especially not with Sandra. I'm sure we'd do it the civilized way—some kind of clinic."

Roby squatted, and I pulled a plastic bag from my pocket. "What if we both did?" I asked, not looking at Mike. "Then we wouldn't know whose sperm it was, and we'd both be the dads."

"Can they do that?"

"I'm sure."

"We'd have to think about it," Mike said. "Even being part-time dads, it's a huge commitment and it changes your life forever."

I stood up. "Yeah. I've seen that with my brothers."

"Imagine my parents as grandparents," Mike said, laughing. "My dad would be giving the kid junior doctor kits before he could read."

"Well, being a grandparent is a chance for our parents to redo all the things they did wrong with us."

Roby looked up at Mike and tried to take the stick from him. I reached down and unhooked his leash. "You gonna throw that thing or what?" I asked.

Mike threw it, and Roby went bounding ahead. I wanted to take Mike's hand, but I had that bag of poop to get rid of. So instead we just chased the dog together.

≈≈≈

Sunday afternoon, Greg Oshiro called my cell. "I heard from Anna," he said. "She won't tell me where she is, or why she's hiding, but at least she's okay."

"Did you get a phone number?"

"Nope. She said she was calling from a pay phone. I asked her about her cell but she just said she had it shut off."

"Okay. Let me know if you hear from her again. See if you can get her to meet you somewhere to see the girls."

"I don't want to use the girls as bait," he said. "Not now. Not ever."

We went over to Lui's that afternoon for a barbecue, and surrounded by all my nieces and nephews, I kept thinking about the conversations I'd had with Sandra and with Mike. I could see us bringing Sandra and Cathy into our family circle—what we call *ohana* in Hawaiian. There would be a new baby or two for my parents to fuss over.

But what would it mean for Mike and me? I'd heard my brothers complain about feeling ignored by their wives. What if Mike and I got so caught up in taking care of our kid, or kids, that we lost the connection that we had?

It was just too complicated a question. But no matter how I tried to ignore it, every time one of the kids ran past, with a scrape or an empty plate or a ball to play with, I kept coming back to it. It was a relief when we finally left and returned home, just Mike and me and Roby.

Monday morning, Ray and I got roped into helping round up a guy suspected of robbing one of the downtown branches of the Bank of Hawai'i. He lived in a crappy apartment in Mo'ili'ili, and we were lucky to get out of there just in time to make it to Wave Power Technologies for our eleven o'clock appointment.

It was the first time I'd been to Levi's office, which was filled with bits and pieces from his past life—framed diplomas, including the one from Harvard Business School; photos of him at conferences and groundbreaking ceremonies; a gold CD that seemed to represent a million copies sold of some software product.

I was happy to see that along with the photos of his daughters, Ilana and Susan, there was a candid shot of him with Terri and Danny. Ray and I sat down across from his desk. "You've got some questions about alternative energy?" he asked.

I gave him a quick rundown of the case so far, and what Selena had suggested. He pursed his lips and twined his fingers together while I spoke.

"I hate to hear this kind of thing," he said. "Not just because two women lost their lives. But because these kind of shenanigans give the industry a bad name. Can I see the spreadsheets?"

I gave him the flash drive, which was certainly getting a lot of use. I'd have to thank Harry again for it.

Levi's secretary stuck her head in the door and asked if we wanted anything to drink.

"Try the pineapple coconut smoothies with açai berries,"

Levi said, still facing his computer. "Another one of my little investments. Lots of antioxidants."

I looked at Ray and we both shrugged. "Sure," I said. "Is there anything trendy you don't have your fingers in?"

"Nope," he said.

The secretary returned with a pair of round bottles for us. There was a nice sort of berry and chocolate aftertaste once you got past the coconut and pineapple flavors. "Not bad," I said.

We were about halfway through the smoothies by the time Levi turned back to us. "Your cousin was right," he said. "These numbers represent about a year's worth of energy production from a prototype system. And if the bad numbers are correct, the project is tanking."

He shook his head. "It's incredibly expensive to put together a prototype and test it. It takes a few years before a company can make money from one of these technologies. That's where Uncle Sam comes in." He leaned back in his chair. "The government has all these programs to encourage the development of alternative energy technology. Wave power is just a small part of it. You've got wind power, biomass, alternative fuels... the list goes on and on. Eventually the industry's going to shake out, and there will be a couple of major players. The downstream potential is huge."

Ray and I finished our smoothies, and Levi took the empty bottles from us and tossed them into a recycle bin next to his desk. "Let's get to your numbers," he said. "Every company has to demonstrate that their technology is successful in order to keep getting more money from the government. But not every project is going to be a winner. Sometimes the science just doesn't work, or it doesn't work well enough to justify the expense."

"Somebody's fudging the numbers," I said.

"Exactly. Harry was on the right track when he said these looked like two sets of books."

"Do you know which company we're looking at?" I asked.

"I can't tell—but I'll bet you can."

"How?"

He flipped to another spreadsheet. "These are the true records of what they spend," he said. "See this? If I'm not mistaken, that's a VIN number. It looks like these are lease payments on a car. Track the VIN number, you know who's using the car. And then you figure out where that person works."

He read the number out, and I wrote it down. I used my cell to call a friend at the DMV, who checked the number out for me and promised to text it back to me.

While we waited, Levi said, "The Business, Economic Development and Tourism department is responsible for monitoring these projects. The company I invest in sends them quarterly reports. Based on how we're doing, they disburse additional grant money, and monitor what we're using the money for."

My phone buzzed with the incoming text. "What a surprise," I said. "Néng Yuán." I explained to Levi who Wyatt was.

"I know a little about Néng Yuán," he said. "I've met Dr. Zenshen a couple of times. She's even smarter than she is beautiful."

"What do you know about the company?"

"The company I invest in uses point absorbers." He clicked a couple of keys and brought up a PowerPoint presentation. "Watch this for a minute."

We looked at the animation, which showed the way a farm of buoys captured the wave energy and transferred it to a generator.

"Néng Yuán has a different approach," Levi said, when the presentation was over. "They use what are called attenuators." He showed us another clip, in which long, worm-like segments moved with the waves, and as they flexed, the energy moved into a hydraulic pump.

"Nobody knows which technology is going to be the best," Levi continued. "We're still taking baby steps. Néng Yuán's approach to attenuators is based on research Dr. Zenshen did in

China. She moved here a couple of years ago to take advantage of the offshore waves. She has big plans for an attenuator project on the North Shore. You know what the waves are like there."

I did. They were among the best in the world for surfing. "What happens to Pipeline or Sunset if something's offshore catching the waves?" I asked.

"They did a study in England. A company wants to put in this project called the Wave Hub off the Cornwall coast. Some reports say that waves will be cut by up to eleven percent."

"That could screw a lot of people. Look how much money comes in from surf competitions and surf touring on the North Shore. And if the project does knock down the waves, it could be bad news for a lot of other places, too."

"Don't get ahead of yourself," Levi said. "No one has built anything on the scale Néng Yuán is proposing yet, so no one knows what the true effect will be on the waves."

"Would somebody kill over a surf beach?" Ray asked. "Don't you think this is all about the money? How can we figure out how much money we're talking about here?"

"Let me run the numbers. I'll call you when I've had a chance to fiddle around."

"Remember, whoever is behind this has already killed two women. Don't tell anyone that you have this data, all right? Don't call anyone at the Department of Business, Economic Development and Tourism. Don't call anyone at Néng Yuán, or any other company."

"I didn't just fall off the turnip truck," Levi said. "I'll be careful."

Ray and I grabbed lunch on our way back to headquarters at a Chinese cafeteria around the corner from Levi's office. "I feel like we're making progress," Ray said, pushing his tray through the line, serving himself white rice and honey chicken. "I just hope this doesn't turn into another dead end."

"It's possible that we're on the wrong track," I said. "Zoë's death still could have been a result of a home invasion gone wrong, and Miriam's just a traffic accident. But I think they're connected, and that means we're going in the right direction."

I used a pair of tongs to grab some barbecue spare ribs, ladled some salad on my plate, and took a bowl full of won ton soup. We paid the cashier, a wizened old woman with missing teeth, and sat at a table by the front window.

As we ate, we watched the passing parade of trucks, tourists and teenagers. "Does it mean that I'm getting old because I want to go out there and pull that kid's pants up to his waist?" I asked, nodding to a Hawaiian guy who thought he was some kind of rap star, with jeans down to his hips, showing off six inches of plaid boxer shorts.

"Yeah," Ray said. "Pretty soon you'll be listening to Don Ho sing "Tiny Bubbles" and calling guys my age, Sonny."

"You're a year younger than I am."

Ray speared a hunk of honey chicken. "Your point is?"

"By the time my dad was my age, he was married with two kids and me on the way. He was a foreman for Amfac, one of the biggest companies in the state, and he was almost ready to start his own business. I can't imagine what that must have been like, all that pressure, all those people depending on him."

"Our generation is definitely spoiled," Ray said. "My dad was like yours. He worked his ass off trying to provide for me and my brothers and sisters. You think two kids was bad; imagine having six."

We finished eating, and pushed the trays away from us. "So where do we go from here?" I asked. "I guess we start with the people Zoë worked with."

"But how do we get in there without tipping them off?"

"Gladys Yuu already knows something's up," I said. "You saw the way she was looking at us when we checked out Miriam's cubicle. I say we ask her for a list of employees. She's the secretary, after all. She'd be the logical choice."

When we got back to the office, I called Gladys and asked her to put together a list of those who worked with Zoë and Miriam. "Why?" she asked. "I thought Zoë was killed in a break-in and Miriam died in a car crash."

"Just crossing all the t's and dotting the i's," I said. "You know what bureaucracy is."

I guess she did, because she faxed us a list a half hour later. We started with Franklin Nishimura, who was a career civil servant, the kind who kept his head down, did his work, and made the wheels of state government move forward. We split up the databases, and about an hour later we compared notes. "Salary eighty-K a year," I said. "Owns a house in Aiea, wife and two sons, Jeremy and Jonathan. Nothing jumps out at me."

"Jeremy Nishimura has a record," Ray said. "Possession, possession with intent to distribute, public intoxication, and so on."

I made a note. "If we were just looking at Zoë, I could see Jeremy. He meets this single woman who works for his dad, thinks her house could be easy pickings. But Miriam?"

"Jeremy's been in and out of rehab," Ray said. "Could be Franklin needs some cash to send him someplace expensive, get him clean."

"Could be."

We went down the list. Nishimura had an associate director below him, Maun Li, and then three senior analysts: Zoë

Greenfield, Winston Cheng, and Donna Paulson. Maun Li and Donna Paulson raised no red flags, but Winston Cheng made fifty grand a year and lived in Black Point, one of Honolulu's most expensive neighborhoods.

That in itself was suspicious. Then add to that the BMW 7 series he drove, and you had a guy who looked like he was living above his means. That's always a red flag when you are researching suspects. We made a note to look into his background more carefully.

There were also two junior analysts—Miriam Rose and Alan Stark—and two secretaries, Gladys Yuu and Penny Stillwater.

While researching Alan Stark, I stumbled across a picture of him at an official function. He looked very familiar, but I couldn't place him. He was a heavyset haole in his late twenties, with a round, unlined face. I tried Googling his name, but didn't come up with anything. But I was sure I knew him. Was he gay? I knew I'd never dated him, but perhaps I'd run into him at a party.

I called Gunter, who never forgets a trick. "You know a guy named Alan Stark? Big guy, baby face?"

"You mean Helen Wheels?"

"That's it! I knew I recognized him but I couldn't place him."

Helen Wheels was a plus-size drag queen who MC'd events in various gay bars. His drag persona was a roller derby queen, complete with skates, knee pads, bouffant hair, and tight, sequined Capri pants. He moved around pretty well for a big guy and did a passable lip-synch to seventies pop hits.

Could he be a blackmail target, I wondered? Nishimura appeared like a pretty straight-laced guy; suppose he didn't approve of drag queens, and someone had threatened Alan with exposure?

Ray and I split up the two secretaries, Gladys and Penny. I got Penny, a 38-year-old divorced mother of a six-year-old son with autism. She lived in a rental apartment in Halawa Valley and had her son in a private school. That had to be expensive.

I told Ray. "You find anything interesting on Gladys?" I asked.

He shrugged. "She's divorced, lives near UH with her eighty-year-old mother."

"Look like she needs money?"

"Not that I can tell. No kids, no mortgage."

We decided that the three people who needed more investigation were Franklin Nishimura, Winston Cheng, and Alan Stark, aka Helen Wheels. I discovered that Helen was the MC for a wet jockey short competition at the Rod and Reel Club, a gay bar in Waikiki, that night. "I'll take that one."

"Yeah, like I was going to fight you for it," Ray said. "I'll go out to Aiea and nose around Nishimura's house, see if the neighbors have anything to say."

"We'll do Winston Cheng together. I know a great deli in Black Point. We'll meet up there tomorrow morning for coffee and malasadas and then check out Cheng's place."

Gunter was working until nine, and I offered to buy him a beer if he'd go with me to the Rod and Reel Club when he got off. "I don't know," he said. "You might cramp my style."

"It would take a crowbar to cramp your style."

"Is that a crowbar in your pants or are you just glad to see me?" He laughed. "You can park in my driveway and we'll walk over together. Give me a few minutes to get home from work and get changed, though."

I was cooking up a quick stir-fry when I told Mike I was going out that night. He was not happy that I was going to the Rod and Reel Club. "You're not going to take your pants off, are you?" he asked.

"I don't know. You think I could win a wet jockey short competition?"

"If Gunter wasn't such a tattletale, I'd worry about you," he said, draining the rice and portioning it out between us. "But I know that he'll tell me whatever you do."

"You could always come with us."

"I have a date. Me and Roby and the TiVo."

I got to Gunter's about nine-thirty and rang the bell of the single-story house he shares with an ever-changing series of roommates. When he answered he was naked.

Now, that's not unusual. Gunter's life is a clothing-optional one. He wears a uniform to work, and then as little as he can get away with everywhere else. He is six-three, rail thin, and muscular, with a blond buzz cut. Before I met Mike, Gunter and I had fooled around occasionally, and I knew that he was an imaginative, athletic lover, with a dick that would have pleased any size queen.

"I think you need to wear jockey shorts if you want to enter a wet jockey short competition," I said.

"I need your advice. Come on in."

I am usually the last guy Gunter asks for fashion advice. I live in aloha shorts, khakis and deck shoes. I wear boxers, usually in wild patterns, like ice cream cones, flamingoes, or fire trucks. Gunter long ago gave up trying to make me over.

I followed his tight, hairless butt across the living room and into his bedroom. "So which do you think?" he asked, holding up a pair of bright red jockey shorts. "These? Or these?"

The second pair were barely-there bikini bottoms. "I can't tell without seeing them on you," I said, sprawling on his bed. "Try them on."

There was a method to my madness. My dick had sprung to attention as soon as Gunter answered the door, and I figured that I could adjust myself more surreptitiously if I did it while falling to his bed. And getting his dick under cover would only help.

We decided on the bikini bottoms. Gunter pulled on shorts, Crocs, and a t-shirt that read "I'm not glad to see you. I just have a big dick."

When we got to the Rod and Reel Club, Helen Wheels was lip-synching to "My Baby Takes the Morning Train," by Sheena

Easton, including some very impressive kicks and spins. I admired her ability to stay balanced on those roller blades, especially in such tight pants.

Helen took a break after that, announcing that the wet jockey short competition would be starting at ten out on the patio. "We'll see if we can get you all wet!" she said.

The house music picked up, and I waved her over as she was leaving the stage. She skated to a hard stop and dropped into a chair at our table with a boom. "Well, well," she said. "Officer Hot and his sexy sidekick."

"Detective Hot, if you don't mind. You want something to drink?"

"I would kill for a lemonade. But then you'd probably arrest me, wouldn't you?"

I handed Gunter a twenty and asked him to get Helen a drink. "I'll make this quick," I said, when Gunter had left. The music had changed to Katy Perry singing about kissing a girl—something I thought most of the men in the Rod and Reel Club had never done. "I need to talk to you about your office."

"You're making me frown," Helen said. "That's not good for my face."

"You knew Zoë Greenfield?"

He nodded. "Poor thing. I heard somebody broke into her house and killed her."

"That's true. You know anything more about it?"

He backed his chair away. "What do you mean?"

"They know about you at work?" I asked. "I mean, about your sideline?"

He laughed. "Are you kidding? Frankie loves me. He even got me a gig at this Japanese New Year party." He narrowed his eyes. "You don't think…"

I shrugged. "Just chasing down leads. You know she was friends with Miriam Rose, right?"

"Oh, sure." His eyes widened as Gunter returned with his lemonade. "Oh, my God!" he said. "You mean what happened to Miriam wasn't an accident?"

"I don't think so. Zoë ever say anything to you about irregularities? Companies reporting incorrect data?"

Alan had turned pale under his makeup. "She wasn't the chatty type. The only one she talked to in the office was Miriam. I mean, yeah, we'd say hello, how was your weekend, that kind of thing. But I work on overall energy conservation statistics, and she worked on alternatives. We didn't overlap."

"Don't tell anybody I was talking to you, all right?" I said. "Not yet, at least."

"Am I in danger? I have some vacation time coming. I could just stop going to work."

"If you don't know anything, there's no reason to worry. But is there anybody in the office you think I should look at? Anybody who's in a position to fudge statistics?"

"I work with those people," he said, his voice going up an octave. "You think somebody in my office killed Zoë and Miriam?"

"Keep your voice down and your wig on, Helen. Like I said, I'm just chasing down leads."

"The only person in that office who's really evil is Gladys," Alan said. "She's like this malevolent dragon, with her tail curled around Franklin. God forbid you should ever need anything from her. Just getting her to process expense reimbursements is a nightmare."

Fred, the bartender, was waving at Helen. "I've got to go on. Oh my God, I'm so upset. I can't believe somebody in my office might be a killer."

"Come on, sweetie," Gunter said, standing up and extending his hand to Helen. "The show must go on, right? And the pants must come off."

Helen took Gunter's hand and rose to his feet, wobbling on

his roller blades. He looked down at me. "You competing?"

"Sorry. I retired from competition years ago. But Gunter will represent."

Helen stole a glance down at Gunter's endowment, and some of the color came back to her cheeks. "Yes, I guess he will. Well, come on, then, honey, let's get the hose out."

"I thought we were keeping our shorts on," Gunter said.

Helen giggled, and the two of them went off to the patio. I took my beer outside and watched Helen hose down Gunter and a half-dozen other guys. After Gunter had been crowned the champion, I left the bar and walked back alone to where I'd parked at his house; he was enjoying his celebrity too much to drag him away.

If Alan Stark wasn't a good suspect, that narrowed the field. I just hoped that I hadn't put him in danger by talking to him.

Mike was waiting up for me when I got home, sitting in bed with his reading glasses and a fire magazine, Roby on the floor next to him. I leaned over to kiss his forehead, and he took my head and brought it down so that we could lock lips. "Mmm," I said as I pulled away. "Did you miss me?"

"I was thinking of you," he said, pulling back the covers and showing me just how much he had me on his mind. "You and that wet jockey short competition."

"Don't worry, I dried off before I got into the Jeep," I said, pulling my shirt off and tossing it toward the laundry hamper.

"You did not," he said.

"Dry off?"

"You did not let them hose you down in your jockey shorts," he said, closing the magazine and putting his reading glasses on the bedside table.

I kicked off my deck shoes and shucked my khakis, turning my boxer-clad butt toward Mike and hanging the pants up in the closet. "Are you kidding?" I said. "You think I could compete with Gunter?"

"Gunter entered the contest?"

I turned back to him and dropped my shorts. I was hard already. "Gunter won the contest."

"Come here, you," he said, turning on his side and reaching around to my butt to pull me closer to him. He licked his tongue up the length of my dick, and my whole body shivered with anticipation.

We made love for a while, in various positions and combinations, and then we relaxed next to each other in the king-sized bed. "You could have won that contest," Mike said, resting one hand on my chest.

"That's sweet. But only if you were the judge."

"We could always run our own little contest. In the back yard, some sunny Saturday afternoon."

I leaned over and kissed his cheek. "I'd get to hose you down?" I said. "I'm up for that."

He looked down the length of my body. "You're up for something, all right."

And I was.

The next morning, I met Ray at the deli in Black Point, where we left his Highlander and rode up in the Jeep to Winston Cheng's house, surrounded by black iron gates. We parked across the street, under the shade of a spreading kiawe tree, and while we waited for him to leave the house on his way to work, we traded information. Ray had gone around Franklin Nishimura's neighborhood the night before with Julie, pretending that they were considering moving into the area.

"We spoke to a bunch of the neighbors. This one lady was very forthcoming on the Nishimuras."

"Got to love a gossip," I said.

"Yeah. She went on about the boy with the drug problems, but it turns out he's in a residential program in California, something state-run. Everybody else only had good things to say."

I told him about Alan Stark's relationship with his boss. "So that's a dead end, too."

Winston Cheng's garage door opened, and the BMW 7 series convertible backed down the driveway, with the top down. He was waiting for the gate to open behind him when a dark-haired woman opened the front door and stepped out. "You forgot this!" she called, holding out a briefcase.

Ray whistled softly. "What a babe."

The woman was probably ten years older than either of us, but the years had been very kind to her. She had a luscious figure, wrapped in a light blue sheath that hugged every curve, and wore high heels that accented her long legs.

Cheng parked the convertible, leaving it running, and walked up to get the briefcase. "Thanks, sweetheart," he said, kissing her cheek.

"Don't forget we're having dinner with my parents at Roy's," she said. "I think they're finally going to give us the deed to the condo in Beaver Creek."

"Wouldn't miss it. Actually, couldn't miss it, could I?"

"Not if you want them to keep giving us money," she said, laughing.

He got into the convertible and backed through the gates and into the street. The woman went back inside, and the gates closed.

"Where's Beaver Creek?" Ray asked as I drove him back to the deli.

"Colorado, I think. Ski resort."

"So maybe all the money comes from her parents?"

"We can check."

It didn't take much time, once we knew what we were looking for. Diana Cheng got her name in the social pages a lot, and we discovered that her father was C.K. Chu, a Hong Kong industrialist who had retired to Honolulu a few years before.

We were running out of people with motives. Everyone we'd checked on seemed to have no more than the ordinary quotient of secrets and troubles. I've found that you need a strong motivation to go against the social order and take another life. Unless you're some kind of psychopath, you need to be pushed to the edge. And none of Zoë's co-workers seemed like they'd go that far.

Around ten, I got an email from Levi that he was still looking into the stuff in the spreadsheets, and he'd get back to me soon. There was a link to Wave Power's website at the end of the message, and I clicked through. I started watching an animation of their technology, and then I remembered our conversation about how surfers were objecting to the use of wave energy.

I started Googling and clicking on links, finding individual surfers and groups that opposed sapping the strength from waves to provide electricity. I remembered the photo of Zoë Greenfield surfing on the wall of the house on Lopez Lane, though I hadn't seen a surfboard anywhere.

I called Greg Oshiro. Two could play his game, I thought, and when he answered, instead of saying hello, I said, "Did Zoë Greenfield surf?"

"Before she met Anna, I think," Greg said. "Why?"

"Just asking." I hung up before he could get anything else in.

I tried Googling her name, this time looking for any connection to surfing or to groups that were protesting the use of wave energy. It took a while, but I found an online petition sponsored by a group called Save Our Beaches for Surfing (SOBS). The specific petition was against the construction of a sewage plant on the North Shore, but when I went to the main SOBS web site, I found that they had also organized protests against the use of wave capture technology.

I paged through the site, looking for any other mention of Zoë. Her name didn't appear, but a familiar one did. My cousin Ben was a member of the organization's board of directors.

Ben was a competitive surfer, better than I'd ever been. He spent much of the year following the waves, entering, and often winning, competitions around the world. I hoped that the cell number I had for him was still good, and that he wasn't in one of those dead zones they're haunting people with in those TV ads.

The call went to his voice mail. "Hey, brah, it's cousin Kimo," I said. "I've got a question about a case. Can you call me as soon as you get a chance? I don't know where you are now, but I hope you're surfing well."

I was going over my idea with Ray when my cell rang. "That was quick, brah," I said. "You in town?"

"Yeah, getting ready to leave on Sunday for Costa Rica. What do you need?"

"You're on the board of a group called SOBS, right?"

"Bunch of nutcases," he said.

"Can we meet up somewhere? I want to talk to you about them."

"I'm in Haleiwa. Got a sponsor meeting later in the afternoon. How about over dinner?"

"Let me check with Mike and call you back."

Mike was up for a quick trip to the North Shore. "I should go look at a fire scene up there anyway. How soon can you get away?"

"Meet you at the house in an hour?"

"I'll be there."

Lieutenant Sampson agreed that Ray and I had put in enough unbilled overtime on the case to let us sneak off for the afternoon. "You think this could be a lead?" he asked, half paying attention to us and half reading something on his computer.

"It's a chance," I said. "We're running out of other options."

"You've got 'til Friday. After that, I'm putting you back in the rotation."

He went back to the computer, and Ray and I left his office. I called Ben to confirm our dinner, then left for home, feeling like a schoolboy playing hooky. I was loading surfboards and rash guards into the back of the Jeep, Roby jumping around like a demented kangaroo, when Mike pulled into the driveway.

He looked at all the gear. "I thought you were going to Haleiwa for a meeting." He reached down to scratch under Roby's chin.

"Not 'til dinner. I figured I can get some surfing in. The waves should still be pretty strong."

The big waves on the North Shore start in October, and start to fizzle by March. That's why Ben was on his way to Costa Rica. But I knew I could still do some quality surfing at Pipeline or

Sunset.

We zoomed along the freeways, then climbed up Kam Highway through the center of the island, blasting "Island Girls' by Fiji and singing along. It was breezy up there, and I didn't trust Roby not to jump out if he saw some other dog, so we left the flaps down and just opened the side windows. We passed the Dole Plantation, driving through endless fields just coming green in the springtime.

"You think this will all be developed some day?" Mike asked, leaning back in his seat.

"Hope not." I spent a lot of time on the North Shore just after I came out of the closet, working undercover to find out who had killed a trio of surfers, and I could see more and more development encroaching the closer we got to the traffic circle where Kam Highway turned right toward Haleiwa.

Instead of turning right toward Haleiwa, I followed the circle around to Waialua Beach Road, and then to Haleiwa Road. I dropped Mike at Fire Station 14 in Haleiwa, where he said he'd get one of the firefighters to drive him out to the scene of the fire, off the Cane Haul Road. Roby and I continued up through Haleiwa, connecting back with Kam, cruising along looking for a good break.

I found a parking space near Alligator Rock, between Leftovers and Marijuana's, and pulled in. It's not one of the toughest, or the easiest, breaks, so it wasn't too crowded. I pulled on my rash guard then tied Roby's leash to a stake in the sand, opened a beach umbrella for shade, and left him a towel to curl up on. But he sat at attention, watching me walk down the beach.

The water was cold, and the swells looked about five feet. I dropped my board in and then turned to look back at him. I made a downward motion with my hand, and he went down on his haunches, though I could see he was still watching me.

I duck dived through the incoming surf, setting myself up beyond the breakers to wait for a good wave. I could just make out Roby on the beach towel, a golden blob on a field of blue, surrounded by sand the same color as his fur.

I surfed for about an hour, then rode the last wave in to the shore for a good landing. As I walked toward Roby, he jumped up and strained against the leash.

We were all alone in our little stretch of beach, so I let him loose, and raced him down to the water. We romped in the surf for a few minutes, him tearing back and forth and all around me, and then we went back to the towel, where I'd left his leash. I walked him up to the street, let him empty his bladder, and then took him over to the pole shower.

We both rinsed off as best we could, and he rewarded me with a spray of cold water as he shook. I put some water in a bowl, which he slurped up. Then we went back to the towel and lay down to dry off in the sun. He dozed, but I sat there, letting the warmth roll over me, and thought about the deaths of Zoë Greenfield and Miriam Rose.

I had to believe that the spreadsheets held the key. But what did they show? Was Néng Yuán cheating the state, and was Zoë killed to prevent that information from being made public? Or had Zoë planned to release that information to a group like SOBS, to damage the wave power movement? In that case, the list of potential suspects could grow—even to include Levi Hirsch, who had invested a lot of cash in Wave Power Technology.

I didn't suspect Levi, or I would never have given him Zoë's spreadsheets. But as I sat there and watched the never-ending surf, I couldn't help but think about how much energy was out there for the taking. Between the heat generated by the sun above me, the gusts of wind that occasionally whipped the sand around us, and the waves, there was a lot of force that could be tamed.

I remembered the old saying that power corrupts. In this case, it was a different kind of power than whoever first said it had meant. The sun, wind and waves could generate energy, and then that energy could be sold to people and businesses who needed it. And didn't having a commodity that others wanted, and were willing to pay for, generate power in the marketplace?

I sat there for a while, watching the waves, until the sun went behind some clouds and I realized it was getting late. I called my friend Ari, who owns and manages property up on the North Shore, and asked if he had a place I could shower and get cleaned up.

"If you don't mind something a little messy, I've got a time-share you can use. The last set of guests checked out yesterday, and I don't have a new set 'til the weekend, so the maid hasn't gotten over there yet."

"Thanks. That'd be great." He gave me the address and the code for the lock box on the door. There were even a couple of clean towels, and I was able to shower, change, and get Roby pretty dry before Mike called.

I picked him up at the fire station, and Roby was so glad to see him you'd think the poor dog had been abandoned for days. Mike leaned down and sniffed the dog's fur. "He smells like strawberries."

"Don't tell Ari, but I dragged him into the shower and shampooed him," I said. "We went into the water for a while, and he was salty and smelly. They had a maximum strength blow dryer at the time share, so it was like a puppy salon treatment."

We got a patio table at Jameson's, where Roby could sprawl at our feet, and ordered frozen daiquiris while we waited for Ben. It was nice there with Mike and Roby, a family outing in the midst of all the confusion. I was sad that Zoë Greenfield would never spend time like that with her daughters again, and wondered how they would grow up—with Greg? With Anna, who was still hiding out somewhere? Would the loss of their mother leave a hole behind, or would they grow up never even knowing that there had been another mother in the first years of their lives?

I thought again of Greg and Anna, and their possible motives. Suppose Ray and I were running off on the wrong track, chasing down energy companies and disgruntled surfers, when Zoë's killer was right in front of us?

"Earth to Kimo," Mike said, nudging me. "Are you here with

us, or off somewhere?"

I raised my glass. "I'm here with you, sweetheart. And very grateful for that."

As Mike and I were finishing our daiquiris, Ben arrived, deeply tanned, wearing a polo shirt with the logo of a waterproof sunscreen company. "One of my sponsors," he said. "I had to meet with them this afternoon."

Ben's dad was a Kansas-born gambler Aunt Pua met and married in a quickie ceremony in Vegas, where she was working for a short while as a cocktail waitress. I don't think he ever knew that she had two other kids back in Hawai'i, and the marriage lasted only long enough for her to become pregnant with Ben.

He looked a lot like me, the haole from his dad coming out on top of the Hawaiian-Japanese mix from his mom. He had short, straight black hair, a tall, wiry frame, and biceps that bulged out of his pale blue polo shirt.

We made small talk until after the waiter had taken our orders – I got Portuguese bean soup, and the opakapaka, a Hawaiian pink snapper, poached in white wine and topped with a Hollandaise sauce. Mike and Ben ordered salads and fish as well, grilled ahi for Ben and the sautéed mahi-mahi for Mike. I was salivating just thinking about what a great meal it was going to be. The waiter even offered to bring some steak tidbits for Roby.

"So tell me about SOBS," I said, after I drained the last of my daiquiri. "You said they were nutcases?"

"They're well-intentioned." Ben leaned back in his chair. "The guy who founded the group is named Steve Hendrix, and he tends to get excited about stuff. There was this sewage plant thing, and then parking along Kam Highway, and then he wanted more showers installed. Now he's got a bug up his ass about wave power."

"How big a group?"

Ben shrugged. "They turn out a crowd for demonstrations. Mostly because he's smart, and he schedules things when the weather's bad for surfing. He runs a surf shop, and he's always giving away free stuff, too, so people show up. Like I said, he's the main guy, but he's got three or four other people who help him out."

"How'd you end up on the board of directors?"

Ben grimaced. "One of my sponsors. They do a lot of business with Steve's store, and they pressured me to let him use my name. I didn't have much choice."

I told him the bare facts about the case—that a woman who analyzed alternative energy statistics had been killed, and we were tracking down all angles. "You think there's anyone at SOBS who might want to sabotage some of these energy companies?"

"You mean kill somebody?" he asked. "I don't think so."

"I know this woman, Zoë, surfed a little. What if she was handing off energy data to a group like SOBS, and somebody from an energy company found out?" I suggested. "Maybe this Steve guy made some threats to some company, and they had Zoë killed to prevent the information getting out?"

Even as I said it, the idea sounded dumb. I could see I was getting way out. Zoë's killer wasn't some anonymous energy company executive trying to protect market share.

The waiter brought our entrées, including the platter of steak tidbits for Roby, who immediately began to wolf them down, as if we never fed him at home.

The fish platters were beautiful, like works of art. "As my mother used to say, Gladys Yuu couldn't have carved this better," Mike said, looking down at his.

For a moment I thought I'd misunderstood him. "What did you say?"

"It's an old family joke," he said. "When my parents moved to Hawai'i, my mother took cooking lessons from this Chinese woman who was an expert at carving meat, trimming fish, all that knife stuff. My father used to tease my mother, when she did a bad job. 'Didn't you learn anything from Gladys Yuu?' And then when something was good, he'd say, 'Gladys Yuu couldn't have done it better.'"

"I need to talk to your mother when we get home," I said.

Mike's eyebrows raised. I'd had a rocky relationship with his parents, mostly with his father, who still believed I was a bad influence on his son, and it was rare that I initiated any contact with them. It was awkward sometimes, but I managed to avoid them most of the time.

Usually we ran into each other in the driveway, waving and saying hello, maybe sharing a comment about the weather. Even Mike wasn't that friendly with his folks, certainly not to the degree I was with my family. He had spent so many years hiding his sexuality from them that lack of communication had become a habit.

After dinner, we said good night to Ben and I got a plastic bag from the restaurant. Mike and I walked Roby down along Kam Highway. There were a million stars out over the ocean, and a cool breeze blowing in. "What do you need to talk to my mother about?" Mike asked.

"I wonder if the Gladys Yuu who taught your mother how to cut up meat and fish is the secretary in the office where Zoë Greenfield worked."

Roby stopped to squat next to a hibiscus bush, the bright red flowers already closed up for the night. In the morning, though, new blossoms would open up. I wondered if new ideas would open up with the case the next morning, if the middle-aged Gladys Yuu we'd met at Zoë's office would turn out to have the skill to put a knife into someone.

"Middle-aged Chinese woman," I said, turning to look at Mike.

He stuck his hand into the take-out bag, reached down, and grabbed Roby's poop. "Excuse me?" he said, standing up.

"Gladys Yuu is a middle-aged Chinese woman. At least the one at Zoë's office is. And that fits the profile of the person who pawned Zoë's jewelry at Lucky Lou's."

We turned back around toward the Jameson's parking lot as I explained how Ray and I had traced Zoë's dragon pendant to Lucky Lou's. "But we were thinking that it was a home invasion then," I said. "And that kind of person didn't fit with what we were expecting, so we pushed it aside."

"But now you think it might connect," Mike said.

I was so excited about the possibility of a new lead that I probably drove too fast on Kam going home. "Slow down, Kimo Andretti," Mike said once, as I sailed around a convertible full of tourists.

We pulled into our driveway just before nine. There was still a light on in his parents' living room when Mike knocked on the front door.

His father answered, wearing a khaki t-shirt, denim shorts and reading glasses that looked just like Mike's. If you saw Mike and his dad together, you'd know they were father and son. Mike was a couple of inches taller than his father, and he had a mustache and a slight epicanthic fold to his eyes, but otherwise, his facial structure and bearing were just the same as his dad's.

Roby went nuts seeing his grandfather, and before he said anything to us, Dominic Riccardi knelt down to rub behind the golden retriever's ears. "This is a nice surprise," Dom said, standing up. "Come on in."

He stepped aside to let us all in the house, and called out, "Soon-O. Mike and Kimo are here."

Mike walked ahead of me and leaned down to kiss his mother's cheek as she sat on the sofa doing a Sudoku puzzle. Even though I have Japanese blood, I think the gene for number puzzles was strained out of my makeup somewhere along the way. I love crosswords, but I can't figure Sudoku out at all.

Soon-O put the puzzle book aside and motioned Mike to sit beside her. She was a tall, slim, Korean woman, a nurse who had met her future husband when he was her patient in an Army field hospital during the Korean war. She wasn't a great beauty; her face was flat and almost circular. But her eyes revealed a deep intelligence, and she was quick to grasp a situation and deal with it.

Her husband still harbored a grudge against me for dumping his son when we broke up the first time, and driving Mike to drink. But Soon-O had more faith in Mike and his ability to control his own life, and never blamed his problems on me.

I sat in one of the wing chairs across from the sofa, and Dom sat in the other. Roby sprawled at Dom's feet, the traitor.

"Kimo has a question about Gladys Yuu," Mike said.

"It was something Mike said at dinner," I began. "About a woman you studied cooking with?"

Soon-O nodded. "When we moved out here from New York so that Dom could start work at Tripler, I decided to take a couple of months off to help us all get settled."

Tripler was the big Army hospital just ewa of downtown, where Dom Riccardi was a doctor and Soon-O a nurse. I knew that Soon-O had been very unhappy on Long Island, where Asian-Caucasian marriages were a rarity, where she hadn't been able to buy the foods that reminded her of home, or hear her native language other than through the long-distance lines.

"A friend of Dom's at Tripler knew a woman who taught Chinese cooking classes out of her house, and I signed up," Soon-O continued. "Her name was Gladys Yuu." She smiled. "I did learn a lot about using knives from her. I guess Mike said something about that."

"Gladys Yuu couldn't have carved the fish better," Mike said. "We had dinner at Jameson's, up on the North Shore."

"Such a long way to go for dinner on a work day," Dom said. He'd put aside his reading glasses, on top of a hardcover Tom Clancy novel on the wooden table next to his chair.

"I was chasing down a lead. My cousin Ben is on the board of a surf group that I thought might be tied into my case."

Dom was a sports nut. Like my brother Haoa, he followed UH football, baseball and basketball. He watched golf and

NASCAR on TV, and even followed surf competitions. "Ben Melville?" he asked.

I nodded. "I think you met him at our house once. He's my Aunt Pua's youngest son."

"So how does this relate to Gladys Yuu?" Soon-O asked.

"The two women who were killed worked in the Department of Business, Economic Development and Tourism. There's a secretary there named Gladys Yuu. I wondered if it was the same woman."

Soon-O frowned. "This was a long time ago, you understand. Mike was only seven, so that was more than twenty-five years ago. But I did keep up with a few of the women I studied with, for a while. I remember Gladys's husband died, and she took a job with the state. I don't know more than that."

"Thanks. That's helpful."

Dom Riccardi wasn't ready to let go so easily. "What makes you think this woman could be connected to your case?"

"The first woman who was killed was stabbed. You probably know it's hard to kill someone with a knife." As a doctor and a nurse, I figured the Riccardis had seen their share of stab wounds. "The person who killed Zoë Greenfield knew how to use a knife. When Mike said that Gladys had taught knife skills, I made the connection."

"How was she killed?" Dom asked.

"Dominic," Soon-O said. "You're not a detective."

"I have some background in this area, Soon-O." He turned back to me. "Well?"

I tried to remember the autopsy report. "Zoë was slender, about five-seven. Her assailant was about the same height, and the first cut came from behind, right about here." I pointed to where my neck met my right shoulder.

"As if he was trying to cut the jugular," Dom said, nodding.

"Or she," I said. "Then it looks like Zoë turned around to

face the assailant. There were a couple of defensive wounds to her hands." I held my own up in front of me, as if warding off the knife. "The final cuts were to her stomach, and it looks like she died from loss of blood."

"Or shock," Dom said. "Was she on any medication?"

"Dom, that's enough," Soon-O said. "Mike and Kimo don't come over enough. We shouldn't talk about murder when they're here." She patted her son's hand. "So, tell us, Mike, what's new?"

Dominic Riccardi grumbled but let it go. Mike told them about the case he'd gone up to investigate. "Stupidity, as usual," he said. "This teenaged kid who'd been grounded was mad at his father. He knew that his dad kept a stash of dirty magazines in his bureau, so he dug around until he found them, then stacked them on the kitchen table and set them on fire."

Soon-O looked like she was unhappy that she had changed the subject. "Of course, the house caught on fire," Mike continued. "At first the kid said that the stove had shorted out but I could tell from the fire pattern that it had started at the table. Eventually he confessed."

I'm fascinated by the technical aspects of Mike's job, the way he can use the evidence to track back to how everything began. But Soon-O said, "Can't either of you talk about anything happy?"

"Saturday afternoon we went to this kite festival up in the Ko'olaus," I said. "My friend Terri's son was flying in the competition."

She turned to Mike. "In school we studied Admiral Yi of the Joseon Dynasty of Korea. When the Japanese invaded Korea in the 16th century, he used kites with special markings to command his fleet." We spent a few minutes talking about the competition, and about the kites Soon-O had flown as a girl in Korea. "That must have been beautiful," she said. "So many kites."

I felt that sting in my eyes again as I told her how Danny had eventually let his go, sending it to his father in heaven. "I would like to go to a festival like that," Soon-O said. "Will you let us know if you go again?"

We said we would, and left a few minutes later. "That was nice," I said to Mike, as we walked into our own house, next door. "Your father didn't bite my head off, and your mother got to enjoy a memory. We should do more with them. Maybe we'll have them and my parents over for dinner sometime."

Mike started to strip down. "If you want. I'm going to watch TV for a while and then hit the hay. How about you?"

I checked my email, surfed to a couple of websites, and then joined Mike in bed by ten. We snuggled up together, Roby on the floor by the bed, and my last thoughts were about how comfortable I felt there within the center of my family.

The next morning, I told Ray what I'd discovered about Gladys Yuu. "I went online and found some photos taken a few years ago, of Gladys teaching a cooking class. I'm pretty sure it's the same woman."

I showed him the album I'd found online. I printed a couple of the pictures, including a good shot of Gladys's face. There was a photo of the students in front of what I figured was Gladys's house. I popped her address into Google Maps and pulled it up on my screen, and what I saw there quickened my pulse.

But before I jumped the gun, I did some fiddling with another search engine. I found the address I was looking for—and I wasn't surprised to find it wasn't too far from Gladys's. I hunted for a different picture and printed it. When I was finished I said to Ray, "Come on. Field trip."

"Where are we going?"

"You'll see when we get there."

He raised his eyebrows, but tagged along. It had rained while we were inside, and the air was fresh with negative ions. I didn't even mind sitting in traffic on South Beretania Street, because it was fun to pretend to be a tourist, spotting green coconuts nestling in the crooks of palms, the bright red bursts of hibiscus blossoms alongside an office building, all the little things that make our visitors feel like they're in the tropics. The high-rises and stores in downtown could be in any US city, but few cities beyond Miami or LA can match us for tropical splendor.

A young woman zipped past us on a scooter, a small boy perched behind her. She wore a simple white helmet, but the boy's was bright blue, with a red Mohawk strip in fake hair blowing in the wind. A troop of schoolchildren walked in double-ranks down the sidewalk, holding hands in pairs, with what looked like a teacher or a mom in front and at the rear.

I took University Avenue until the commercial buildings faded and we were in a residential neighborhood. We passed an elderly woman in a baseball cap and sweat pants, walking backwards on the sidewalk, a harried Japanese mom pushing a tandem baby carriage, and an enormously fat man walking a very tiny Yorkshire terrier on a bright red leash.

When we came to Hillside Avenue, I said, "Recognize where we are?"

"The cat?"

"Yup. We brought her back to that house over there." I pointed, and turned onto Hillside Avenue. Then I made a left, and pulled up in front of a single-story bungalow. "And this is where Gladys Yuu lives."

"So Gladys could have picked up the cat and taken it up to Nuuanu Pali Drive," Ray said.

We sat there for a few minutes, looking at Gladys's house and thinking. Just as I put the car back in gear, the front door of the house opened, and a young Filipina in a nurse's uniform pushed an elderly woman in a wheelchair outside.

As they got closer to us, I could see the Filipina wasn't so young; she was about forty, with a snaggle-toothed smile. The old woman was bundled up in a sweater, despite the morning heat, and her white hair blew around her like a halo. She was Chinese, and I heard her complaining loudly in a guttural voice as the aide bounced her down the broken walkway toward the street.

"That must be Gladys's mother," I said. "I remember she said something about her mother having an aide."

"That's tough," Ray said. "Living so long that you end up in a wheelchair, some stranger wiping your behind."

"Well, at least Julie's growing a little stranger for you who'll wipe your butt when you get old," I said.

"Don't even go there. We'll be wiping the kid's butt for the first few years." He made a face.

"It's not so bad. I pick up after Roby every day. I don't usually wipe his butt, though, unless he has diarrhea."

"TMI."

We watched the aide, smiling grimly, as she pushed the old woman down the street. "Must be expensive to have an aide like that," I said.

"And I'll bet Gladys doesn't make that much as a secretary."

"I want to show you one more place." It was only a couple of blocks to Puuhonua Street, which backed up against the lower reaches of Round Top. "See that house there?" I pointed to a ranch-style with overgrown foliage in the front yard.

"Who lives there?"

"Dr. Xiao Zenshen."

Ray gave a low whistle. "So both of them live close enough to pick up the cat. We know if Dr. Z needs money?"

"You run a science project like she's got, you always need money. Whether you get it from the state or from investors like Levi Hirsch." I put the car back into gear. "Let's see if Lucky Lou remembers either of them." We drove out to Salt Lake and had to wait while a crew-cut soldier pawned a digital camera. He kept looking over at us nervously, and as soon as Lou gave him the money and the claim ticket he was out of there fast.

"You guys are great for business," Lou grumbled. "What do you want now? Want to confiscate more of my merchandise? I could go bankrupt the way you guys keep coming back here."

"Just want to see if you recognize someone." I showed him the photo of Gladys Yuu.

He shrugged. "Looks like any Mama-san you'd see at the grocery," he said. "I'm supposed to know her?"

"How about this one?" Dr. Zenshen's photo was a headshot from Néng Yuán's website.

Lucky Lou didn't recognize her either.

"You think either of them could have pawned that dragon pendant?" I asked.

"That was like a two weeks ago. You know how many customers have been through here since then? They don't have big knockers, I don't pay any attention."

A shy-looking young woman entered the pawn shop, carrying a rifle case. I didn't want to get involved, so we left.

"How are we going to get Gladys's fingerprints, to see if they match the one on the pendant?" Ray asked. "And we need a cast of her tires to see if they match the tracks we found where Miriam Rose got run off the road."

"I don't know if we've got enough evidence yet. We can ask Sampson, but I think that's what he's going to tell us."

And that's exactly what he said. We sat in his office and presented what we had. "She worked with both the victims," I said.

"But the pawnbroker can't ID her?"

"Nope."

"What's her motive? She have money problems? A history of beefs with the defendants? Any connection to this power company, what's it called?"

"Néng Yuán," I said.

"We'll get into her," Ray said. "A day or two, we'll have all the answers to those questions."

"And then maybe you'll have enough for a warrant," Sampson said. "Maybe."

"We should have anticipated that," I grumbled, as we walked back to our desks. "We're not a pair of rookies."

"We got over excited," Ray said. "I'll run the credit check. You see what else you can find out about Gladys and Dr. Zenshen. Maybe Harry can do some searching."

"Good idea." I called Harry and told him what we knew about both women. "Nothing illegal," I said. "Just see if you can dig up anything on her that we can use to get a search warrant."

I called Levi and asked if he had anything on Néng Yuán

yet. "We're trying to connect the company to a secretary in the Department of Business, Economic Development and Tourism," I said.

"I found a guy you can talk to," Levi said. "His name is Mike Cheng, and he used to work with Néng Yuán, but now he runs his own consulting business."

Cheng agreed to meet with us, so we went over to his office, in a four-story building out Ala Moana Boulevard beyond the Kewalo basin, almost at Honolulu Harbor. It was some kind of office co-op, with a single receptionist out front. Cheng himself was a short, stocky Chinese guy, about fifty, with an accent almost as heavy as the receptionist at Néng Yuán.

He led us back to his office, a single room with a desk, a plan table, and a couple of visitor chairs. "Levi said you wanted to talk about Néng Yuán?" he asked.

We sat across from him. "You worked there?"

"I knew Xiao Zenshen back in Shanghai," he said. "At the university. I was a lecturer and she was very smart graduate student. Both of us interested in wave energy. So when she come here and start business, she ask me to come, too. Get me visa and everything."

"How come you're not still working with her?" I asked.

He wrinkled his nose like there was a bad smell in the room. "I don't like how she do business. If you scientist, true scientist, you go up and down with your experiments. Ride the wave, they say. But Xiao, she want to succeed, big time. When numbers don't work her way, she make them work."

He shook his head. "Not good way to do business. The hand that is always open never hold on to what matters."

I looked at Ray. He didn't seem to understand that either, so I pushed on. "Could Dr. Zenshen be giving incorrect data to the state government?"

When Mike Cheng smiled, I could see he had terrible teeth—some missing, some broken, others stained by tobacco. "Xiao do that all the time."

"And nobody ever caught on?" Ray asked.

Cheng rubbed his fingers together in the universal sign for money. "Easy to look other way when money involved."

"Who did she pay off?" I asked. "Franklin Nishimura?"

Cheng shook his head. "His chair always empty. Woman who make everything go in that office is secretary. Gladys. She hand reports to Nishimura to sign, he say, okay, Gladys."

"So Dr. Zenshen paid Gladys to get Nishimura to sign off on false data," I said.

Cheng smiled again.

"You have any proof of this?" Ray asked.

Cheng shrugged. "Xiao, she always keep two sets of records. Actual data, and data reported to state. You find those records, you have proof."

I pulled the little flash drive Harry had given me out of my pocket. "Can you take a look at the data on here?"

He put on a pair of reading glasses, stuck the drive into the side of his computer, and focused on the screen. He made a bunch of sounds in Chinese as he flipped from page to page. Then he took the glasses off and looked at us again.

"Where you get these from?" he asked.

"A woman at the Department of Business, Economic Development and Tourism," I said. "She had this file on her computer. We found it while we were investigating her murder."

Cheng closed out the file on his computer and returned the drive to me. "You have to give to lawyer, make demand for wave attenuator results. Then you compare to milestones Xiao met, and payments state gave her. Those your two sets of data."

"Where do you think she could have gotten these?" I asked.

"Xiao very careful about her data," Cheng said. "When I work there, only she and I have access. When I leave, she replace me with other analyst. Must be him."

When we were back in Ray's Highlander, I said, "So Wyatt saw something fishy at Néng Yuán, and he must have told Zoë about it. He gave her the data."

"And she knew there was something hinky going on," Ray said. "That's why she hid the files on her backup drive with different names."

"I think we need to talk to Wyatt again," I said. "You can get back onto the H1 at the Pali Highway on-ramp."

It took us a while to get all the way back to Hawai'i Kai, and it was lunch time when we pulled up in front of Néng Yuán's building. Wyatt Collins was standing out in front of the building, smoking a cigarette and talking to a dark-haired young woman in a severe black skirt and white blouse.

"Hey, Wyatt," I said through the window, as Ray pulled up at the curb. "Why don't you join us for lunch?"

He looked at the woman and then back at us. "Why not," he said, and he got in the back seat.

"There's a good burger joint in the Koko Marina shopping center," I said to Ray. "Down the street a couple of blocks."

"Got a new girlfriend already, Wyatt?" I asked, turning my head to face him.

"She works down the hall," Wyatt said. "It a crime these days to talk to a pretty girl?"

"No crime," I said. "Now, stealing confidential data from your employer, that might be a crime." I turned back to Ray. "Left in there, at the shopping center."

I let Wyatt stew until we were parked and waiting in line at the burger place. "Go wild," I said to him, motioning to the menu. "My treat."

He looked like a dog that had been beaten and then offered a treat. But he ordered himself a burger and fries, and Ray and I did the same.

While we waited for the burgers, we took a table by the window. The shopping center was busy, cars pulling in and out, moms and kids and whole tourist families in matching T-shirts. "It's not like I stole the data," Wyatt said. "I mean, it was something Zoë should have seen anyway."

Ray and I nodded, sucking on our drinks. Wyatt took in a

deep breath, then let it out. "When you told me she was dead, I got scared. I thought if I told you about giving her those spreadsheets, you'd arrest me. And I don't have anything but this job anymore."

"Let's start from the beginning," I said. "How did you figure out there was something fishy going on?"

Wyatt laughed. "I may have turned over a new leaf when I came out here, Detective, but I still recognize a scam when I see one. I put together all the statistics for Dr. Z to submit to the state. I knew we weren't meeting our targets, and I was worried that if we didn't get the next installment of money from the state, Dr. Z might not have the money to pay my salary."

They called our number, and Ray went up and got the platters, bringing them back along his arm like a seasoned waiter. "Your range of skills constantly surprises me," I said.

"I worked my way through college waiting tables," Ray said. "Baseball cap, skinny tie, all those little badges. Don't have the crap any more, but I have the pictures."

We started to eat, the three of us just making casual conversation about past jobs we'd had. Wyatt had worked with his uncle fixing lawn mowers and farm equipment back in Tennessee. "In a way, that was what started me on my life of crime," he said. "Couldn't stand going home every day with my hands full of grease."

I'd finished my burger and was working through the rest of the fries by the time I asked, "You talk to Zoë about Dr. Z not meeting her targets?"

"I did. Like maybe a week before Zoë got killed." He pushed his half-eaten burger away from him, as if he'd lost his appetite. "She was surprised. She said she'd just finished looking at the data, and Dr. Z had made every target. That's when we figured out there was something strange."

"Who else had access to the data?" I asked.

"Me. Dr. Z. She had a couple of investors who knew what was going on, too."

"Did you worry that Dr. Z would track the data back to you?" Ray asked.

Wyatt shook his head. "I wasn't supposed to know there was a second set of results. All I had was my data. Zoë put it together with the data Dr. Z had submitted to the state. That's when we started to see what Dr. Z was up to."

"Did Zoë talk to anybody about the discrepancies?" I asked.

"Miriam. This girl she worked with. You should talk to her. Cute Filipina chick."

"Miriam Rose is dead, too," I said. "Last week."

Wyatt's face paled. "You're shitting me."

"Nope. We went over to the office last week, showed her the data, and she said she'd take a look at it. The next day she called to say she needed to talk to us. We were on our way up to her house when somebody ran her off the road."

Wyatt slammed his hand on the table so hard other people in the restaurant turned to look at us. "Goddamn mother fucker," he said, way too loud.

"Inside voice, Wyatt," I said.

"This is what you get when you try to go straight," he said, lowering his voice. "See? What the fuck good is it trying to play by the rules when nobody else does?"

"We do," I said. "And we catch the people who don't, and put them behind bars. You know that."

He gave a short, choked laugh. "The cops back in Tennessee were no better than the crooks. You know how many times I got the shit beat out of me, for no reason? How many days I did in jail when I didn't do nothing?"

"Yeah, yeah, the prisons are full of innocent men," I said. "Let's get back to Zoë and Miriam. You have any ideas about who could have killed them?"

"No fucking idea," he said. "Back in prison, I knew these guys, looked like choirboys, who were stone cold killers. And I knew this one guy, could have been in ZZ Top with the beer gut and the long pointing beard. Sweetest guy you'd ever want to know."

"How about Gladys Yuu?" Ray asked. "You know her?"

"Gladys? Secretary at Zoë's office?"

Ray leaned forward. "That's the one. A middle-aged Chinese woman pawned some of Zoë's jewelry. And it looks like somebody picked up a cat from Gladys's neighborhood and threw it in front of Miriam's car, to make her go off the road."

"Jeez, Zoë always said the woman was a bitch, but you think she murdered Zoë? And Miriam?"

"Don't know yet. Xiao Zenshen's also a middle-aged Chinese woman. And she could have picked up the cat, too."

We drove Wyatt back to his office. "Watch your step," I said, as I let him out of the car. "If one of these women killed Zoë and Miriam, you could be next."

Wyatt smirked. "All due respect, Detective, I know how to take care of myself. I couldn't have lasted in prison otherwise."

"You're not in prison now," I said.

Wyatt said, "We're all in some kind of prison, one way or another." Then he turned and went into the office building.

When Ray and I got back to headquarters, we went over what we had. "Somehow, Dr. Zenshen found out Zoë had the spreadsheets," I said. "Maybe Zoë didn't realize Gladys was working with her, and she went to her."

"Or she went to Nishimura, and Gladys heard about it."

"That means we need to talk to Nishimura. But without Gladys knowing about it."

"We could go to his house," Ray said. "But I'm doing special duty tonight. Some foreign dignitary coming into the airport, needs a motorcade."

"I can do it myself. You have the address?"

It was close to quitting time, so I drove up to Aiea Heights and took Roby for a long walk. Mike was working late, so Roby and I had dinner, and then I drove down to Nishimura's place, a small ranch house on a corner lot.

The Japanese woman who answered the door was tall, with iron-gray hair, wearing a simple white kimono patterned with black bamboo, tied with a black obi. "Mrs. Nishimura?" I asked.

"Whatever you're selling, we're not interested," she said, and started to slam the door.

"HPD," I said, holding up my badge. "I'd like to talk to your husband."

She frowned and tried to take my ID from me, but I held on to it so that she had to lean out the door to see it. "Franklin!" she called back into the house. In Japanese, she said, "What did you do now, you stupid idiot? Why do the police want to talk to you?"

It can be convenient, looking the way I do. People don't assume I can speak Japanese, not knowing that my mother spoke it to my brothers and me when were small. Her father never spoke English, so whenever we wanted to talk to Oji-san we had to speak Japanese to him. I'd even taken a couple of years of it at Punahou, as my mandatory foreign language.

"What do you mean, woman?" Nishimura said, coming out of the kitchen with a dish cloth in his hand. He was still wearing his suit pants, and a white shirt, though he'd taken off his tie and undone the first couple of shirt buttons. "What are police doing here?"

He saw me and switched to English. "Oh, it's you." To his wife he said, "This is about work. A woman who was killed."

He put the towel down on the dining room table and motioned me to the living room. "Why didn't you just come to the office, detective? I was in all day."

"I need to talk to you about Gladys Yuu. I thought it would be best if she didn't know."

Mrs. Nishimura continued in Japanese. "I told you that woman was bad. Why don't you ever listen to me?"

"Your behavior is embarrassing me in front of my guest," Nishimura shot back to her in Japanese. To me, he said, "Please sit down, detective. May I offer you a cup of tea? Coffee? Soda?"

"No, thanks, I'm fine."

He sat across from me, while his wife hovered in the background.

"How long has Gladys been working for you?"

"Ten years. I'd be lost without her. She's my right hand." He paused. "What's this about?"

"When we were going through Zoë Greenfield's belongings after her death, we found some very interesting spreadsheets," I said. "First, confusing, because Zoë had given the files strange names, and hidden them in a folder with an odd name as well. Once we started to look into it, we discovered that the data in the spreadsheet relates to contracts administered by your office."

Nishimura's face paled. "You are saying someone killed her because of what was in those files? Gladys?"

"We don't know yet," I said. "That's why I wanted to talk to you. How closely do you look at the invoices presented for payment?"

"My husband is a very good man," Mrs. Nishimura said. "You cannot blame him for anything those idiots at his office do."

Nishimura held his hand up. "You'll have to excuse my wife. She is a good woman, but very protective." He sighed. "I admit, there is so much going on at the office that sometimes I simply sign off on things that my staff presents me with. That is the purpose of staff, isn't it? There is no way I could check the data in every report. I would never get anything done."

"I know what you mean. There's an awful lot of paperwork at the police department." I could see his wife was ready to interrupt again, so I said, "Maybe I could use a cup of tea."

"Very good," Nishimura said. "We have just received some delicious *karigane* green tea from my cousin in Tokyo. Fumiko-san? Can you make us tea, please?"

I knew enough about the rules of hospitality to know that there was no way Fumiko Nishimura could turn down such a request, and I knew it would give Franklin and me a few minutes to talk.

"Who gives you the paperwork to sign off on?" I asked. "The analysts?"

He shook his head. "Everything goes through Gladys. She receives the materials from the companies we supervise, and logs them in to our system. Then she gives the analysts the materials to review. When they sign off, she brings me the paperwork to issue the checks."

I began to take some notes. "Which company do you suspect is involved?" Nishimura asked.

"Néng Yuán. Zoë had a friend who worked there, and he says he told her that the experiments were failing, and asked what would happen to the company's payout. She was surprised, because the data she had received indicated everything was fine."

"I would have to check," Nishimura said. "But I believe Néng

Yuán is current on its progress and its disbursements."

I nodded. "Zoë compared the data presented to the state with what her friend had collected, and put them together into a spreadsheet. She never showed that to you?"

He shook his head. "Each month, there are many contracts to review. I have been very busy. I don't think I spoke with Zoë in at least a week before she died."

I heard Fumiko clattering cups and saucers angrily in the kitchen. I figured she had failed in learning the grace of the tea ceremony. "Is it possible that Zoë confronted the management of Néng Yuán?" Nishimura asked. "That someone there might have killed her?"

"Yes, it's possible," I said. "But then there's Miriam Rose."

"Miriam?" He looked surprised. "But she was killed in a traffic accident."

I nodded. "As she was on our way to meet with me and my partner. We had asked her to look over the data and give us some insight."

Fumiko Nishimura entered the living room carrying a tray with a black ceramic teapot and two tiny cups, as well as a small platter of Japanese chocolate-covered cookies. She bowed briefly to her husband and placed the tray on the coffee table between us. She kneeled at one end of the table, and then poured the tea into the two cups.

She nodded to her husband, who picked up one cup and passed it to me. I brought it up to my nose. "The aroma is most pleasant," I said, smiling to Nishimura first, and then to his wife. I took a small sip, and made an appreciative sound. It was very good tea.

I sipped the tea. "Thank you very much for your kindness. I have just a few more questions. Do you think Miriam might have asked Gladys about Néng Yuán's account?"

He shrugged. "I don't know. But I do know that Gladys watched the analysts very closely. It's possible she was monitoring

Miriam's work and recognized what she was looking at."

Even as he spoke, it looked like the idea caused him physical pain. "You think Gladys might have killed Miriam? But how? She had already left the office when Miriam said good night to me."

"My partner and I went up to the scene of the accident," I said. "We found a white cat there, a cat from a home near Gladys's, which was many miles away. It's possible that Gladys left the office early, drove up to Miriam's exit on the Pali Highway, and when she saw Miriam's car coming towards her, she threw the cat in front of Miriam's car, causing her to swerve."

"Miriam would never have run over a cat," Nishimura said, shaking his head.

"How was the first woman killed?" Fumiko asked. "Zoë."

"She was stabbed with a kitchen knife."

"Then you must arrest Gladys," Fumiko said. "She knows how to use knives very well."

"I understand she used to teach cooking classes. Did you ever study with her?"

"I learned to cook from my mother and my grandmother. I had no use for Gladys."

I finished the rest of the tea, and declined another cup. "Please accept my apologies for disturbing your evening," I said. "And I must ask you not to mention this interview to Gladys."

"My husband is stupid, but not that stupid," Fumiko muttered in Japanese.

"Smart people still do stupid things," I said to her, watching the surprise on her face as she realized I had been understanding her all evening.

"I'll let myself out," I said, standing.

Levi Hirsch called as I was driving home. "Listen, I was thinking I could make this clearer to you if I took you and Ray out on my boat," he said. "Show you what the wave attenuators look like, and help you put those numbers into perspective."

"I'll never pass up a chance for a boat ride," I said. "When were you thinking of going out?"

"How about tomorrow afternoon? I need to swing past and look at the stuff my company has out there as well. Say four o'clock?"

"Sounds good. I'll check with Ray in the morning and let you know."

Mike was home by the time I got there, and we compared notes on our days, then walked Roby together just before bedtime.

"Nestor's wife is pregnant," Mike said. "He's kind of freaking out."

Nestor Matsuoka was one of the analysts at fire department headquarters, a guy Mike sometimes had lunch with. "Really? Why?"

Mike shrugged. "It's their first. He goes from stressing about not being able to sleep once the baby comes to worrying about paying for college."

"Sounds like he's getting ahead of himself."

"Yeah. But you've got to admit, things change a lot when you have a kid."

We stopped so Roby could sniff a couple of bracts someone had cut off a palm tree. "I think as long as you really want to have the baby, everything else fades away." I took a deep breath. "I'm just not sure I want a baby, even if someone else is raising it and we're only the weekend dads."

Mike looked at me. "I was afraid to say that myself. I thought maybe you would really want to be a dad."

"We're already dads," I said, as Roby tugged me forward. "And uncles. And nobody's shutting the door yet. Sandra said she's not ready to get pregnant for a while anyway."

I leaned over and kissed him. I felt the tickle of his mustache, which always made me smile. "I think we'd both make terrific dads. When we're ready."

When I walked into headquarters the next morning, Sampson was standing in the doorway of his office, motioning us in. His polo shirt, like his mood, was dark.

"Where do you stand on your two murder cases?" he asked.

"We've been making the connection between the spreadsheets Zoë Greenfield had and the murder," I said. Sampson made no motion to us to sit, so we stood awkwardly just inside the door of his office. "Right now, we have two strong suspects, but we're not sure yet which one did the killings."

"We're leaning toward a secretary in the Department of Business, Economic Development and Tourism," Ray said. "She had the means and the opportunity for both killings."

"And the motive?" Sampson asked.

"Right now, we're assuming that she was paid by the company who was fudging the data," I said. "But there's also the woman in charge of the company."

"A middle-aged Chinese woman pawned a piece of jewelry we traced back to the first woman who was killed," Ray said. "Both the secretary, and the head of the company, fit the description, but the pawn broker can't be more specific."

"Both women live near each other, in Manoa," I said. "Someone picked up a cat from that area last Thursday, and we found it near where Miriam Rose's car ran off the road. So either of the two women could have been the one to manipulate the accident."

"This case is going on too long," Sampson said. "Wrap it up. If you have to, bring both women in and question them."

"Will do, chief," Ray said, and I nodded along.

"Let's step back," I said, when we were back at our desks. "Zoë and Wyatt are talking one day, and they figure out there's something screwy going on with Néng Yuán—they're not getting the results they're reporting to the state."

"Either Dr. Z or someone working for her broke into Zoë's house and killed her, and took her laptop, not realizing that Zoë had an online backup, too," Ray said.

"But how did anyone besides Zoë and Wyatt know that Zoë had the data?"

"Must have been Gladys," Ray said. "Nishimura said that Gladys monitored the analysts very closely."

"But there's no connection between Gladys and Dr. Zenshen. Gladys works for the state. Why wouldn't she be happy that Zoë uncovered a problem?"

Ray crossed his arms. "Dr. Zenshen must have been paying Gladys."

"I wonder if Harry dug up anything on either of them. Let me call him."

Harry apologized that he hadn't gotten back to me. "More drama with Brandon last night. He had another test today, and he was sure he was going to fail. I had to spend a couple of hours going over the material with him before he could settle down and go to bed."

"Ah, the life of a father," I said, looking over at Ray as I did.

"Give me an hour, and I'll have something for you," Harry said. "Why don't you come over here?"

"Remember, Harry, nothing illegal," I said.

"You're breaking up. Gotta go. See you later."

"We're both on land lines. Nobody's breaking up." But he had already hung up.

We spent the next hour doing paperwork, then drove up to Harry's. "Don't get mad at me, Kimo," he said, as he led us back toward his office. "You know once I get curious it's hard to shut me down."

"And you know that anything you find when you're curious

can't be used in a court of law, so it does us no good."

"But it can show you where you should be looking," he said.

I looked over at Ray, who shrugged. "He's your friend."

"I looked up the first woman, Gladys Yuu," Harry said, sitting down at his computer. "Up until about a year ago, she was pretty broke. She had a savings account with about a grand in it, and she was always overdrawing her checking account. She even took out a home equity line against her house, drawing down about twenty grand." He turned to face us. "A lot of her money was going to this company called Island Care, so I looked them up."

"She has an elderly mother living with her," I said. "Must be some kind of nursing agency."

Harry looked deflated. "Yeah, that's it. She pays them close to four grand a month, which swallows up almost all her take-home pay."

"You said up 'til a year ago," Ray said. "What happened then?"

"She started getting transfers from an offshore account," Harry said. "The first deposit was $25,000. Then six months later, another twenty-five grand. A couple of weeks ago, she got an extra boost—fifty grand. She paid off the home equity line and closed it out."

"Interesting," I said.

"So then I switched over to that other woman you asked about, Xiao Zenshen. That was harder, because she has all these connections back to China. But I kept digging. And then I hit pay dirt."

"What? What did you find?"

"She gets payments from the same offshore account," he said. "Nothing like Gladys Yuu, but more regular. A couple of grand a month."

"There's the connection between the two of them," Ray said. "Somebody's paying them both."

"Hold on, cowboy," I said. "Dr. Z comes from China. Maybe

that's her offshore account, and she's drawing down living expenses for herself, and paying Gladys, too."

"You can't deny that it's a connection," Harry said, siding with Ray.

"Yeah, but we can't do anything with it."

"We can use it to confront Dr. Zenshen," Ray suggested. "We should bring her in for questioning."

"She's a smart woman. We need something more, some detail we can catch her on."

"And those spreadsheets aren't enough?" Harry asked.

I shrugged. "I think we could get her on fraud. But murder? No. We don't have enough to get a warrant for either woman's tire treads or fingerprints yet."

"You're a real party pooper, you know that?" Harry asked.

We went back to headquarters, but even after laying the case out again and again, we still couldn't come up with enough to justify a warrant. And we didn't want to tip our hand by bringing either Gladys or Dr. Zenshen in for questioning until we had something more.

Later that afternoon, Ray and I met Levi at the Koko Marina shopping center in Hawai'i Kai, adjacent to where he kept his boat. "It's nice of you to take us out like this," Ray said.

"I thought it might help you to see the different kinds of technology," Levi said, as he swung up onto the boat. "Kimo, untie that bow line, would you?"

I walked up to the line at the front of the boat, just as my cell phone rang. I didn't recognize the number and I was tempted to let it go to voice mail, but I gave in to my obsessive nature and answered.

I could barely understand the woman on the other end of the phone, because her Chinese accent was so heavy. "Wyatt?" I asked. "You're calling about Wyatt Collins?"

"*Shi, shi.*" That was yes in Chinese. "He go out on boat, with doctor."

I didn't understand, so I repeated what she'd said.

"Shi, shi," again. "I think she have gun."

Gun is a word I always understand. And then it clicked. "Dr. Zenshen," I said. "She held a gun on Wyatt and made him get on a boat?"

"Shi, shi," she said.

I remembered the boat we'd seen when we talked to Wyatt. "The boat docked behind the office? What's its name?"

She didn't understand. I struggled to remember the little bit of Chinese I had learned from Uncle Chin, my father's best friend, who had enjoyed teaching me and my brothers a few phrases. "*Nei giu mut ye meng,*" I said. That meant *What is your name?* but I hoped that by adding "The boat" at the end she'd understand.

"Shi, shi," she said. "Wave Walker."

Well, that's what I figured out she meant—but it took a while.

I hung up and told Ray and Levi what I'd heard. "Come on," Levi said. "She's probably going out to the wave articulators. We can head her off there."

I hustled to cast off the bow line while Levi started the boat, and both Ray and I jumped on board. We weren't sure where Dr. Zenshen was going, and we didn't even know for certain that Wyatt Collins was an unwilling passenger, so I didn't want to call for official backup. I could just imagine what the dispatcher would say if I did.

We powered slowly out through the marina, and then under the Kalaniana'aole Highway bridge, and then Levi revved the engines up and we almost hydroplaned out into the ocean. I climbed up to the flying bridge, where Levi stood at the boat's helm. "You know where you're going?" I shouted over the noise of the engine.

He held up a chart. "Always good to know what the competition is up to."

I picked up a pair of binoculars and climbed back down. I walked around to the bow of the boat, where Ray was sitting with his back against the window into the lounge. "Might as well enjoy the ride," he said. "Damn nice boat."

I sat next to him and put the binoculars up to my eyes. I couldn't see anything except open ocean, and I hoped that Levi knew where he was going. I hoped, too, that it was where Dr. Zenshen was going, and that we'd be able to get there before she did anything to hurt Wyatt Collins.

He might have been an ex-con, but I hadn't seen him do anything yet to make me think he hadn't reformed. Chances were pretty strong that he had worked hard to make a new life for himself, come out to Hawai'i on the word of an Internet friend, and then found himself on his own once again, this time in a strange place. Hell, the receptionist at his office could barely speak English. That had to be tough for a guy from Kentucky.

Following some unseen marker, Levi turned the boat to starboard, keeping the engines at full, and then, in the distance,

I could make out another boat. I handed the binoculars to Ray. "Can you make out the name on the transom?"

He squinted for a while, until we got closer. "Yup, that's it. Wave Walker."

"Damn." I was impressed. Although I spent a lot of time in the water as a surfer, I never got more than a few hundred yards off shore, and considered the open ocean an unknown territory. Levi, though, had been able to find a boat out there, with nothing more than a guess to its destination.

As we got closer, I saw that the Wave Walker was holding steady near what looked like a bunch of pontoons strung across the waves. I remembered how Levi had tried to describe Dr. Zenshen's research into wave articulators.

Levi cut the engines down, and we moved more slowly toward the stationary boat. Ray and I traded the binoculars back and forth; he was the one who saw the man and woman first, standing together at the boat's stern. "That must be them," he said, handing the glasses to me.

I was watching Dr. Zenshen when she looked up and spotted us approaching. She was holding a long, bright blue pole in her hand, and as we got closer I saw that it had a wicked hook at the end. I recognized that it was a gaff, used to help bring sport fish into the boat.

She swung the gaff toward Wyatt, and the hook slammed into his mid-section. Wyatt stumbled backward from the impact. With her left hand, Dr. Zenshen pushed him, and he went back over the edge of the boat, into the water. Then she disappeared into the boat.

I handed the glasses to Ray. "I'm going to tell Levi what I saw. Keep an eye on her."

I scrambled around to the stern of the boat and started to climb the ladder. As I did, I heard the engines of the Wave Walker start up.

"Want me to chase her?" Levi asked, as I got up to the flying bridge. He looked like he was enjoying himself.

"She hit Wyatt with a gaff and then pushed him over the transom." The Wave Walker took off, its wake rattling the wave articulators. "Can you get us in there to try and save him?"

Levi nodded, his enthusiasm gone. I went back down the ladder, and found Ray standing at the stern. "I should tell you, I'm not the strongest swimmer in the world," he said.

"I'm good." I unbuttoned my aloha shirt, kicked off my deck shoes, and pulled off my khakis. It was cool there in only my boxers, especially as I leaned around the port side, scanning the waves for Wyatt.

Ray looked out the starboard side. The closer we got to the wave articulators, the slower Levi took us. I spotted Wyatt in the water, tilting his head back and flapping his arms to try and keep his mouth above water.

I yelled up to Levi, pointing, and he slowed the boat to a crawl so our wake wouldn't swamp Wyatt as we approached.

There was blood in the water around him. He went under, then struggled back to the surface. He was unable to keep his mouth above water long enough to breathe properly. Without air, he couldn't wave or shout at us.

I knew that his lungs must be filling with water, making him less buoyant. And he was a skinny, muscular guy, without a lot of body fat, which would make him more prone to dropping below the water than a fat guy.

Ray was scanning the horizon. "Uh, Kimo?"

I clambered up on the transom, ready to jump in the water. "Yeah?"

"Is that a shark?"

I looked in the direction he was pointing and saw the telltale dorsal fin knifing through the water.

"Yeah. Keep an eye on it and shoot it if you have to."

I jumped into the water, feeling the cold all over me, and swam overhand to Wyatt, trying to ignore the fact that we were miles off shore and the bottom was way, way below us.

I heard Ray's gun go off and hoped that if he was shooting at the shark he'd hit it, or at least scared it away. But I was too intent on keeping an eye on Wyatt to look around. If Wyatt went under again I might not be able to find him.

He sank again just before I reached him. I took a deep breath and ducked under the surface. I bumped into him, then reached out and grabbed him under the arms. Then I pushed upward, breaching the water and taking deep gulps of air.

Wyatt was gasping for air, too. I hooked an arm around him and turned back toward the boat. "Kimo! Behind you!" Ray called.

I didn't want to waste the energy to turn around, but I knew I had to. I twisted my head and saw the shark approaching. "Shoot him!" I called to Ray, my voice hoarse.

The air rang with the sound of the gun, and I saw the shark flip backwards with a huge splash that covered Wyatt and me and left us winded again. I backstroked with my free arm, kicking with my legs, until we were close to Levi's boat.

He and Ray leaned over the transom, and I let Wyatt go when I felt them begin to lift him up. I held onto the dive platform for a minute until they were clear, looking back to where the shark was still thrashing in the water, blood spreading on the gentle waves. I knew I needed to get in the boat before a dozen more like him showed up for the feast.

I hoisted myself up on the dive platform, my legs still in the water, scanning the horizon. I didn't see the Wave Walker anywhere, but I did see another dorsal fin approaching fast. I swung my legs into the boat.

I picked up a big towel from a pile Levi had left on the deck and as I huddled into it I watched him and Ray wrap Wyatt up, leaving only his wound open. Ray took over with the first aid kit, working to patch him up, as Levi went up to the flying bridge and turned us back toward shore.

As we were going back under the highway bridge, my cell reception returned, and I called for an ambulance to meet us at the marina. "How's he doing?" I asked Ray.

"Holding a pulse. He's still pretty cold, and I think he's in shock."

By the time we docked, we could hear the ambulance siren approaching. I was dry enough to get back into my clothes, though I had to go commando, balling up my soggy boxers and tossing them into the back of the Jeep.

We arranged for a unit to head over to Néng Yuán's office and see if the Wave Walker had returned to the dock. As the EMTs were loading Wyatt into the ambulance, the patrol cop called said that the boat had been returned. "We're on our way over there," I said.

As I drove, Ray got the license plate for the Lexus registered to Dr. Zenshen, and we had the patrol cop check the parking garage for it.

"No dice," Ray said, when he hung up. "She must have flown."

The receptionist was just closing down the office when we arrived. She swore that Dr. Z had not returned after leaving with Wyatt.

Based on what we'd seen, we put out an APB for Dr. Zenshen's Lexus, and we also stationed a unit near her house in Manoa. "Let's go over to Gladys's house," I said. "With Dr. Z on the run, it may be the time to break her."

We drove slowly past Gladys Yuu's house. The sun was setting, its last rays glinting off the windshield of the champagne-colored Toyota Camry parked in her driveway. "Who owns the car?" I asked Ray.

He called the tag in as I cruised down the street. The houses were mostly single-story fifties style, though occasionally someone had slipped a lot-hugging McMansion in between.

"It's Gladys's car," Ray said, as I slowed to let some kids playing kickball scurry out of the way.

"So where's the doctor?"

"Maybe we got here before she did," I said.

We reached the end of the street, and as I was making a U-turn in a rutted driveway, Ray said, "There's a black Lexus over there on the side street. Go past it slow so I can get the tag."

The car was empty, but the tag matched Xiao Zenshen's registration. "Not good," I said. "Where is she? Why didn't she park closer to Gladys's house?"

We called for backup, and parked down the street. Two kids were practicing skateboard tricks in the intervals between traffic, two houses down from Gladys's. An elderly woman across the street was watering her yard with a hose.

I was just about to get out of the Jeep when Ray grabbed my arm. "Hold up. Look up there, by that yellow house. There's a woman moving under that big tree."

She was tall and slim, walking through the shadows and under the trees toward us. We strained forward to see if it was Dr. Zenshen.

And then the world erupted in a blast of heat and light. The flash blinded us both for a moment, and when we got our vision back, the woman had disappeared. Ray jumped out. "I'll go for the house, you see if you can catch that Lexus."

I put the Jeep in gear and swung around, fumbling for my cell phone. In the rear view mirror I could see Gladys's house, engulfed in flames, and Ray running toward it. I dialed 911, identified myself and reported the fire. "You'll need an ambulance, too," I said. "I think there were at least two women in the house."

Ahead of me, the black Lexus pulled away from the curb and accelerated down the street. I used my radio to report that I was in pursuit, giving the dispatcher the tag number, vehicle description, and the direction we were heading.

There were two cars between me and the Lexus as I grabbed my flashing light and stuck it up on my roof. The car in front of me immediately pulled off to the side, but the one in front of him was slowing for a turn and didn't seem to care that I was coming up fast on his tail.

My pulse was racing, and I tried to remember the advanced driving skills I had learned at the police academy. It had been years since I'd been in a car chase, and the experience felt surreal, like I was an actor in a movie and at any minute the director would call "Cut!"

Advanced driving is the art of controlling the position and speed of a vehicle under any conditions. I felt every sense was heightened, as I had to be sure of everything around me, every car, traffic signal, and pedestrian. That training, which had lain dormant for years, kicked in and I found myself intuitively considering the road around me.

At the same time, I couldn't help remembering that the Jeep was the first new car I'd ever owned, and that it was only a year and a half old. I was going to be plenty pissed if I wrecked it.

Dr. Z had the advantage, because she lived in the neighborhood and knew the streets, and she had about a block and half head start on me. She swung onto Manoa Road, heading makai, toward where Manoa connected with Punahou Road, and an on-ramp to the H1 expressway.

That was good for me, in a way. First of all, I thought I knew where she was going, and could anticipate her moves. And second, I had learned to drive in the streets around the Punahou School, and even now I could see every corner in my head. I heard on the radio that other cars were responding, aiming to close off her options and force her toward Berwick Field, where she could be shepherded into an area free of homes and businesses.

A Smart car came speeding out of the intersection with Aleo Place, turning onto Manoa Road in front of Dr. Z's Lexus, but when the driver saw my flasher behind her, she swerved right off into a semi-circular driveway.

Dr. Z ran through the intersection where Manoa Road met up with East Manoa, narrowly avoiding a crash with a minivan, which ran off the road and into somebody's front yard. I heard on the radio that cops were blocking Manoa where it met up with Ahualani on one side and Piper's Pali on the other. They hoped to run her into the tennis courts on the makai side.

Dispatch said that the courts were being cleared, and I recognized Kitty Sampson's car number among those that were being positioned around the courts. I kept up with Dr. Zenshen, trying not to cause any accidents but at least keep her in view. It wasn't easy; the cars around us didn't seem to care about getting out of our way. Dr. Z pulled up behind a couple of tourists in a convertible and blasted her horn, then swerved around them.

A late model Nissan pulled right in front of me off of Linohau Way, despite my flashing lights, and I could see the driver on his cell phone, oblivious to the chase going on around him.

Suddenly there were cop cars everywhere, pulling in off the side streets with sirens and flashers, all in pursuit of Dr. Z. The guy in front of me dropped the cell and grabbed his steering wheel with both hands, veering quickly off to the side of the road.

Our shepherding techniques worked, and we forced Dr. Z to turn into the tennis courts behind Berwick Field, where she blasted through the shrubbery in front of the middle court, smashing into the chain link fence. She brought the car to a stop and jumped out, looking right and left.

There were a couple of patrol cars between me and her, and the officers in those cars jumped out and pulled their weapons on her. She looked down at the gun in her hand and realized she had been outmaneuvered. She tossed the gun away from her and put her hands up in the air.

I didn't wait around for formalities. There were plenty of cops there to cuff Dr. Zenshen and take her downtown. I made a U-turn and headed back up to Gladys Yuu's house, listening to the radio for any report of damage or injury. All I heard was that there were fire engines on the scene. Well, duh.

Traffic was a mess in the wake of Dr. Z's chase. I took East Manoa Road, because it would bring me up to Hillside, and even with getting away from Dr. Z's original route it took a lot longer than it should have to climb back into Manoa. I wove in and out of residential streets until I reached where Gary Saunders and his patrol car were blocking the turn.

He waved me through, but I still had to park a block and a half away from Gladys's house because of all the fire trucks. As I jogged toward the house I passed Mike's truck, with its distinctive flames painted down the side. He'd never admit it, but he loved that decoration.

Parents and kids were standing in clusters on the street. I saw the skateboards the kids had been playing with, abandoned beside a mailbox, and a black slash in the grass where some fiery debris must have landed.

Overhead I heard the whirr of one of the news station helicopters. In a gesture of brotherly solidarity, I called Lui as I dodged around another family group, a mom and dad and three kids sharing a big bowl of popcorn, as if they were watching a movie.

"You have somebody out here in Manoa you want me to talk to, brah?" I asked, when Lui picked up.

"You're a prince, Kimo. My truck is stuck a couple of blocks away but I have Ralph Kim and a cameraman on their way on foot. I'll tell him to call you."

Ray was leaning against one of the trucks as I ran up. He was sweating and his face and shirt were streaked with black soot. He shook his head. "I tried to get in there but the place was already an inferno. I heard a woman screaming."

I grabbed him into a bear hug. "We can't save them all, brah," I said. "All we can do is try."

He hugged me back, and then pulled away. "Your partner's up there," he said. "I talked to him for a minute. They found two bodies in the house, both women."

"Most likely Gladys and her mother." I told him about the car chase, how I'd turned around once I saw cops taking Dr. Z down. "You okay?"

He nodded. "Still a little shaky, but I'll manage. Go see what you can find out."

I walked toward the house. One wall was completely gone, sections of the roof had been destroyed, and there was still smoke coming from the interior.

Mike was in conversation with one of the firemen near the ruined wall. He spotted me, and motioned me over. "I'm not quite sure what we're looking at here," he said. "The explosion was localized on the exterior of the house, on this side."

The fireman walked away, and Mike continued, pointing at the ground. "There are fragments of glass and metal there, and there. I think they might have been part of the electric meter. I looked at a couple of other houses on the block, and they all had exterior meters mounted on this wall."

"The woman I chased down is some kind of electrical engineer," I said. "So she probably knows her way around a meter."

I filled him in on Dr. Zenshen and what we suspected.

"It's going to take me a while to figure it all out. I'll get you a copy of my report when I have it done."

"She's a smart woman," I said. "You may be looking at something pretty sophisticated."

"I can do sophisticated." He looked over to where Ray was slumped against a kiawe tree, still sweating heavily. "You'd better go look after your other partner."

I snagged a couple of bottles of water from one of the EMTs I knew through Mike and carried them over to Ray. As we were drinking, my cell rang, and a couple of minutes later I was on camera with Ralph Kim, a newscaster I'd had a couple of run-ins with in the past.

He set up the shot with the ruined house in the background, the last fire truck still hosing down the embers. I gave him a quick sound bite on the explosion. "There are at least two potential victims," I said.

"Any idea what was going on?" Ralph asked.

"Right now, all I can say is that this is connected to an open investigation, as well as to the car chase through Manoa earlier today. But I believe you'll see a resolution very quickly."

"As always, Honolulu's finest are on the job," Ralph said, turning to the camera. "We'll have a full report on the late news."

Ray was feeling better by then, and we drove downtown. I was hyper-careful in traffic, figuring I'd used up all my good driving karma earlier in the chase with Dr. Zenshen.

As we drove, we talked about the interrogation. "There are a lot of parts to this case, so we're going to have to start in the right place in order to get the information we need," I said.

"So where do you think that is?" Ray coughed and hacked up something from his throat, then opened the window and spit it out. When he pulled his head back in he said, "Not with Zoë Greenfield's murder. That came later."

"I agree. But how far do we go back? Her coming here from China? The technology her company uses?"

He shook his head. "I'm thinking we start with Wyatt. We get her to talk about him and how he got hold of the information he had. From there, maybe we can get her to talk about taking him out on the boat."

"Sounds like a plan. You want to take lead?"

He coughed again. "My voice is still raw from the smoke. You take it and I'll jump in when I think I should."

Lidia Portuondo and Kitty Cardozo had teamed up to shepherd Dr. Z through the booking process, and they were almost done by the time we arrived. Dr. Z was quiet and poised as we walked her to an interview room before transporting her to the jail.

She sat down in a wooden chair, and I sat across from her and switched on the tape recorder. Ray lounged against the wall behind me. I read her rights; since it was clear that she couldn't just pick up and walk out, it was important that we got everything on the record and followed the rules.

"Do you understand these rights?" I asked.

She nodded.

"I'm sorry, but I have to ask you to speak out loud for the recording."

"Yes, I understand," she said. "I am just glad to get a chance to explain what has happened. You will see that I am the victim here."

I love a suspect who's willing to talk. "Then let's get started." We went through the formalities, getting her name, address and so on.

Then I jumped in, where Ray and I had decided we would begin. "You have an employee named Wyatt Collins?"

"That is correct. He works for my company, Néng Yuán."

"Tell us what happened this afternoon."

She smiled. "My company owns a boat, so that we can go out into the ocean regularly to check on our research projects. One of the wave attenuators has been returning anomalous data, so I went out to see what was wrong. I invited Mr. Collins to accompany me."

Her back was erect, her hands folded in front of her on the

table. She was a very cool customer, I had to give her that.

"When we reached the wave attenuators, Mr. Collins made some threatening remarks. He indicated that he had been working with a woman at the state Department of Business, Economic Development and Tourism, the agency that regulates our research. That he had been feeding her false data, and that he was going to put the blame for that onto me if I didn't pay him a very large sum."

"That must have been upsetting," I said.

She nodded. "And then he began threatening me, physically. I grabbed the first thing I could find, a gaff we use to pull in the attenuators to check them. In defending myself I hit him with the gaff, and he fell overboard."

"What happened then?"

"There was another boat approaching. I was frightened for my safety, Detective, so I left the area immediately. I worried that the approaching boat might have had friends of Mr. Collins, and that I would be in danger if I remained there."

"What did you do after that?"

"I returned the boat to the slip behind my office," Dr. Zenshen said. "And then I determined to go and speak directly with the woman Mr. Collins had implicated."

She spread her hands out then. "I know it was not the wisest decision, but I was very upset. I should simply have called the police and reported Mr. Collins. Did you know that he is an ex-convict?"

"Yes, I am aware of that fact."

"Well, I was not aware, when I hired him. I can assure you that I never would have hired such a person if I had known."

"Why did you hire him?"

"He came very highly recommended," she said. "By the woman who I learned was working with him. Gladys Yuu."

"So Gladys recommended him? Not Zoë Greenfield?"

She played her part well. "I don't recognize that name."

"Really? She's the analyst at the state bureau who reviewed your data."

"Ah, that is the reason, then," she said. "There are safeguards, you see, to keep the reviewers separate from those who are being reviewed. All my contact with the office went through Gladys Yuu. The same was true for my employees, including Mr. Collins."

"Let's get back to this afternoon," I said. "You went to speak with Gladys Yuu?"

"Yes. But I never got the chance. As I approached her house, an explosion occurred. I ran away, once again, frightened for my life. I was chased by a man in a Jeep, and I thought he was another associate of Mr. Collins and Ms. Yuu."

"Even with the blue police light on the roof of the Jeep?" I asked.

For the first time, her confidence faltered. "Excuse me?"

"I was the one chasing you, Dr. Zenshen. In my Jeep. With the blue light flashing on the top."

"I was very upset," she said. "I had just discovered that my employee had been stealing from me, and then I was physically threatened."

She leaned forward. "He told me that he had killed Zoë Greenfield and Miriam Rose, and that he would kill me, too."

"Miriam Rose?" Ray asked. "Who's that?"

We could tell from Dr. Zenshen's face that she knew she'd screwed up. How would she know Miriam's name, if she had pretended not to know Zoë because she was shielded from the state employees?

"He told me," she said, her voice becoming more shrill, her accent even stronger. "He told me that he had been working with Gladys, and that Zoë and Miriam had discovered what he was doing. He killed them, detective. He would have killed me."

My cell phone rang, and I could see from the display that it was Mike. "I have to take this call," I said, standing up. "Detective Donne will stay with you until I return."

I flipped the phone open as I walked out the door. "What's up?"

"I'm still up at the blast site. But one of the guys here spoke to a crime scene tech working on your suspect's car. They found fuses and ammonium nitrate. It looks like that stuff will match what was used in the blast."

"Thanks. I'll probably be home late."

"Me, too. I'll call my dad and get him to walk Roby."

We both said that we loved each other before we ended the call. I walked back into the interview room and asked, "What is ammonium nitrate used for, Doctor?"

She looked confused for a moment, then recovered. "I suffer from migraine headaches, detective. I carry ammonium nitrate with me in my car because you can mix it with plain water to make a cold pack, which I used to relieve the migraine pressure."

"It can also be used as an explosive, can't it?" I asked.

"I have no idea," she said.

"Come now, Doctor. You have a PhD in electrical engineering. I'm sure you're quite familiar with the properties of most common chemicals."

She just smiled at me.

"I think we're done for now." I turned off the recorder, and Ray and I stepped outside. We got an officer to escort Dr. Zenshen to the holding cells, where she would wait for her arraignment.

"She's smart," Ray said.

"You bet. But we're smarter. We'll catch her."

We went over to the Queen's Medical Center, where Wyatt Collins was resting in a private hospital room after a doctor had stitched up the wound from the gaff. "Guess I'm unemployed, huh?" Wyatt said.

"A gaff in the chest is a pretty harsh termination notice," I said. "You want to tell us what happened this afternoon?"

"I was working at my desk around three, when Dr. Zenshen came in. She said that she had to go out and check on some of the wave attenuators, and it would be good for me to see what it was I was working on."

He shifted in the hospital bed and I could see the pain etched on his face. "I didn't want to go. I'm a lousy swimmer, and I just didn't trust her. But she was very persistent, and, well, up 'til then I figured I had to do whatever I could to hold on to my job."

"Did she have a gun?"

"No. Why?"

"The receptionist thought she might have," I said. "That's what convinced us you were taken onto the boat against your will."

"Good for her." He sighed. "She didn't talk much as we rode out toward the wave attenuator area. But then when she shut the engine down, she started asking me all these questions. About Zoë, and about the numbers we submitted to the state. I was trying to dodge around things, but she was on to me."

"What do you mean, she was on to you?"

"She knew that Zoë had two different sets of data, and she was sure that I'd given her the second set, the true numbers. She started cursing at me, first in English and then I guess what was Chinese. I just kept denying it, and darting around the boat."

"And then?"

"Then we heard this other boat coming up. Neither of us knew who was in it, but it made her even jumpier. All of a sudden she grabbed this fishing pole with a hook on the end and stabbed me."

"A gaff," I said. "They use it to bring fish in."

"All I know is that it hurt like a son of a bitch, and I was doubled over with the pain. She dropped the pole and pushed me, and I went over into the water. I was sure I was going to drown until you grabbed me."

We went back over his story a couple of times, even asking him to repeat the events backwards to be sure he wasn't making stuff up or leaving stuff out. He came through pretty well every time.

The assistant district attorney was waiting for us at headquarters. She was a young haole woman, only a few years out of law school, but she seemed to know her stuff. We went over the case, and everything we had on Xiao Zenshen. Finally, she said, "I have enough for the arraignment. I'll be back in touch with you tomorrow."

It was late, and neither Ray nor I had gotten dinner. I sent him home to Julie, then grabbed takeout from Zippy's on my way home. While I ate, Mike and I traded information. "You going to be able to nail her?" he asked, when we were done.

"Hard to say," I said. "Like I said, she's a smart woman. I still don't know if she killed Zoë Greenfield and Miriam Rose, or if Gladys Yuu did. And if Gladys did, was Xiao Zenshen pulling the strings? But it's up to the ADA to make the case, now. Ray and I just have to testify."

"What's your gut reaction?"

"My gut says that Dr. Z was behind it all, but I think Gladys did the actual killing."

"She was Chinese, right?"

I nodded.

"She had to do whatever she could to keep her mother going," he said. "It's what good children do, especially when they come from cultures that demand that kind of behavior." He looked at me, as I was crumpling up the paper from my dinner. "We haven't shut the door on kids yet, have we?"

"No, I don't think we have. But I think the next move has to be Sandra's. When she's ready to have a baby, she can ask us again, and then we'll decide."

"I don't like leaving big decisions about life up to other people," Mike said. "We have to know what we want first. Then we decide if we want to work with Sandra and Cathy, or go on our own—with some other woman, or adoption, or maybe even fostering."

"You'd want to do that? Raise a kid who's not biologically either of ours?" I asked.

"What does it matter, in the end? You and I both know that families come in all shapes and sizes. Whether we adopt or foster or donate sperm or whatever, we'd still love the kid the same."

"I agree. I mean, you look at Aunt Mei-Mei, and how she took in Jimmy Ah Wong. To see her with him, you could never tell he wasn't her blood." I hesitated, not sure how to say what I meant.

I sat down on the far end of the sofa from him, and lifted his feet into my lap. "I love you, you know. I feel like my life is here, with you. But we've only been living together for what, eight months? We've still got some adjusting to do before we bring someone else into our lives."

"You're right," he said, as I started to massage his feet. "And nobody says we have to have kids to be complete as a family."

Roby came up to sniff Mike's hand. "Roby will look after us in our old age," he said. "He'll be our seeing eye dog. He'll open doors for us and dial 911 with his nose when we fall and break our hips."

Roby put his front paws up on Mike's thighs and looked back and forth between us. "You going to do that, boy?" I asked, scratching behind his ears.

He nodded his head vigorously, and Mike and I both laughed.

Over the next few weeks, Ray and I pulled together additional evidence in the deaths of Zoë Greenfield and Miriam Rose. Gladys Yuu's only surviving relative was a distant cousin on Maui, and she gave us permission to take Gladys's fingerprints and compare them to the one on the stolen pendant, and to make a cast of Gladys's tires. The print matched, and so did the tire track.

The DA had to get subpoenas for both women's bank records to verify what Harry had found, that there were payments going from Dr. Z's offshore account in China to Gladys's account in Honolulu. Because of the difference in banking laws between the US and China, that was taking a long time.

The only evidence we could count on pointed toward Gladys Yuu, rather than Xiao Zenshen. The good doctor was too wily to admit to anything, and we couldn't find that one thing that would conclusively put her behind the two women's murders. The ADA had to settle for fraud in the payments Néng Yuán had collected from the state, and assault on Wyatt Collins. It wasn't going to be much, but at least Dr. Zenshen would serve some time, and then be deported back to China.

A few days after Dr. Z's arrest, Anna Yang surfaced again. She petitioned for the right to stay in the US, based on her long-standing marriage to Greg Oshiro. Because Zoë's murder was still an open case, Ray and I spoke up on her behalf in front of an immigration judge, who reinstated her visa and gave her a year in this country, during which time she could apply for permanent status.

She and the girls moved in with Greg, and they seemed like a pretty happy family. Both of them were committed to raising the girls. "I'm not saying I'll never find a guy," Greg said, as we sat in a Kope Bean a few weeks later. We'd just traded information on another case, the murder of a newlywed by his wife of less than a week. "But if I find someone, he's got to be willing to have the girls in his life."

"Anna feel the same way?" I asked.

He nodded. "She was hurt pretty bad when Zoë broke up with her—especially since Zoë went for that guy. It was like their whole life together had been some kind of sham. I think it's going to be a long time before she's ready to date anybody."

Ray's cell phone rang, and he stepped away from us to take the call.

Greg took a sip of his cappuccino. "What happened to that guy, the ex-con?"

"My friend Levi Hirsch gave him a job," I said. "He already knew all the stuff about energy statistics. And Levi collects wounded cases, anyway."

"Like your friend Terri?"

"Yeah, I guess so." Terri and Levi had announced they were getting married in the fall, and Levi had already asked Harry, Mike and me to be his groomsmen.

"I'm glad," Greg said. "I was so scared when Zoë took up with Wyatt, because I was afraid it meant she was going to take the girls and go to the mainland, and I'd never see them again. But once I got to know him, I felt sorry for him. He seems to be trying to turn his life around."

Ray came back to us then. "Gotta go," he said. "Julie's getting her first sonogram. We're going to see if they can tell what kind of creature she's carrying inside there."

"I hope it's human," Greg said.

Ray pretended to trip and spill his coffee on Greg, but the cup was empty. It was still kind of funny to see Greg jump back.

When Ray was gone, I asked Greg, "So, how do you like being a full-time dad now, having Anna and the girls live with you?"

"It's not what I signed on for, and it gets rough sometimes, but you go with the flow, you know? I mean, what was I going to do? It's important for Anna's citizenship petition that we live together. And the girls are great, when they're not screaming or crying or fighting with each other. Having them around all the time is a lot different from taking them for a weekend, with my mom and dad around to help."

He sipped his coffee, then looked at me. "How about you and Mike? You guys thinking of kids?"

I blew out a big breath. "Yeah. But neither of us are ready for such a big commitment. We both love my nieces and nephews and our friends' kids—but we like being able to say goodbye to them, too."

"It's a different world today," Greg said. "Imagine when we were teenagers – we couldn't even imagine that gay couples could get married, have kids—all that stuff we thought was restricted to straight people."

"It makes things tougher, though," I said. "I mean, right now, Mike and I could get married in a couple of different states on the mainland, but it wouldn't make any difference back here, or to the Feds, either. But soon? I'll bet we see same-sex marriage everywhere. And then we'll all have to decide if we get married or not—something we didn't even have to worry about just a few years ago."

I crumpled up my coffee cup. "And this whole baby thing? I mean, even ten years ago, who thought about it? Now everywhere I look gay and lesbian people are having kids. It puts that much more pressure on a relationship."

"There have always been pressures, brah," Greg said. "They're just different ones today. Ten years ago, neither you nor Mike could have been comfortably out at work, but today? Maybe not a cake walk, but it's doable."

I sat there for a minute, thinking about all the changes. But I kept circling back to kids—to Julie's pregnancy, and Pua's. And to Sandra's open-ended offer.

Greg stood up. "We should both get back to work," he said.

I stood up, too. "One thing that doesn't change is that people keep on killing people."

"Gives us writers something to write about, huh?" Greg said.

"That it does," I said. "That it does."

OTHER PEOPLE'S CHILDREN

An exclusive Mahu Investigation short

A call from the boss on your way to work on Monday morning is never a good way to start the week. "Jogger found a body at an empty lot off Ahui Street about half an hour ago," Lieutenant Sampson said. "Call Donne and go right over there." He paused for a moment. "Sounds like a bad one."

Ray Donne was my partner in the Honolulu Police Department. I called him and arranged to meet him at the site, a short road that ran parallel to the cut leading into the Ala Wai Yacht Basin, where Gilligan and the Skipper left for their three-hour tour so many years ago.

There were two police cruisers already on the scene, blue lights flashing. Across an empty lot I saw the back of the Children's Discovery Center, with school buses already pulled up out front disgorging a flow of little keikis on a field trip.

Lidia Portuondo, a patrol officer I'd known for years, was standing next to her car with a twenty-something Asian man in a sweat-soaked tank top, nylon shorts, and expensive-looking running shoes. "This is Wing Bing-Bing," Lidia said, introducing us. "He found the body." She turned to the man and said, "Detective Kanapa'aka."

"Can you tell me what you saw?" I asked.

"I live Kaka'ako," he replied in a heavy Chinese accent, pointing behind us to a row of high-rise condos a few blocks away. "I run here every morning. This morning I run past and I see pile of big plastic trash bag. I think bad people to dump trash here. Then I see foot." He shivered. "I don't do anything more, I just call police."

I thanked him, and made sure Lidia had his contact information. By then Ray was pulling up. He looked like he hadn't slept in days, which was probably true, since his wife, Julie, had given birth two weeks before. Little Vinnie had a big set of lungs and didn't mind using them.

Ray and I walked over to where another beat cop, Gary Saunders, was standing guard over a haphazard tumble of black plastic trash bags. The foot Mr. Wing had mentioned was clearly visible sticking out of a hole in the bottom bag. The toenails were painted pink and the heel was callused. The bags were already beginning to smell in the early morning heat.

I got my digital camera, portable tripod, and an L-shaped measuring scale from the glove compartment. I made sure the date and time stamp was on, and began taking pictures of the scene, beginning with the widest angle. You never know what may show up in the background of a shot, after all. Then with Ray's help I began shooting pictures closer and closer, positioning the measuring scale to document how close I was.

When I was sure I had all the angles covered, I popped the memory stick from the camera and uploaded the pictures to my netbook computer. While we waited for the Medical Examiner's van to arrive, I created a new folder on the desktop with the case number and put the files in there, as well as blank copies of many of the forms we'd have to fill out.

A steady stream of fishing boats left the marina to head out in search of marlin, tuna and wahoo, rigged with fishing poles and gaffs. A half dozen cattle egrets pecked the barren land near the water's edge, and a huge black frigate bird soared on a thermal around us. When I was a kid, my father told me that the old Hawaiians believed that the appearance of a frigate bird meant someone had died. I guess they were right.

The ME's van pulled up a few minutes later, and we let the techs load the bags onto the van, to be opened and inventoried back at the lab. When they were done, Ray and I walked around to the couple of businesses in the area to see if anyone had been around to notice the bags being dropped off, but we had no luck.

By the time we got to the ME's office, a low-slung off-white building on Iwilei Road, Doc Takayama had the body parts removed from the bag and laid out on a table. We dabbed some Vicks Vapo-Rub under our noses and walked in to the examining room.

"You brought me a jigsaw puzzle this morning," he said. "I don't like jigsaws."

"We'll keep that in mind for the future," Ray said.

The body parts had been laid out in a rough sort of order, and we could see the victim was a Hawaiian woman in her late teens or early twenties, nearly six feet tall and close to three hundred pounds. Her skin was pockmarked with acne, and her hair was lank and greasy. She had the start of a mustache on her upper lip.

"Cause of death?" I asked.

"Right now I'm saying evisceration," Doc said. "Most of her internal organs are gone."

"Some kind of ritual killing?" Ray asked.

Doc shrugged. "I'll have more information for you once I finish the autopsy."

"No ID on the body, I assume," I grumbled. "That would be too easy."

"Can't help you with that. But she had a couple of tattoos." He rolled her arm so we could see the words "da kine" on her upper back, and a dolphin on her right ankle.

I snapped pictures of the young woman's face and tattoos and then once again moved pictures from the camera to the netbook. Then we drove back to headquarters to try and track our mystery woman down.

"Didn't look like a prostitute," Ray said, when we were at our desks. "And she looked plenty strong. So most likely she knew her attacker."

There was no missing persons report, so we were stuck until we got an ID. I emailed a good head shot of the girl to Greg Oshiro, a reporter I knew at the Star-Advertiser, and asked him to put something in the paper. I did the same thing with my oldest brother, Lui, who manages KVOL, a local TV station. Their motto was "Erupting News All The Time," and they loved anything with a hint of sensation. I was sure that a "help us find out who this dead girl is" appeal would get us something.

There wasn't much else we could do without an ID, so we worked on other cases, slogging through reams of paperwork and making follow-up calls. I checked the TV in our break room at noon, and saw the girl's photo broadcast on the KVOL news. A few minutes later, the tip line transferred a call to my desk.

"Eh, brah, I t'ink I know da kine girl," a man's voice said. "Her name Alamea, and she work at da kine drugstore on Prospect Street in Papakolea."

"Thanks, brah." I hung up and dialed the drugstore. I identified myself and asked if a girl named Alamea worked there.

"Yeah, but she no come to work today," the man who answered complained.

I described the dead girl, and the man verified that sounded like her.

On our way up to the drugstore, Ray pulled into a Kope Bean, our local island-based coffee shop. He pulled up at the drive-through window. "Gotta have some caffeine to stay awake," he said, while we waited in line. "You want?"

"Might as well. My usual."

He ordered himself a Longboard sized Macadamia Nut Latte, and a raspberry mocha in the same size for me. Then he turned the big SUV uphill to where the drugstore sat, at the foot of Mount Tantalus.

We carried the coffee inside and sipped while we waited for the manager to come out from the back. He was a slim, slight Filipino named Luis. "Yeah, that's her," he said, when we showed him the dead girl's picture. He stepped back and crossed himself.

He led us to the office, where he pulled her original application from a file cabinet, and I copied her full name and address into the file I was building on the netbook.

"What kind of girl was she?" Ray asked while I typed.

Luis shrugged. "Slow. Not like retarded, but always take her longer to get things and do things. She work photo counter most of the time because it was same thing over and over, you know? Take film, scan, ring up."

"She have a boyfriend?"

"Alamea? No way. Not even friendly with other staff."

We established that Alamea had worked her shift on Saturday, but she hadn't shown up Sunday. Luis had called her cell phone and gotten no answer. "Now I think, she look sick on Saturday," he said. "She keep shifting foot to foot, squeezing her lips together like something hurt."

Ray bought a monster-sized pack of dried mixed fruit sprinkled with li hing powder, a spicy treat he had become addicted to, and we drove the few blocks to the first-floor apartment where Alamea lived, in what looked like a converted motel. Ray knocked and we waited. No answer.

He knocked again. We were about to start canvassing the neighbors when the door opened slowly to reveal a huge Hawaiian woman in an extra-wide wheelchair. We showed our badges and Ray asked, "Does Alamea Kekuahona live here?"

"She my daughter, but she no home."

Ray broke the news to her about Alamea's death. "She always babooze, dat one," the woman said, meaning stupid. "What happen? She walk in front of bus?"

"May we come in, Auntie?" Ray asked. It was awkward talking like that in the doorway.

She backed the chair up and let us into a small, dark living room, partitioned down the middle with a faded floral-print bed sheet hung from the ceiling. There was a single bedroom to the left, a galley kitchen and a small bathroom. There was only one chair at the table.

Her name was Betty Kekuahona, she said, and Alamea was her younger daughter. The older one had gotten married and moved out years before, and when Alamea turned sixteen, she had rigged up the curtain to give herself some privacy.

Betty's hair was pulled back and twisted into a bun that looked like the face of a small, yappy dog, like a Brussels Griffon or an Affenpinscher. Her forearms were massive and lightly dusted with brown hair.

We put on gloves and searched the small space, but there were no clues as to what had happened to Alamea. "She had a cell phone, right?" I asked.

Betty gave us the number. I pulled out the netbook and added it to the list.

"Any friends?"

"None she talk about. Alamea always too big and stupid to make friends."

We gave her the phone number for the medical examiner's office. "How I gonna bury her?" Betty asked. "I got no money. And I got the diabetes bad. Can't work, got to get my medicine from the free clinic."

I brought up the name and phone number for the department's victim advocate from the netbook. I gave that to Betty. "She can help you out," I said. "We're sorry for your loss, Auntie."

She shrugged. "I always knew dat girl would do something stupid one day."

We got in Ray's SUV and he backed out of the parking space. "Not exactly broken up, is she? That was her daughter."

"Makes me feel bad for Alamea," I said. "Fat, homely, no friends, a boss who thought she was slow and a mother who thought she was stupid."

"Not the kind of person you'd think would end up the way she did," Ray added.

When we got back to headquarters we put together a subpoena for Alamea's cell phone records, and went through a dozen more calls and emails from people who thought they had information on the dead girl. None of them panned out, though.

One man insisted that Alamea had been killed by the Night Marchers. "I saw them take her," he wrote, in an email. "They're going to come for me next."

Ray looked up at me. "Who are the Night Marchers? Sound like a punk rock band."

"The ghosts of ancient Hawaiian warriors. They come out on certain nights to walk around battlefields. And some people think they come to escort the dead to the next world."

Another woman who left a voice mail said she was a psychic. "I didn't see any mention on the newscast of her baby. Make sure someone takes care of the baby."

Ray shook his head. "These people come up with the craziest things."

The subpoena for Alamea's phone records was signed and faxed over to the phone company, and the woman I spoke to promised to have them together by the next morning.

By the end of our shift we were no closer to finding out who killed Alamea. Ray looked at his watch. "I've gotta go. We're meeting the priest at the church to go over the details of the baptism."

Ray and Julie were practicing Roman Catholics, and Vinnie was to be baptized on Saturday, at a Catholic church near their home in Salt Lake, near the Aloha Stadium.

Ray and I had been working together for three years, and we'd become close friends off the job as well. My partner Mike and I often went to dinner with him and Julie on the weekends, and just before Vinnie was born they had asked Mike if he would be one of the baby's godfathers.

"My youngest brother is flying in from Seattle to be one," Ray said. "But we'd like to have someone local, too. Has to be a Catholic, as you know."

Mike was flattered. His father was Italian and his mother Korean, and both of them were practicing Catholics. Mike had grown up in the church, though he didn't attend except for the occasional holiday mass. By coincidence, the church closest to Ray and Julie's house, St. Filomena's, was the one Mike's parents attended, because they offered Mass in Korean. So it all worked out very nicely.

"Have fun," I told him. I drove home, fed and walked our golden retriever, Roby, then joined Mike next door for dinner with his parents. He had grown up in that half of the duplex, and then when he was a working fireman he had bought the other side. I'd moved in with him when we finally decided to settle down together.

I had developed a real taste for Korean barbecue since I met Mike, and no one made a better marinade for the beef than Soon-O. Her special mix of soy sauce, garlic, sugar, sliced onions and some other spices was better than any restaurant's.

Dominic and Soon-O were so proud that Mike had been asked to be Vinnie's godfather, and they were looking forward to the ceremony on Saturday morning. "Almost like having a grandchild," Soon-O said. "But not quite."

Mike and I had been approached by a lesbian couple we knew to be their sperm donors, and he and I had been going back and forth on the question. I thought I was happy being Uncle Kimo to my nieces and nephews, while Mike was leaning toward becoming a father. Mike was an only child, and his parents, now that they were comfortable with his being gay, were eager to get themselves a grandchild however they could.

I was determined to resist the pressure. "Poor Ray looked like walking death this morning," I mentioned, between bites of the succulent beef. "Vinnie's keeping them both up all night."

"Mike slept through the night as soon as we brought him home from the hospital," Soon-O said. "What a good baby!"

"He does have a knack for sleeping," I said. Mike's favorite hobby was dozing on the sofa, with the TV going in the background. I was the more active one, always ready for surfing, jogging, or a more horizontal form of recreation.

"Your parents are probably too busy with all their grandchildren," Soon-O said. "But Dom and I would always be available to help you out."

I smiled, nodded, and kept eating. That night, Mike and I walked Roby together just before eleven, giving him a last chance to empty his bladder before sleep. The dark sky was clear and spangled with stars, and I wondered what kind of wish Mike was making on them. Was it really that important to him to have a child of his own? Why didn't I feel the same way?

We walked back inside and Mike surveyed the living room. "You're a pig, you know that?" he said. I'd left my aloha shirt on the sofa when I switched to a T-shirt, and the morning paper was still strewn around the kitchen table in sections.

"Oink, oink." I grabbed for his hand. "Leave it. Let's go to bed."

He disengaged from me. "I can't go to sleep when the house is a mess."

I almost said that we couldn't make a baby together if we didn't have sex—but then I remembered the plumbing problem. I left him in the living room to clean up. I stripped down and slid between the covers, and I was asleep before he came in to join me.

The next morning I called the Medical Examiner's office soon after I got to work. "Hey, Alice," I said to the ever-cheerful receptionist. "Doc have the report together on the jigsaw puzzle girl?"

"He didn't like that one," she said. "You should have seen him. Grumbling and complaining all day. I'll transfer you."

I sat through some gloomy elevator music until Doc finally picked up. "Cause of death was massive blood loss due to internal hemorrhaging," he dictated. "Time of death was sometime between ten o'clock and midnight Saturday night. I don't have the full toxicology results back yet but she had consumed a massive amount of sedatives shortly before death."

"So the killer knocked her out first?"

"That's not the best part. Your victim gave birth shortly before her death."

"Excuse me?"

"You heard me. All the results are correct. Where's the baby?"

"Great question, doc. I have no idea."

I did have an idea, though. I went back through the phone records from the day before. The psychic had left her phone number, and I called her back. I introduced myself and asked if Ray and I could come over and talk to her. She agreed, and gave me her address.

It was my turn to drive, so we hopped in the Jeep and opened up the flaps. It was a sunny, cool morning and it felt great to be outdoors. We trailed behind an elderly man with a long gray ponytail, riding a slow-moving scooter, and I didn't mind because I knew we'd get where we were going too quickly anyway.

The old guy pulled in at a low-rise office building, and I continued at the same sedate pace until we reached a run-down house in the shadow of the H1 expressway, beside a sign that read "MADAME OKELANI. TAROT CARDS, PSYCHIC READINGS, 'AUMAKUA." The 'aumakua were also known as spirit animals in the Hawaiian tradition; they were the spirits of our ancestors, who had chosen to take physical form in the body of a particular creature.

Ray made a disgruntled noise in the back of his throat, like the one my father used to make when my brothers and I were kids and we were trying to put one past him.

An elderly Hawaiian woman opened the door. Her gray hair flowed down to her shoulders, and she wore an oversized muumuu in a rainbow of bright colors.

"I'm so glad you came, detectives," she said. "Sometimes law enforcement is distrustful of psychic abilities."

Madame Okelani sat down at a square table, and motioned us to the chairs opposite her. "How did you know the young woman who was killed?" I asked.

"I didn't know her. I just had a vision." She looked at us. "Do either of you have any experience with psychics?"

"I had my tarot cards read in college," I said. "That's about it."

"I think everyone has some level of psychic talent." She smiled. "I teach workshops on how to get in touch with your own ability, and one of the exercises I give people is to consider a news report, often one about a crime."

"I don't understand," I said. "Why crimes?"

"Because there will usually be follow up reports, and those reports can verify information you might sense. For example, last week I saw a report about a burglary just down the street. I was upset by that, because it was so close. I meditated, and I saw something very unusual—a mop and a pair of rubber gloves. I didn't know what to make of that. Then the next day I learned that the maid had been involved in the robbery."

"Did you report that information to the police?" Ray asked.

She shook her head. "Detective. If I called you about that you would have just laughed and said I was crazy."

"But you did call us about this vision."

"Here's what I did. I saw the piece on the TV news about the girl you needed to identify. As soon as I did, I turned the TV off and went into a meditative state. I closed my eyes, lowered my heart rate, and tried to focus on the girl's energy."

"And you did this why?" Ray asked.

"I make my living this way, Detective. It's important that I be able to do as much as I can for my clients. And that requires discipline and practice."

"What did you see when you focused?" I asked.

She shuddered. "A lot of blood. But also a very tiny baby, like a newborn, red-faced and crying."

"Where was this?"

She motioned to a laptop on the table between us. "I use Google Maps. I open the program and then continue my meditation, hoping to be directed to a particular place on the map." She looked up at me. "The violence was too strong for me to focus. All I could tell was that the place I was seeing was near the water, with fishing boats. Perhaps a marina."

We hadn't released the location of the body to the press or

the public, so it was interesting that Madame Okelani was able to get so close. Was she really a psychic? Or was she the one who had killed Alamea?

I could tell Ray was thinking the same thing. "Where were you Saturday night?" he asked.

"Why?"

Neither of us said anything, just looked at her.

"I attended a psychic fair at the Blaisdell Center on Saturday." She turned and retrieved a flyer from a counter near her, and passed it to us. "The fair went until eight o'clock at night, as you can see. An event like that can be very draining for a psychic, with so many people and so much to interpret. Several of my colleagues and I went out for dinner afterward, to regroup."

"What time would that have been?" I asked.

"Let me check my purse." She got up and left the room, and returned a moment later with a leather wallet. She pulled a receipt out from a restaurant at the Ward Center, time stamped 11:30 PM. "I guess we were there later than I thought," she said, showing it to us. "I can give you the names and numbers of the people I was with. And the server will remember me, too. She's a client."

I opened my netbook and took down the information. She had an unsecured wi-fi connection, and while I had the computer open I checked my email and downloaded Alamea's cell phone record.

"How is the child?" Madame Okelani asked when I was finished.

I shook my head. "We don't know. We didn't even know there was a child until we got the autopsy report this morning. Which was why we were surprised that you knew yesterday." I hesitated for a moment, unsure of how to proceed.

Like Mike, Ray had been raised a Catholic, and he had an innate distrust of anything that didn't fit within his set of beliefs. But I was more open in what I was willing to consider.

My parents were a polyglot mix of religion and ethnicity. My mother was half-Hawaiian and half Japanese, and had little training in either culture. My father's father was a full-bloodied Hawaiian who married a haole, or white, missionary from Montana and converted to her Presbyterian religion. My father had grown up believing in what he learned from both parents. He and my mother married in the Kawaia'aho Church in downtown Honolulu, and we'd been taken to services there occasionally as kids, usually for the big holidays like Christmas and Easter.

But like my father, I'd taken it all in and remained independent in my beliefs. I had a strong set of spiritual beliefs, about treating your fellow man the way you'd like to be treated, and I respected the ancient gods and goddess of Hawai'i—Pele, who ruled the volcanoes; Kanaloa, the god of the seas; and Lono, who brings rains, fertility and harvest, among them.

"Can you try to focus on the baby again?" I asked. "With the computer?"

"Kimo," Ray said. "Can I speak to you outside?"

"I'll boot up the computer," Madame Okelani said. I stood up and followed Ray outside to her front lawn.

"Why are we wasting time here?" he asked. "The woman's a crackpot who had a couple of lucky guesses."

"You have any other ideas?" I held up my hand. "We have a dead woman who had no friends, and a little baby out there somewhere. Madame Okelani may be able to help."

"What about the records from Alamea's cell phone. We can work on those."

"Just humor me, all right? Let's see if she can come up with anything."

We went back inside. Madame Okelani's eyes were closed, and her fingers rested lightly on the laptop's keyboard. We watched her for a moment. Then she opened her eyes.

"I'm sorry," she said. "I can't get anything. There's some kind of interference." She looked at my netbook. "Is your computer on, detective?"

"Hibernating. Is that the interference?"

"May I?" she asked, holding out her hand.

I gave her the netbook, and immediately she put it down on the table, as if it had burned her fingers. "Makiki," she said. "The baby is in Makiki." Beads of sweat appeared on her forehead. "I'm sorry, I'm not feeling well. I need to lie down."

"Thank you for your help," I said, taking the computer back. Ray and I turned toward the door.

"Oh, and detective? You're not a pig, you're a dolphin."

It took me a minute to process that. "Yes, you're right. Thank you."

"What the hell was that about?" Ray asked, as we got into the Jeep.

"Which part? Makiki? Or the dolphin?"

"Whichever part makes sense."

I opened the netbook and turned it back on. "I had an argument with Mike last night. The living room was messy, and he called me a pig."

"And?"

I pointed to Madame Okelani's sign, as the netbook came back to life. "You know what an 'aumakua, a spirit animal, is?"

Ray shook his head.

"The ancient Hawaiians believed that their ancestors remained around them, often taking shape in a particular animal. A family would be protected by that particular animal. A family that lived in up in the mountains might have an owl for an 'aumakua. One that lived by the water, like my family did, might have a shark or a dolphin.

"My father always told us this story about how he was surfing when he was a teenager, and the wind came up very strong, suddenly, and he got knocked off his board. He was floundering in the water, couldn't keep his head up out of the waves. Then he felt something nudge him from below, pushing him toward land. It was a dolphin."

I opened the PDF file of phone numbers Alamea had called.

"He told us that dolphin was our family's 'aumakua, and it would always protect us when we were out in the water."

"And did it?"

"We're all here, aren't we? My brothers and I have all been caught by waves, tossed around and banged up. But we all survived."

"Uh-huh. What do the phone records say?"

I looked down. "On Saturday afternoon, Alamea called a cell phone several times." I flipped to another page. "That number is registered to a woman named Charlotte Montes, with an address in Makiki. I think that's our next stop, don't you?"

"We could have figured that out without the crazy lady."

"Just because you don't believe doesn't mean she's crazy."

We drove down to Makiki, to a small stucco house on a tiny piece of land, with a chain link fence all around. The gate into the small front yard was locked.

I called the number from the printout, and through the open front window I heard a tinny rendition of Israel Kamakawiwo'ole's "N Dis Life." As the phone rang, a baby began to cry.

No one answered the phone, and the baby inside continued to cry. "I think we have reason to believe that Alamea's baby is inside this house and may be in danger," I said. "We need to take whatever measures necessary to check it out."

"I agree." Ray grasped the top rail of the fence, testing it. Then he climbed up and over, dropping lightly into the front yard. I followed him, a little less gracefully.

I unholstered my gun. "If we're right, the woman inside killed Alamea."

Ray nodded, and pulled his gun out as well. I stepped up and rapped on the front door. "HPD. Open the door, please."

There was no answer. All we heard was the baby continuing to cry.

I tried the handle. The door was locked. I nodded to Ray to go around the left side of the house, and I went right, toward the open window. I approached it carefully, peeking in from the side.

Through the screen I saw a baby in a crib in the middle of the room. And on the floor, a young dark-haired woman sat with her legs out in front of her. She was crying, too, though more quietly than the baby. "Charlotte Montes?" I asked.

She nodded.

"Can you open the door, please?"

"He won't stop crying," she said. "No matter what I do."

"We'll help you," I said gently. "If you can just get up and open the door."

She took a deep breath and stood up. Without a backward look to the baby she walked out of the room, and a moment later she was opening the front door.

We both holstered our guns and followed her inside. The baby was still crying, and Ray walked over and picked him up from his crib. He began rocking the baby and cooing to him, and soon had him calmed down.

In the meantime, I sat down at the kitchen table across from Charlotte. Up close I could see she was a bit older than I had thought, probably late twenties or early thirties. "How did you know Alamea Kekuahona?" I asked.

"From the drugstore. I used to talk to her sometimes. One day I saw her checking out pregnancy tests, and she told me she didn't believe she was pregnant."

Ray stood behind her, holding the baby in his arms and swaying gently.

"She didn't even want the baby. And I did."

I nodded.

"She wouldn't go to the doctor or anything. Finally one day

I told her that I was a midwife, and I would deliver the baby for her, and no one had to know."

"But you're not a midwife, are you?"

She shook her head. "I thought I would help her deliver, and then she would give the baby to me. But she started bleeding, and she wouldn't stop, and then she passed out."

She looked up at me. "I didn't know what to do. I wanted to call 911 but I knew if they came, they would take away the baby."

"So you just let her die?"

"We were both so stupid. We thought the baby would just come out and she could go home. When she passed out I got scared, and I took the baby and went for a walk. By the time I got back she was dead. I didn't know what to do—she was so big and I couldn't carry her anywhere. So I had to cut her up in pieces." She shivered and began to cry.

I sat there with my arm around Charlotte's shoulder as Ray called Social Services to take custody of the baby, and a squad car to take Charlotte downtown. Lidia Portuondo answered the call, and I knew she'd be kind, yet careful, with Charlotte.

As Lidia was driving away, the crime scene techs showed up and sprayed a mix of luminol and a chemical activator in Charlotte's bathroom. The luminol reacts with the iron in blood to show traces of any blood residue, even after the surface has been cleaned, and the activator causes the luminescence that reveals the traces. It works best on non-porous substances, like the nubby tile on the bathroom floor. They turned the lights out, and we saw a blue glow where Alamea's blood had spattered. They took some long-exposure photographs that documented the traces.

Fortunately Charlotte wasn't a great housekeeper; if she had scrubbed the entire bathroom with bleach or some copper-containing substance, the whole room would have reacted with the luminol, giving us a false positive and effectively camouflaging any of the blood traces.

When the crime scene techs were finished we locked up the

house and drove down to headquarters, where we read Charlotte her rights and she gave us a full statement.

≈≈≈

Alamea had never told Charlotte who the baby's father was, and no one else even knew she was pregnant. As next of kin, Betty signed the papers so the baby could be put up for adoption. Charlotte was arraigned on charges of negligent homicide, and released on bail.

We moved on to other cases, but I couldn't help thinking about Charlotte Montes, and the lengths some people went to in order to have a baby.

Saturday morning, Mike and I drove to St. Filomena's with Dominic and Soon-O. It was our first opportunity to meet both Ray's and Julie's parents, who had flown in for the occasion, and it was funny to me how quickly Dominic and Mike blended into the crowd of exuberant Italian-Americans from Philadelphia. I was left on the sidelines with Soon-O.

"Was this what it was like when you guys lived on Long Island?" I asked her.

Dominic and Soon-O met in Korea, when he was a wounded soldier and she was his nurse. After some opposition on both sides of the family, they had married, and she had worked to put Dominic through medical school, living near his big family in New York.

"Yes," Soon-O said. "Except there was a lot more talk in Italian. Dom's parents were born there, you know."

I knew that Soon-O had been unhappy in New York, far from her family and her culture, and that Mike had been uncomfortable as a mixed-race kid. The Riccardis had moved to Hawai'i when Mike was seven, in an effort to make both of them happier. As far as I could tell, it had worked.

"I'm sorry Michael couldn't grow up around his cousins, on both sides," Soon-O said. "And now Vinnie will be the same, so far from family."

"We make our own family." I took Soon-O's hand. "Look at us."

"I know," she said. "I almost feel like your mother is my sister. And now, Michael will be connected to Vinnie, and to Ray and Julie and their families. That means we all will be, too."

I looked up and saw Ray at the door of the church, trying to get everyone to go inside. "Well, then, we'd better go in and join them," I said.

I gave one last thought to Alamea Kekuahona and her baby, and hoped that both of them would find loving families, in Heaven and on Earth, and then I joined my family of choice for the ceremony to welcome our newest member.

NEIL PLAKCY is the author of *Mahu, Mahu Surfer, Mahu Fire, Mahu Vice, Mahu Men, Mahu Blood , Zero Break* about openly gay Honolulu homicide detective Kimo Kanapa'aka. His other books are *Three Wrong Turns in the Desert, Dancing with the Tide, The Outhouse Gang, In Dog We Trust, Invasion of the Blatnicks,* and *GayLife.com.* He edited *Paws & Reflect: A Special Bond Between Man and Dog* and the gay erotic anthologies *Hard Hats, Surfer Boys* and *Skater Boys.* His website is www.mahubooks.com.

ACKNOWLEDGMENTS

A writer needs an ohana, a family and a community, in order to put out a book—and I've been lucky to have a very supportive ohana during the years of the Mahu series. Christine Kling, Sharon Potts, Mike Jastrzebski, and Miriam Auerbach all critiqued parts of this book, and their help has been invaluable.

Cindy Chow once again provided invaluable service by reading the manuscript and pointing out so many mistakes I'd made about Hawai'i, though any remaining errors are my fault, not hers. She has been a wonderful tutor into the intricacies of life in the Aloha State.

For their personal support I am grateful to my mother, to Eliot Hess and Lois Whitman, Fred Searcy, John Spero, Steve Greenberg, Eileen Matluck, Andrew Schulz, Elisa Albo, and Lourdes Rodriguez-Florido. And as always, gratitude is due to my other colleagues in the English department at Broward College's South Campus for their support and encouragement, and to the college's Staff and Professional Development program, which has allowed me to attend conferences and conventions.

For professional advice and encouragement I want to thank Wayne Gunn and my fellow members of the Florida chapter of Mystery Writers of America.

A big mahalo to Laura Baumbach, Kris Jacen, J.P. Bowie, Lisa Edwards and Victoria Landis, for all their help in bringing this book out.

The author acknowledges the trademark status and trademark owners of the following wordmarks mentioned in this work of fiction:

7-11: Southland Corporation

Aloha Stadium: State of Hawaii

Bank of Hawai'i: Bank of Hawaii

Barbies: Mattel Inc.

Blackberry: Research in Motion Limited

Bluetooth: Bluetooth Sig Inc.

BMW: BMW of North America LLC

Brooks Brothers: Retail Brand Alliance

Camaro: General Motors

Cartier: Cartier International

Children's Discovery Center: Children's Discovery Centers of America, Inc.

Crocs: Crocs, Inc.

Denny's: DFO, Inc.

Dole Plantation: Dole Food Company, Inc.

Excel: Microsoft

Facebook: Facebook, Inc.

Fire Rock Pale Ale: Kona Brewery LLC

Foodland: Foodland Super Market, Ltd.

Google: Google, Inc.

Gucci: Gucci Shops, Inc.

Harvard: President and Fellows of Harvard College

Hawai'i Five-O: CBS Productions and Leonard Freeman Productions

Hilo Hattie: Pomare Inc.

Honolulu Community College:

Jeep: Chrysler Group LLC

Kawasaki: Kawasaki Motors Corp., U.S.A.

Maui Divers: Maui Divers of Hawaii, Ltd.

Mini Cooper: BMW of North America LLC

MIT: Massachusetts Institute of Technology

NASCAR: Turner Sports Interactive, Inc.

Nissan: Nissan Jidosha Kabushiki Kaisha TA Nissan Motor Co., Ltd.

Old Navy: Gap Inc.

PowerPoint: Microsoft

Roy's: OSI Restaurant Partners, LLC

Royal Hawaiian: Starwood Hotels & Resorts Worldwide, Inc.

Sears: Sears Brands, LLC

Shirokiya: Shirokiya International

Star-Advertiser: Honolulu Star-Advertiser

The Wizard of Oz: Metro-Goldwyn-Mayer and Warner Bros.

TiVo: TiVo Inc.

Toyota Camry: Toyota Motor Sales, U.S.A., Inc.

Toyota Highlander: Toyota Motor Sales, U.S.A., Inc.

UH Warriors: University of Hawaii

Vicks Vapo-Rub: Proctor & Gamble

Word: Microsoft

Zippy's: Zippy's Inc.

Rainbow Romance Writers

Raising the Bar for LGBT Romance

RRW offers support and advocacy to career-focused authors, expanding the horizons of romance. Changing minds, one heart at a time. www.rainbowromancewriters.com

The Trevor Project

The Trevor Project operates the only nationwide, around-the-clock crisis and suicide prevention helpline for lesbian, gay, bisexual, transgender and questioning youth. Every day, The Trevor Project saves lives though its free and confidential helpline, its website and its educational services. If you or a friend are feeling lost, alone, confused or in crisis, please call The Trevor Helpline. You'll be able to speak confidentially with a trained counselor 24/7.

The Trevor Helpline: 866-488-7386

On the Web: http://www.thetrevorproject.org/

The Gay Men's Domestic Violence Project

Founded in 1994, The Gay Men's Domestic Violence Project is a grassroots, non-profit organization founded by a gay male survivor of domestic violence and developed through the strength, contributions and participation of the community. The Gay Men's Domestic Violence Project supports victims and survivors through education, advocacy and direct services. Understanding that the serious public health issue of domestic violence is not gender specific, we serve men in relationships with men, regardless of how they identify, and stand ready to assist them in navigating through abusive relationships.

GMDVP Helpline: 800.832.1901

On the Web: http://gmdvp.org/

If you're a GLBT and questioning student heading off to university, you should know that there are resources on campus for you. Here's just a sample:

GLBT Scholarship Resources

http://www.hrc.org/resources/entry/tell-us-about-an-lgbt-scholarship

Syracuse University

http://lgbt.syr.edu/

Texas A&M

http://glbt.tamu.edu/

Tulane University

http://tulane.edu/studentaffairs/oma/lgbt/index.cfm

University of Alaska

http://www.uaf.edu/woodcenter/leadership/organizations/active/index.xml?id=61

University of California, Davis

http://lgbtrc.ucdavis.edu/

University of California, San Francisco

http://lgbt.ucsf.edu/

University of Colorado

http://www.colorado.edu/GLBTQRC/

University of Florida

http://www.multicultural.ufl.edu/lgbt/

University of Hawaii, Mānoa

http://manoa.hawaii.edu/lgbt/

University of Utah

http://www.sa.utah.edu/lgbt/

University of Virginia

http://www.virginia.edu/deanofstudents/lgbt/

Vanderbilt University

http://www.vanderbilt.edu/lgbtqi/

Say Aloha to the Islands...
Kimo Style

Print ISBN # 978-1-60820-261-4
eBook ISBN #978-1-60820-262-1

Print ISBN # 978-1-60820-381-9
eBook ISBN #978-1-60820-301-7

Print ISBN # 978-1-60820-371-0
eBook ISBN #978-1-60820-302-4

Print ISBN # 978-1-60820-378-9
eBook ISBN #978-1-60820-379-6

Print ISBN # 978-1-60820-306-2
eBook ISBN #978-1-60820-307-9

Print ISBN # 978-1-60820-129-7
eBook ISBN #978-1-60820-130-3

MLRPress.com